ב"ה

YESHURUN PARENTS ASSOCIATION

Presented to
Sarah Chaplin

for attendance and achievement

on
Sunday 14 July 2002

Chairman: Jonathan Holmstock
Treasurer: Paul Koslover

ArtScroll Youth Series®

Rabbi Nosson Scherman / Rabbi Meir Zlotowitz

General Editors

Published by

Mesorah Publications, ltd

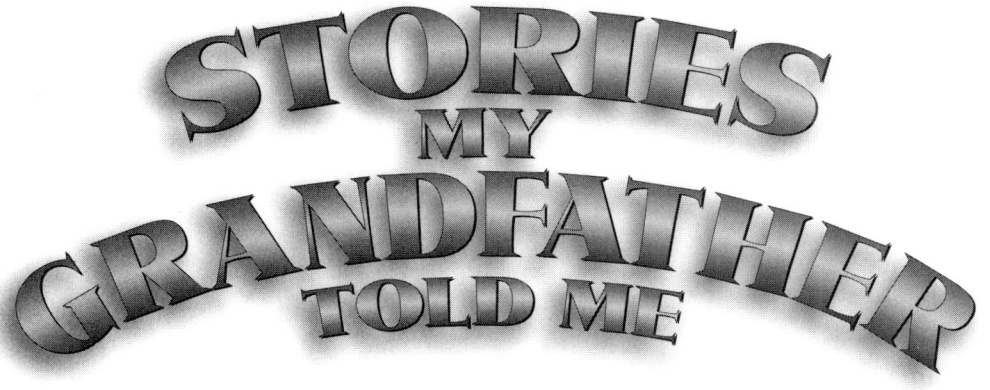

STORIES MY GRANDFATHER TOLD ME

Memorable tales arranged
according to the weekly *Sidrah*

DEVARIM / דברים

by
Zev Greenwald

Translated from the Hebrew *Maasei Avoseinu* by
Libby Lazewnik

Illustrations by
Tova Katz

FIRST EDITION
First Impression … July 2001

Published and Distributed by
MESORAH PUBLICATIONS, LTD.
4401 Second Avenue / Brooklyn, N.Y 11232

Distributed in Europe by
LEHMANNS
Unit E, Viking Industrial Park
Rolling Mill Road
Jarrow, Tyne and Wear, NE32 3DP England

Distributed in Australia and New Zealand by
GOLDS WORLD OF JUDAICA
3-13 William Street
Balaclava, Melbourne 3183
Victoria Australia

Distributed in Israel by
SIFRIATI / A. GITLER
6 Hayarkon Street
Bnei Brak 51127
Israel

Distributed in South Africa by
KOLLEL BOOKSHOP
Shop 8A Norwood Hypermarket
Norwood 2196, Johannesburg, South Africa

ARTSCROLL SERIES®
STORIES MY GRANDFATHER TOLD ME
VOLUME V — DEVARIM
© Copyright 2001, by MESORAH PUBLICATIONS, Ltd.
4401 Second Avenue / Brooklyn, N.Y. 11232 / (718) 921-9000 / www.artscroll.com

ISBN:
1-57819-533-0 (hard cover)
1-57819-534-9 (paperback)

Typography by CompuScribe at ArtScroll Studios, Ltd.

Printed in the United States of America by Noble Book Press Corp.
Bound by Sefercraft, Quality Bookbinders, Ltd., Brooklyn N.Y. 11232

Table of Contents

Parashas Devarim

Parashas Va'eschanan

Parashas Eikev

Parashas Re'eh

Parashas Shoftim

Parashas Ki Seitzei

Parashas Ki Savo

Parashas Nitzavim

Parashas Vayeilech

Parashas Ha'azinu

Parashas Vezos Haberachah

פרשת דברים

Parashas Devarim

A Child's Honor

אֵלֶּה הַדְּבָרִים אֲשֶׁר דִּבֶּר מֹשֶׁה אֶל כָּל יִשְׂרָאֵל בְּעֵבֶר הַיַּרְדֵּן

"These are the words that Moshe spoke to all Israel, across the Jordan"

(Devarim 1:1)

"Because they are words of rebuke, and [because Scripture] lists here all the places in which they caused anger before the Omnipresent — this is why it put 'the words' vaguely, and mentioned them through intimation, because of the honor of Israel."

(Rashi)

A group of students from Talmud Torah Eitz Chaim once went with their teacher to visit the *rosh yeshivah*, R' Isser Zalman Meltzer. The *rosh yeshivah* tested the boys, asking them questions on the Gemara they were learning.

When R' Isser Zalman asked for the explanation of a certain *Tosafos*, one of the boys answered in a way that showed he did not correctly understand it. R' Isser Zalman tried to spare the boy humiliation.

"Maybe," the *rosh yeshivah* suggested, "you really meant this and this." And he himself began to explain the *Tosafos* to the boy.

But the student protested, "No! That's not what I meant." And he went back to his incorrect explanation.

R' Isser Zalman tried to explain the *Tosafos* in a different way, always making sure to add, "That's probably what you meant to say."

But the boy stubbornly stuck to his own explanation of the *Tosafos*.

The student's teacher lost all patience with the boy, but R' Isser Zalman continued for ten minutes to try to spare the boy more embarrassment — but in vain.

Finally, the *rosh yeshivah* apologized to those present, saying

that he had to leave the room for a few minutes. He walked into the hall, closed the door behind him, and began to pace to and fro. As he paced, R' Isser Zalman was heard repeating to himself, over and over, "Honoring one's fellow man includes children, too ... honoring one's fellow man includes children, too."

After a few minutes, R' Isser Zalman returned to the room. He behaved as though the students had just walked in. With fresh enthusiasm and warmth he turned to the boy and began explaining the *Tosafos* once again, until the boy finally grasped his meaning and was saved from total embarrassment.

❧❧

R' Avigdor Halberstam, brother of R' Chaim of Sanz, was once a guest in a rich man's home. In those days, the custom was for an honored guest to dole out the *cholent* on Shabbos. R' Avigdor's host, therefore, placed the *cholent* pot in front of R' Avigdor at the table.

R' Avigdor put some *cholent* on his plate and tasted it! Then he took another taste. Instead of handing out the *cholent* to the rest of the family, R' Avigdor continued to eat spoonful after spoonful, until there was no *cholent* left for anyone else!

When the *cholent* pot was empty, R' Avigdor asked if there was another pot, or whether there was any more *cholent* left in the kitchen. The rich man hurried to bring everything that was left — and R' Avigdor ate every bit of it. He left nothing at all for the others.

The rich man and his family were dumbfounded. They understood that their honored guest must have his reasons for his actions, but they could not fathom what those reasons could possibly be.

A few days passed — and the reason for R' Avigdor's actions came to light. The widow who cooked for the rich man had made a mistake. Instead of pouring oil into the *cholent* pot, she had poured in kerosene. R' Avigdor, after that first taste, realized her error — but did not want the maid to be embarrassed. Mastering his distaste, he finished his own portion, and then made sure that no one else would get a chance to taste that awful *cholent*.

When all was found out, R' Avigdor explained, "Better that they think me a glutton, and better that I suffer with eating kerosene-flavored *cholent*, than to let the widowed maid feel humiliated."

Horse Talk

וַחֲצֵרֹת

"And Chatzeros"

(Devarim 1:1*)*

*"[Moshe] said to them, 'You should have learned from what I did
to Miriam at Chatzeros because of lashon hara.'"*

(Rashi)

R' Aharon of Karlin started out on foot to visit his rebbe in Mezritch. On the way, a group of wagon drivers picked him up on the road to give him a lift. As soon as they were on their way, they began to speak disparagingly about the Jews of the city. Their talk was filled with slander and *lashon hara.*

R' Aharon broke into the conversation to ask a question about horses. Distracted, the drivers went on to discuss horses enthusiastically all the way to Mezritch.

As the wagon pulled into the city, chassidim flocked around from all sides. The drivers were astounded. Turning to R' Aharon, they demanded, "If you are a rebbe, why did you discuss horses with us all this time?"

R' Aharon replied, "I saw that you were murdering people with the words you were speaking, and I said to myself, 'It is better to let them murder horses.'"

The Chofetz Chaim once met a well-known philanthropist in Moscow. The two began to discuss various matters. In the course of the conversation, the Chofetz Chaim sensed that they were on the brink of speaking *lashon hara.* He stood up and told the wealthy man, "Look how careful people are when sending a telegram. They count every word and make every effort to reduce the number of words they use. Why? Because they know that every word will cost them money. If people are so careful with something that involves only money, how much more so should we be careful to scrutinize every word to see if we're coming close to the serious sin of speaking *lashon hara.*"

One of Warsaw's foremost citizens came to see the Chofetz Chaim and ordered all his *sefarim* — except for the *sefer* "*Chofetz Chaim.*"

Surprised, the Chofetz Chaim asked his reason for this.

The businessman replied that because he had dealings with so many people in the course of his business transactions, there was no way he could be careful about speaking *lashon hara*. So there was no use buying that particular *sefer*.

Hearing this, the Chofetz Chaim told his visitor, "That same thought occurred to me before I printed the *sefer*, and I brought it up to R' Yisrael Salanter. R' Yisrael told me that it was worthwhile for me to publish my *sefer*, even if it succeeded in nothing more than making one Jew sigh from his heart because of *lashon hara*. Even that sigh has value."

Then the Chofetz Chaim added, "It's worthwhile for a person to learn *mussar* all his life, even if all it does is prevent him from speaking *lashon hara* just once."

The Rebbe's Prediction

וַחֲצֵרֹת וְדִי זָהָב
"And Chatzeros and Di-zahav"
(Devarim 1:1*)*

A certain *talmid chacham*, a disciple of R' Shlomo of Radomsk, was destitute. He went to see the Rebbe and told him that his daughter had reached marriageable age but he had nothing to give her. How was he to marry off his daughter?

"Do you have bread?" the Rebbe asked.

The chassid stammered a "yes."

"You make the *berachah 'Hamotzi lechem min ha'aretz'* every day," the Rebbe persisted. "Where do you get the bread from?"

The chassid told him that his wife went to the noblemen's courtyards selling vegetables, and she used the money she earned to buy bread for their home.

"In that case," said R' Shlomo, "the *pasuk* says, 'And Chatzeros and Di-zahav.' Go home in peace — Hashem will light your way!"

When the chassid returned home, his wife asked him what the Rebbe had said. The man did not know how to answer her, because he had not understood the meaning behind R' Shlomo's enigmatic words.

One day, the wife excitedly returned home and handed her husband a mud-splattered sack. "Look what I found today in one of the noblemen's courtyards!"

The chassid opened the sack — and his eyes flew wide open with shock. In the sack were three hundred gold coins.

The Rebbe's prediction had come true: "Chatzeros (courtyards) and Di-zahav (gold)!"

Always Thinking of Others

ד׳ אֱלֹקֵי אֲבוֹתֵכֶם יֹסֵף עֲלֵיכֶם כָּכֶם אֶלֶף פְּעָמִים וִיבָרֵךְ אֶתְכֶם
כַּאֲשֶׁר דִּבֶּר לָכֶם

"May Hashem, the G-d of your forefathers, add to you a thousand times yourselves, and bless you as He has spoken of you."

(Devarim 1:11)

The last year of the life of R' Chaim Meir of Vizhnitz was filled with sickness and suffering. But, despite his great weakness, he was as devoted as ever to the other suffering people who begged him to pray on their behalf. In his heart there was always room for another's pain. Even when his own illness troubled him, he rejoiced whenever he heard about another sick person who had been cured.

One of his *gabbaim* slept in the Rebbe's room during that final year. He related that, at about 2 a.m. one night, he was awakened by a soft voice. Opening his eyes, the *gabbai* saw the ill, weak Rebbe standing beside his bed.

"Rebbe!" cried the *gabbai*, aghast. "Why is the Rebbe up so late at night? Is something hurting him — is that what woke the Rebbe up?"

The Rebbe gave him a gentle, reassuring glance. "Forgive me for waking you," he said. "But tell me — do you happen to remember the name of the mother of the woman who came here, asking me to *daven* urgently for her recovery?"

Pens and Ink

הָבוּ לָכֶם אֲנָשִׁים חֲכָמִים וּנְבֹנִים וִידֻעִים לְשִׁבְטֵיכֶם וַאֲשִׂימֵם בְּרָאשֵׁיכֶם

"Provide yourselves men who are wise and understanding and well known to your tribes, and I shall appoint them as your heads."

(Devarim 1:13)

R' Shlomo Zalman Porush of Jerusalem was a dedicated worker on behalf of his community. In the year 5630 (1870), he founded the large *Chevras Sha'arei Chesed Gemach* (free-loan fund), which he managed for eighteen years without receiving any salary or reward.

One day, when the fund's *gabbaim* were looking over the books, they noticed that no expenses had been listed for paper or writing implements over a period of five years. They went to R' Shlomo Zalman to ask for an explanation.

R' Shlomo Zalman was forced to reveal that he had paid these expenses out of his own pocket, in order to avoid the suspicion of using community funds. Because he might occasionally make a mistake and use one of the *gemach's* pens, ink, or paper to write a personal letter, he preferred to personally bear the entire expense for such items.

A Judge's Wisdom

וָאֲצַוֶּה אֶת שֹׁפְטֵיכֶם בָּעֵת הַהִוא לֵאמֹר שָׁמֹעַ בֵּין אֲחֵיכֶם וּשְׁפַטְתֶּם צֶדֶק בֵּין אִישׁ וּבֵין אָחִיו

"I commanded your judges at that time, saying, 'Listen among your brothers and judge righteously between a man and his brother'"

(Devarim 1:16)

Two men came to a *din Torah* before R' Binyamin Diskin, *Av Beis Din* of Volkovisk and the father of R' Yehoshua Leib Diskin. Both men gave the Rav the sum of 5,000 rubles to hold until the verdict was handed down.

A few days later, one of the litigants came with an unusual request. Because of an unexpected development, he urgently needed 3,000 rubles immediately. He promised to return the money within two days.

The Rav looked at him, and was silent.

"Doesn't the Rav believe me?" the man pressed. "He can rest assured that the money will be back in his hands within two days!"

"I believe you," R' Binyamin Diskin replied. "But the other litigant in your case was here before you. He came here yesterday — and also asked for 3,000 rubles for a few days, promising to return it without delay."

"*What?*" the man screamed, outraged. "Is it permitted to take money that was left in the Rav's keeping until the *din Torah* is ended?"

"Never!" the Rabbi smiled. "And that's why I didn't give him what he wanted."

Hiding his burning face, the man turned and left at once.

There was a rule in the Hungarian Kollel: Any member of the *kollel* who was about to marry off a child would receive ten gold napoleons as the *kollel's* contribution to the wedding expenses.

When R' Yosef Chaim Sonnenfeld was getting ready to marry off one of his sons, the treasurer forgot to give him the set-upon amount. The wedding date drew near, but R' Yosef Chaim had no money to pay for anything. Although he generally shied away from borrowing money, this time he had no choice. He was forced to go to a number of places in order to secure a loan to pay for the wedding.

On the day of the wedding, the *kollel's* treasurer suddenly remembered that he had not given R' Yosef Chaim the money that was due him for the wedding expenses. He sent the *shamash* to R' Yosef Chaim's house at once, with the money, and instructions to apologize profusely about the oversight.

The *shamash* was astounded when R' Yosef Chaim handed him back the money, saying, "This does not belong to me. This sum is meant to ease the burden of the needy, to help them pay for their children's weddings. But I have already paid all my expenses. So what if I owe money? This grant was not intended for repaying debts."

Justice Is Blind

לֹא תַכִּירוּ פָנִים בַּמִשְׁפָּט

"You shall not show favoritism in judgment"
(Devarim 1:17)

"When litigants stand before you, they should be as wicked men
in your eyes." (Avos 1:8)

R' Shimon HaLevi Epstein of Warsaw had a business partner by the name of R' Koppel Halperin. Once, when they were in Bialystok, a misunderstanding arose between them due to an unclear clause in their partnership contract. The two went to a *din Torah* before the city's Rabbi, the *gaon* and author of the *Mar'os Hatzov'os*.

The two men asked the *shamash* to let the Rav know that they had come to him for a *din Torah*. The Rav permitted them to enter his room.

As they walked into the room, they saw that the Rav had pulled his *tallis* over his head until it covered his eyes. He did not shake their hands or invite them to sit, but merely said coldly, "Shimon and Koppel, which one of you is the plaintiff? Let him state his claims first!"

At this cold reception, the two men became afraid. They were also insulted, as both were well-known supporters of Torah. But they tried to swallow their hurt feelings and stated their claims.

When they were done, the Rav handed down his verdict. Then he said, "Shimon, Koppel, do you accept the judgment?"

Both men said, "Yes!"

Then the Rav lifted the *tallis* from his eyes, thrust out a hand to shake theirs warmly, and called for refreshments for his guests. R' Shimon and R' Koppel were extremely taken aback at this turnaround.

The Rav explained. "Our Sages, may their memories be blessed, told us in *Maseches Avos*: 'When litigants stand before you, they shall be as wicked men in your eyes. And when they are finished with you, they should be as innocent men in your eyes, as they have accepted judgment.' If a judge welcomes litigants as though they are *tzaddikim*, they may take advantage of this and exaggerate their claims beyond the strict truth, thus damaging justice. When something touches upon the honor of the Torah and of maintaining justice, there is no greatness and no importance before Hashem!"

A Greater Fear

לֹא תָגוּרוּ מִפְּנֵי אִישׁ כִּי הַמִּשְׁפָּט לֵאלֹקִים הוּא

"You shall not fear in the face of man, for the judgment, it is unto G-d"

(Devarim 1:17)

During the Ba'al Shem Tov's lifetime, his disciple, the Maggid of Mezritch, once presided at a *din Torah* in which a relative of the Ba'al Shem Tov was suing another man. While the *din Torah* was going on, the Ba'al Shem Tov came into the room. The mere sight of his rebbe made the Maggid of Mezritch fear that there was now a breath of a suspicion of bias in his heart toward his rebbe's relative. Without hesitation, he declared, "With the authority of this court, I decree that anyone who does not have to be in this room at this time should leave!"

Despite his tremendous awe and respect for the Ba'al Shem Tov, the Maggid's fear of Heaven was even greater.

During a year of drought and hunger in Eretz Yisrael, the Jews there decided to send a messenger abroad to ask their brothers in other countries to donate money to help them in their difficult situation. The man they sent was R' Yaakov Shimshon of Shepitovka. He set off at once for Istanbul, Turkey, where he was received with great honor.

The local Rav welcomed R' Yaakov Shimshon, and then related a difficult problem. A certain rich man was engaged in a *din Torah* with another person, and the rich man had produced a letter from the king commanding the Rav to acquit him, even if the Rav judged him to be the guilty party.

"I don't know what to do," the Rav said. "If I judge against the man, I will be acting against the king's orders. And if I acquit him, it may not be true justice according to the Torah."

"Inform the king that a greater rabbi than you has come to town," R' Yaakov Shimshon suggested, "and that I will judge the

case." But the rich man soon brought a second letter from the king, demanding that the second Rav, too, acquit him.

R' Yaakov Shimshon paid no attention. He judged the case, and found the rich man guilty. The king sent for R' Yaakov Shimshon, inviting dignitaries from various foreign countries to come at the same time. When R' Yaakov Shimshon arrived at the palace, the king demanded, "How is it that you were not afraid to act against the king's orders?"

R' Yaakov Shimshon opened a *Chumash* and read from *Parashas Devarim* (1:17): "You shall not fear in the face of man, for the judgment, it is unto G-d." He went on to explain the *pasuk* with wonderful logic, until the king and all the foreign representatives were satisfied. Though they came from different countries and spoke different languages, R' Yaakov Shimshon's words made sense to them all, and found favor in every heart.

First Day on the Job

לֹא תָגוּרוּ מִפְּנֵי אִישׁ

"You shall not fear in the face of man"

(Devarim 1:17)

The book *Madregas HaAdam* tells the story of R' Raphael HaKohen, who was still a young man when appointed Chief Rabbi of Hamburg. On his first day in that city, a woman came to him saying that she had a legal dispute with one of Hamburg's foremost citizens.

"Is it possible for you to wait until tomorrow?" R' Raphael asked her. "I am tired from my journey."

But the woman had a host of reasons why the *din Torah* must be attended to that very day.

The young Rabbi called his *shamash* and said, "Go to So-and-So's house and tell him that he is summoned to a *din Torah* with this woman."

The *shamash* fell into a panic at the thought of the rich man's reaction to the summons. But R' Raphael urged him to go at once.

Trembling and weak-kneed, the *shamash* set out. When he arrived at the rich man's home, his fear grew so powerful that he found it impossible to go in. He began pacing to and fro in front of the courtyard, until the owner of the house saw him and came out.

What are you doing here?" the man asked.

The *shamash* stammered out his mission: "The Rabbi sent me to summon your honor to a *din Torah*."

The rich man sent back a message of his own: "Go tell the Rabbi that I'll come another time."

The messenger returned to the Rabbi with the rich man's answer. R' Raphael turned to the woman and asked if she agreed to a postponement. But the woman said impatiently, "Please do not delay. It's so hard for me to wait!"

The rabbi sent his *shamash* a second time. "Tell him that the woman is not willing to wait, and therefore I command him to come here today!"

The *shamash* was terrified. Hamburg's prominent citizens were not used to being spoken to in this way, and were certainly not prepared to tolerate it. But the *shamash* had no choice. He returned to the rich man's house. Like the time before, the words stuck in his throat.

"Well? What did the Rabbi say?" the rich man demanded.

"The woman does not agree to wait. The Rabbi says you should come to his house today."

The rich man grew furious. Insolently, he told the *shamash*, "Go tell the Rabbi that I am the richest man in Hamburg, while he is still only a guest here. He does not yet know the people in this place. If I say that I'll come when I have time, then I will keep my word!"

The poor *shamash* returned to the Rabbi with this message. The Rabbi stood up, saying, "Go at once and tell him that it is true that he is the richest man in Hamburg. However, if I tell him to come today, he is obligated to come specifically today. If not, I have a means at my disposal. It is called *cherem* — and I can transmit that to him through you!"

Hearing these harsh words, the *shamash* grew limp with fear. He begged the Rabbi to send someone else in his place. But the Rabbi was adamant. The *shamash* was to go, and make all possible haste.

Seeing that there was no way out, the *shamash* collected his courage and went to the rich man's house for a third time. Eyes lowered to the ground in fear and embarrassment, he managed to pass on the Rabbi's message. The moment the words were out of his mouth, he turned and fled, shaking from head to toe.

A short time later, the rich man appeared at the Rabbi's door.

Extending a hand to the young Rabbi, he boomed out, "Mazal tov! Mazal tov! Your honor is indeed worthy of being our city's Chief Rabbi. I can now reveal the truth. I am not being sued, nor is that woman suing me. This whole matter was a kind of test. We, the community supporters, were afraid that the Rabbi's youth would make him incapable of keeping the law of 'Do not fear in the face of any man,' especially since our city has a number of wealthy and powerful individuals. That is why we decided to test the Rabbi by this summons to a *din Torah*.

"Now we have seen that the Rabbi is not deterred by difficulty and unpleasantness. We have seen how he fulfilled the Torah's command without any problem. He is indeed worthy of serving as our rabbi!"

Mud on the Scales

כִּי הַמִּשְׁפָּט לֵאלֹקִים הוּא
"For the judgment, it is unto G-d"
(Devarim 1:17)

R' Yisrael of Ruzhin once visited a certain town, and he stayed at the home of the town's richest citizen. The many chassidim who came to see the Rebbe tracked mud and dirt into the house, making the rich man furious.

"I will tell you a story," R' Yisrael said. "In a certain village, there lived a destitute Jew, the father of six children, who also supported his elderly parents. All winter long he hardly made any money, and when Pesach approached he had nothing with which to prepare for the holiday. He decided to travel to the city and see what he could earn. Hashem helped him, and he managed to earn six gold coins to use for baking matzos for Pesach. He set out at once for his home in the village.

"On the way, the wagon he was riding on sank into the mud. Much as the poor horse struggled, it was unable to pull the wheels out again. Soon a wealthy Jew passed by in his carriage. Seeing the poor man's plight, the rich man took him into his own carriage and drove him home.

"When the rich man saw the hovel that the poor man called home, he gave him the staggering sum of 600 gold coins, to buy a decent house and to make a proper Pesach. Then the rich man traveled on to his own home — where, just a few hours later, he died.

"When that man came to the Heavenly Court, he was asked, 'Were your business dealings honest?' Angels came from all sides to relate various sins that the man had committed over the course of his life. The Court was about to send him to *Gehinnom*, when another angel came along and said, 'How is it possible to send a man like this to *Gehinnom*? A person who sustains one life is considered as though he sustained a whole world — and this man saved tens of Jewish souls from poverty.'

"The Court ordered the man's mitzvos to be placed on one side of the scale, and his sins on the other — and they saw that the sins outweighed the good deeds. What did the good angel do? He hurried to bring the mud in which the poor man's wagon had sunk. That single good deed tipped the scales in the man's favor.

"You see," R' Yisrael told his wealthy host, "sometimes, even a Jew's mud and dirt can save him from *Gehinnom*."

R' Isaac Lefkowitz, who lived in Margareten, traveled to Ratzfert every year to see his rebbe, R' Sholom Eliezer. People from his hometown would give him *kvittlach* (notes with requests for prayers) to take along, asking the Rebbe to bless them and to remember them in his prayers.

Once, just before the outbreak of World War Two, R' Isaac was preparing to set out for his rebbe as usual when R' Chaim Goldberg, a well-known lumber merchant, came to see him. He asked R' Isaac to take along a *kvittel* and to tell the Rebbe that he was in dire straits and needed help in the most urgent way.

"Eight years ago," R' Chaim related, "together with my partner, a fellow lumber merchant, I bought a large tract of forest from one of the local *poritzim* (noblemen). This year, we were about to cut down the trees and sell them all in this country and to neighboring ones as well."

But the Nazis' influence was already strong here in Romania, and among its other evil decrees the government has banned the sale of forest land to Jews. When he learned of this new law, the *poritz* asked the courts to nullify his contract with the Jewish lumber merchants and to make them return all his land to him.

The Jews' lawyer argued that the law applied only from the day it had been put into effect, and did not apply to a business deal that had taken place eight years earlier. But the anti-Semitic judges ruled that the *poritz* was to return the money that the Jews had paid him and that the Jewish merchants were to return the property. This ruling was a terrible one for the Jewish merchants, as the value of Romanian money had dropped greatly. With the amount of money they were to receive, they'd be able to buy no more than a pair of shoes!

The merchants appealed the ruling to the highest court in the land, and were now anxiously awaiting the verdict. Concluding his story, R' Chaim said to R' Isaac, "Please, tell the Rebbe my story and ask him to *daven* that those wicked men will have no hold over me or my property."

When R' Isaac arrived in Ratzfert, he handed R' Chaim Goldberg's *kvittel* to R' Sholom Eliezer and told him the whole story of the lumber merchant's troubles. The Rebbe read the *kvittel*, then turned to R' Isaac and said, "Tell the partners that they should send me a wagonload of wood to heat the *beis midrash* for the winter, and I guarantee that they will win their case."

On his return home, R' Isaac hurried to tell R' Chaim the good news: The Rebbe had promised that he would not be hurt in the lawsuit, but he must send a wagonload of wood for the *beis midrash*. R' Chaim agreed at once, but since he was not alone in this business venture he went to consult with his partner.

The partner, who was not Torah observant, rejected R' Chaim's request at once. "Isn't it enough that I stand in danger of losing everything? Shall I also lose a wagonload of wood? If you want, send all the wood at your own expense. For my part, I won't send a thing!"

Immediately, R' Chaim sent half a wagonload of lumber to Ratzfert. A few days later, the verdict from the high court was handed down: The merchant Chaim Goldberg could keep his half of the forest, while his partner was to be paid his share of the money and return his share of the land. In his explanation of the ruling, the judge wrote that Chaim Goldberg was a longtime lumber merchant who had worked in the business for many years. It was clear that the *poritz* had sold him the forest permanently and could not rescind the deal now. The second partner, however, was a speculator with many dubious lines of business. He had bought his half of the forest only for the moment, in order to speculate with it and turn a quick profit. Therefore, he must return the land and get his money back for it.

This ruling had a powerful impact on the Jewish community, who witnessed firsthand the Rebbe's influence and the power of his blessings.

A Pile of Dirt

וַיִּפְנוּ וַיַּעֲלוּ הָהָרָה

"They turned and ascended the mountain"

(Devarim 1:24)

R' Avraham, son of the Maggid of Mezritch, arrived in a certain city. When the chassidim came to visit him, they found R' Avraham standing by an open window, looking out at a tall mountain standing opposite the window.

An arrogant man turned to the Rebbe and asked, "Why do you stare at a mountain which is nothing more than a pile of dirt?"

"I am amazed," the Rebbe replied, "how a simple pile of dirt like that can be so proud that it has fashioned itself into a tall mountain!"

The man took the hint.

He Couldn't Sleep

אִם יִרְאֶה אִישׁ בָּאֲנָשִׁים הָאֵלֶּה הַדּוֹר הָרָע הַזֶּה אֵת הָאָרֶץ הַטּוֹבָה אֲשֶׁר נִשְׁבַּעְתִּי לָתֵת לַאֲבֹתֵיכֶם

"If even a man of these people, this evil generation, shall see the good land that I swore to give to your forefathers."

(Devarim 1:35)

It is said that whenever R' Mordechai Leib Kaminetzky happened to wake up at night — even if it was just an hour after he had gone to bed — he would immediately get out of bed and sit down to learn Torah till morning. Once, when asked about the meaning of this custom, he replied simply, "What is there to be so surprised about?"

He went on to explain that, in his youth, he was stricken with a serious illness, so serious that he was near death. The doctors despaired of finding a way to save him — but Hashem willed otherwise. R' Mordechai Leib recovered completely.

"I learned an important lesson from that episode," he said. "I deserved to die at that point, but Heaven put off the decree for a later time."

He went on to speak of the generation of the *midbar*, who sinned in believing the spies who spoke badly about Eretz Yisrael. The people dug holes in the ground and laid down in them on Tishah B'Av night to wait for Hashem to take away their lives. Many of them probably fell asleep in those holes. When they awoke in the middle of the night and saw that they were still alive, they understood that they would continue to live for another year.

Did they remain in their holes till morning? Of course not! They jumped out at once, and dedicated to Torah the year of life they had been granted.

"That same feeling comes over me every night," R' Mordechai Leib concluded, smiling. "When I wake up and see that I'm still alive, I can't just go back to sleep. I jump out of my bed at once, and learn Torah till the morning light."

The Plot

לֹא תִּירָאוּם כִּי ד׳ אֱלֹקֵיכֶם הוּא הַנִּלְחָם לָכֶם

"You shall not fear them, for Hashem, your G-d — He is the One Who shall wage war for you."

(Devarim 3:22)

A Jewish villager — a grain merchant by trade — faced stiff competition from a gentile *poritz* who created all sorts of difficulties for him. One day the *poritz* and his assistant came to the Jew's office. The Jewish merchant offered them food and drink. When his host wasn't looking, the *poritz* secretly slipped a few drops of poison into his assistant's drink. Within a few seconds, the man was writhing in pain, and soon died.

The *poritz* jumped up and accused the Jewish merchant of poisoning his assistant and of doubtless having plans to poison him as well. He ran to bring this accusation to the authorities. Knowing the tremendous danger facing him, the Jew fled to Hornsteipel to see his rebbe, R' Mordechai Dov.

The Rebbe listened to the story of the false accusation of murder without blinking an eye. The villager stayed with him for several days, with no idea about how he would ever be able to return home.

"Rebbe," he said, "what will be with me?"

"You will travel home by ship — in a first-class cabin."

No one understood the meaning of these mysterious instructions, but the merchant totally believed in his rebbe's wisdom. He went at once and bought a first-class ticket on a ship bound for his hometown. Only high officials and men of power and authority generally traveled first class. The Jewish merchant climbed aboard, wondering how this trip was going to save him from the danger in which he stood.

With a broken heart, amid a sea of tears, he stood on the first-class deck and *davened Minchah*. In Hashem's mercy, traveling with him in that very same first-class section of the ship were the pathologist and police inspector who had been sent to look into the poisoning of the *poritz's* assistant. Seeing the brokenhearted Jew at his prayers, they went over to him and asked, "What is the matter? Why are you crying?"

In his innocence, the merchant poured out the story. With touching directness, he convinced the two that he was innocent — a victim of the *poritz's* malicious plot to bring him down. The doctor and the police inspector believed him and made up their minds to save the innocent man.

On their arrival in the village, the two officials pretended to be fellow grain merchants. They visited the *poritz*, supposedly to discuss a business deal. The three sat chatting for a long time, until the *poritz* passed the whiskey around. Under the alcohol's influence, the *poritz's* tongue was loosened.

"I've got a Jewish competitor and would love to get rid of him," one of the pretend "merchants" remarked.

"Learn from me," chuckled the *poritz*. "I also suffer from a Jewish competitor, and here's what I did ..."

As soon as they heard the *poritz's* confession, the two men began to do everything in their power to bring the truth to light — until the Jewish merchant was acquitted of all wrongdoing.

פרשת ואתחנן

Parashas Va'eschanan

The Clue of the Mule

כִּי הוּא חָכְמַתְכֶם וּבִינַתְכֶם לְעֵינֵי הָעַמִּים אֲשֶׁר יִשְׁמְעוּן אֵת כָּל הַחֻקִּים
הָאֵלֶּה וְאָמְרוּ רַק עַם חָכָם וְנָבוֹן הַגּוֹי הַגָּדוֹל הַזֶּה

"For it is your wisdom and understanding in the eyes of the peo-ples, who shall hear all these statutes and who shall say, 'Surely a wise and understanding people is this great nation!'"

(Devarim 4:6)

A quarrel once broke out between two Arabs in Tunis. They owned adjoining properties, with a line of fruit trees growing along the border between them. One of the Arabs left town for a few days, and on his return was appalled to find that the trees had been uprooted. His neighbor had widened his own field, taking a portion of the first Arab's land.

The newly-returned Arab was furious. "Thief!" he shouted. "Look what you've done. You have uprooted the fruit trees, and also moved onto my property!"

"I, a thief?" his neighbor exclaimed. "I did not uproot any fruit trees. This piece of land where I have set up my tent has always belonged to me!"

Angry words soon gave way to an actual fist fight. Afterwards, the two Arabs remained locked in a bitter feud. They decided at last to bring their quarrel to the local governor, who found himself at a loss as to how to solve it. The governor, in turn, brought the matter to the king's attention.

The king listened to both sides — and was also stumped. It was impossible to know where true justice lay.

"There is one man who can answer this question," the king declared. "R' Yitzchak Chai Taib, Chief Rabbi of Tunis!"

The king had the Rabbi summoned, and placed the matter before him.

"Do you own a mule?" R' Yitzchak asked the wronged Arab.

"Yes," the man replied, wondering where the Rabbi's thoughts were leading. He went home at once, with R' Yitzchak and a large contingent following. The mule was brought out.

Mules have an interesting trait, of which R' Yitzchak was aware. A mule will only enter a field that belongs to its master. It will simply not walk into a stranger's field! The mule trotted over the field — and suddenly stopped.

"You must dig here!" the Rabbi announced.

Stunned, all those present took up shovels and began to dig. They dug and dug ... until they hit the roots of a tree that had been uprooted on that very spot!

In this way, the innocent Arab had his property returned to him.

Deeply moved by the Rabbi's wisdom, he later went to R' Yitzchak's home to present him with a gift.

"If I were to accept presents from people," R' Yitzchak said, "I would not be fit to render rulings!" And he adamantly refused to accept any gift from the man whom he had helped to find justice.

The Final Journey

וְשַׁבְתָּ עַד ד' אֱלֹקֶיךָ וְשָׁמַעְתָּ בְּקֹלוֹ

"You will return unto Hashem, your G-d, and listen to His voice"

(Devarim 4:30)

R' Moshe Yitzchak Darshan served as the Maggid of Kelm for fifty years. His influence was widespread. Everyone was afraid of his rebuke, and all respected him.

One day, the Maggid came to the city of Dubolon, a health resort near Riga. In the summers, the Jews of Riga would come there to bathe in the sea. Entering the local shul, the Maggid saw that many of the worshipers were not wearing *talleisim.*

The Maggid climbed up to the dais, turned to the assembly, and said, "*Rabbosai,* let me tell you a true story. One Shabbos, I was in Riga. I went to visit a certain Jew there, and was told that he was not at home.

"'Where is he?' I asked.

"'He's gone to Dubolon.'

"Suddenly, I heard the sound of weeping coming from the next room. Going in, I saw that the room was empty, except for a *tallis* lying in one corner. It was the *tallis* that was crying!

"'*Tallis*,' I asked, 'why are you crying?'

"'Wouldn't *you* cry?' the *tallis* said. 'My owner has gone to Dubolon. He took along gold and silver — but left me here, all alone!'

"I comforted the *tallis*, saying, 'Do not cry. The day will come when your owner will set out on a longer journey than this one. Then he will leave behind all his gold and all his silver, and will take only *you* along with him!'"

R' Sholom Schwadron, the Maggid of Jerusalem, told the following story:

There was a student in the yeshivah at Radin who got drunk one Purim. In his intoxication, he went over to the Chofetz Chaim's house and told him, "Rebbe, I am not going to leave you alone until you promise me that I will sit near you in *Gan Eden*!"

The members of the Chofetz Chaim's household tried to remove the boy from the house, but the youth would not budge. Finally, the Chofetz Chaim said, "Listen, my son, I will fulfill your request and promise what you want — on one condition. For sixty years now, I have been scrupulous in staying away from *lashon hara*. If you wish to be near me in *Gan Eden*, promise me that you will do the same thing!"

Hearing these words, the student said a hasty "good-bye" and left the house.

R' Sholom Schwadron ended: "Had that young man considered the matter, roused himself to be better, and declared, 'Rebbe, I will do whatever you command me,' he would have been helped from Above. He would have merited achieving higher and higher levels, and to bask in *Gan Eden* near the Chofetz Chaim himself."

A chassid once came to R' Bunim of Peshischa and asked, "I read in *sefarim* that anyone who fasts for forty days will merit seeing

Eliyahu HaNavi. I have already fasted more than forty fasts and have not had this privilege. Why?"

R' Bunim replied: "The Ba'al Shem Tov often experienced *kefitzas haderech* in his travels. His horses noticed a curious thing. They were galloping right past the places where they usually stopped to be fed, but they did not feel hungry! The horses began to believe that they had turned into human beings. As they continued running and still were not hungry, they began to think that they were angels!

"At last, they arrived at their destination. Entering the stables, they began to eat ravenously. Only then did they realize, to their disappointment, that they were still horses.

"When you sit and fast," R' Bunim continued, "you believe that you have reached the level of a towering *tzaddik*. Another fast, and you feel as though you've achieved the level of an angel ... But stop a moment, and think: How do you behave *after* the fast? You return to your plain, everyday self. The fast, in other words, did not elevate you at all. That is why you have not merited seeing Eliyahu HaNavi.

"The goal of fasting is repentance and elevation — through which it is possible to attain mighty spiritual heights!"

The Rebbe Sings

כִּי אָהַב אֶת אֲבֹתֶיךָ וַיִּבְחַר בְּזַרְעוֹ אַחֲרָיו

"Because He loved your forefathers, and He chose his offspring after him"

(Devarim 4:37)

When R' Yisrael of Modzhitz was hospitalized in Berlin, he was attended to and operated on by a surgeon named Professor Israels. The surgeon remarked to R' Yisrael, "I just gave you a compliment. There's a certain non-Jewish government minister here in the hospital who keeps screaming in pain. I told him that there is a Jewish rabbi here whose suffering is greater than his, yet he sings and is peaceful."

R' Yisrael replied, "I, too, scream in pain. But Jewish cries should not be made in vain. Therefore, I attach them to song — to honor our Creator!"

No Hardship at All

וְזֹאת הַתּוֹרָה אֲשֶׁר שָׂם מֹשֶׁה לִפְנֵי בְּנֵי יִשְׂרָאֵל

"This is the teaching that Moshe placed before the Children of Israel."

(Devarim 4:44)

R' Dovid Moshe of Chortkov was a physically weak man, yet on Simchas Torah he would hold a *sefer Torah* and dance with it for a very long time. Though exhausted, he would not give up the Torah.

His chassidim, fearful for the Rebbe's health, asked him, "Isn't it hard for you to keep holding the *sefer Torah?*"

"Before picking up the *sefer Torah* in my arms," the Rebbe replied, "it was hard for me. But once I am already holding it and dancing with it, it is no longer hard at all!"

R' Yitzchak of Vorka suffered from financial hardship. Because he lacked a large sum of money, he expected to lose his leasing rights. Together with a friend, he searched for a loan. But despite all their efforts, they came away empty-handed.

R' Yitzchak asked his friend to come to the *beis midrash* with him. He opened a Gemara and said, "There is a *Maharsha* here that I'm finding hard to understand. Let's try to get to the bottom of it together." The two sat learning for several hours, until they finally understood the *Maharsha's* meaning.

R' Yitzchak's friend marveled, "How is it possible for you to concentrate on your learning in spite of all your troubles?"

"On the contrary," R' Yitzchak replied, "when all of a person's thoughts and worries are wrapped up in one great concern, it's easy to take them all and devote them to the study of Torah!"

The Chasam Sofer Finds a Way

כַּבֵּד אֶת אָבִיךָ וְאֶת אִמֶּךָ

"Honor your father and your mother"

(Devarim 5:16)

R' Moshe Sofer, the Chasam Sofer, was the spiritual leader of Hungarian Jewry. He taught Torah at his yeshivah in Pressburg, guiding his large community in the ways of Torah and piety.

The Chasam Sofer had an elderly mother who lived in Frankfurt. The two had not seen each other for a long time, as she lived in Germany and he in Hungary. Near the end of her life, the mother asked to see her son before she died.

The Chasam Sofer wanted with all his heart to see his mother and to fulfill the mitzvah of honoring her, but he was afraid of the spiritual damage that might result from his prolonged absence from his community. Unsure of how to resolve his dilemma, the Chasam Sofer sent the question to the *beis din* in Frankfurt-am-Mein.

"What is the opinion of the Torah: Should the Chasam Sofer travel to visit his mother because of the mitzvah of *kibbud em*, or is he not obligated to go because of the *bitul Torah* that will result for many people who depend on him?"

This was the *beis din's* answer:

"The Torah learning of many takes precedence! If R' Moshe leaves Hungary, the yeshivah students are liable to slacken off in their learning, and the community's spiritual needs will also suffer from the Rav's absence."

Thus guided, the Chasam Sofer remained at home. Still, he felt a powerful urge to give his mother *nachas* and pleasure, to honor her and gladden her heart. How could he do this while so far away from her?

Then he found a way. The Chasam Sofer sent a wise and pious man by the name of R' Ber Frank to visit his mother, to ask her how she was faring and to tell her anything she wanted to know about her son.

When the mother saw R' Ber, she understood at once that her son had sent him to her. Shewelcomed him joyously, and asked about the Chasam Sofer's welfare. R' Ber told the aged woman all about her son, about his greatness in Torah and his tremendous goodness.

The mother was very happy with the messenger's visit — and was glad, too, that her son was unable to free himself in order to visit her, being busy day and night with spreading Torah and strengthening *Yiddishkeit*!

Listening to Mother

כַּבֵּד אֶת אָבִיךָ וְאֶת אִמֶּךָ כַּאֲשֶׁר צִוְּךָ ד' אֱלֹקֶיךָ לְמַעַן יַאֲרִיכֻן יָמֶיךָ וּלְמַעַן יִיטַב לָךְ

"Honor your father and your mother, as Hashem, your G-d, commanded you, so that your days will be lengthened and so that it will be good for you"

(Devarim 5:16)

The two holy brothers, R' Shmelke of Nikolsburg and R' Pinchas, author of the *Hafla'ah*, once went to see their mother, who lived in the city of Chernov. They thought it best to travel together, in order to gladden her heart and give her the honor she deserved.

The mother was overjoyed to read her sons' telegram announcing the date of their arrival. The news of their coming quickly spread throughout the town: "Have you heard? The holy brothers are coming! Let's go out and welcome them!"

The Jews of Chernov were gripped with excitement. From everywhere, people began streaming out to welcome the great *tzaddikim*, some on foot, and others by train.

When the mother heard about the tremendous honor that was soon to be heaped on her sons' heads, she sent off a messenger with an urgent message: "My sons, I am ordering you in the name of *kibbud av v'em*: Return home, and do not come to visit me!"

Everyone was aghast at this request. The mother explained: "I do not want to enjoy my sons' honor in this world. I prefer to receive my full reward in the World to Come!"

When the brothers received the message from their mother, they obeyed her at once, without question. Hard as it was for them to give up their visit, they turned around and went home. That was their mother's wish. If a mother orders her children not to come see her, then not seeing her is *kibbud em*!

A Last Request

שְׁמַע יִשְׂרָאֵל ד' אֱלֹקִינוּ ד' אֶחָד

"Hear, O Israel: Hashem our G-d, Hashem is One"

(Devarim 6:4)

A student of R' Yehudah Assad was once walking in the heart of the forest when an outlaw leaped out at him and wanted to murder him. The student pleaded for his life, but the murderer refused to listen.

Believing that his end was near, the student begged the murderer to give him time to prepare for his departure from this world, by saying *Viduy* and *Kerias Shema*. After much pleading, the murderer grudgingly allowed him fifteen minutes.

The student began by closing his eyes and reciting the *Shema* with tremendous concentration and fervor. When he was done, he opened his eyes fearfully — to find that the murderer was gone!

The student hurried away. The first thing he did was to go to his rebbe, to ask for an explanation of this amazing incident.

When R' Yehudah heard the story, he asked, "Tell me, have you recited the *Shema* with such enthusiasm before, even once in your life? You should know that Heaven wanted to teach you a lesson about the proper way to say *Kerias Shema*. Every person must accept the yoke of Heaven as though this were the final time in his life that he could say the *Shema*!"

With All Your Possessions

וְאָהַבְתָּ אֵת ד' אֱלֹקֶיךָ בְּכָל לְבָבְךָ וּבְכָל נַפְשְׁךָ וּבְכָל מְאֹדֶךָ

"You shall love Hashem, your G-d, with all your heart, with all your soul, and with all your possessions."

(Devarim 6:5)

R' Moshe Feinstein once participated in a trip to raise money to build a *mikveh*. The fund-raising tour took several hours. As the time passed, R' Moshe's companion realized that R' Moshe was becoming tired. He suggested that they return home, but R' Moshe wanted to continue collecting money.

Knowing what an effort this was for R' Moshe, the companion searched for a way to persuade him to stop. All at once, an idea popped into his head. "The *Rosh Yeshivah* hasn't had enough time to learn today. Maybe we should go home?"

R' Moshe replied, "In *Kerias Shema* we are commanded to love Hashem with all our heart, with all our soul, and with all our possessions. *Chazal* explain that this means we must serve Hashem with such devotion that we are even prepared to sacrifice to Him that which is most precious to us!

"The most precious thing of all to me is Torah, and learning Torah is my greatest love. Therefore, I must sacrifice my learning when the needs of the Jewish people demand it!"

R' Nachum of Chernobyl once came to a small town and wanted to immerse himself in a kosher *mikveh*. The town's notables told him that there was no *mikveh*, as the town stood on a very high place and it would take a great deal of money to dig deep enough to find water or a spring. The townspeople were too poor to afford the job.

"Do you have just one rich man," the Rebbe asked, "who will be willing to purchase my share in the World to Come — the portion that has been awaiting me from the day of my birth to this moment — in exchange for building a kosher *mikveh* and keeping it warm at his own expense?"

At once, a rich man stepped forward and donated 300 gold coins in return for R' Nachum's share in *Gan Eden*. R' Nachum, in turn, gave the money to the townfolk for the purpose of building a kosher *mikveh*.

"Now I am satisfied," R' Nachum declared, "that I am not serving Hashem in order to receive reward, but only out of love and devotion to Him!"

"But how can a man like you give up your eternal life and sell your portion in *Gan Eden*?" they asked the Rebbe.

Wisely, R' Nachum answered, "On the contrary. Answer me this: How is it possible for a man like me, who has nothing in this world and considers nothing important here, to fulfill the commandment, 'and with all your possessions'? How can I save myself from testifying falsely twice each day when I read the portion, 'And you shall love Hashem, your G-d, with all ... your possessions'?"

He Finished Shas at Twelve

וְשִׁנַּנְתָּם לְבָנֶיךָ

"You shall teach them to your sons"

(Devarim 6:7)

A Jew brought his 8-year-old son to the Rebbe of Nikolsburg.

"Tell me," the Rebbe asked the child, "do you know the six volumes of *Mishnah* by heart?"

The boy, smiling in confusion, hung his head without answering.

"When I was your age, I knew the six volumes of *Mishnah* by heart," the Rebbe remarked.

The father ventured, "I hope that he will know the *shishah sidrei Mishnah* by heart at the age when the Rebbe knew all of *Shas*."

The Rebbe smiled. "It's a deal! Perhaps you are aware that I finished *Shas* for the first time at the age of 12?"

Timely Advice

וְדִבַּרְתָּ בָּם בְּשִׁבְתְּךָ בְּבֵיתֶךָ וּבְלֶכְתְּךָ בַדֶּרֶךְ וּבְשָׁכְבְּךָ וּבְקוּמֶךָ

"And you shall speak of them while you sit in your home and while you walk on the way, when you lie down and when you rise."

(Devarim 6:7)

The Chasam Sofer once traveled to Vienna in the company of a wealthy member of his community, a *talmid chacham* who usually spent a great deal of his time learning Torah. While they were in

Vienna together, the Chasam Sofer noted that his companion, busy with other matters, did not learn Torah at all. He rebuked the man for behaving differently in Vienna than he did at home.

The rich man apologized to the Chasam Sofer, saying that his many business affairs in the big city did not leave him time to learn.

The Chasam Sofer replied, "The Torah has the solution to your problem! It says, 'And you shall speak of them while you sit in your home' — when you, the businessman, sit at home, you must be involved in learning Torah every spare minute you can find. On the other hand, 'while you walk on your way' — when you are away from home on business, the Torah advises, 'when you lie down and when you rise' — devote the time before you go to sleep and the time after you rise from sleep to learning Torah. When you become accustomed to doing this, then all will be well with you!"

The Bonus

וְדִבַּרְתָּ בָּם בְּשִׁבְתְּךָ בְּבֵיתֶךָ וּבְלֶכְתְּךָ בַדֶּרֶךְ וּבְשָׁכְבְּךָ וּבְקוּמֶךָ

"And you shall speak of them while you sit in your home and while you walk on your way"

(Devarim 6:7)

It said that R' Reuven Zelig Bengis, Rabbi of Jerusalem, learned the entire *Shas* 101 times during the course of his life. As he would always review a page of Gemara four times, it turned out that he actually learned all of *Shas* 404 times!

Once, R' Reuven Zelig invited his relatives to a special *seudah* to celebrate his completion of learning *Shas*. His guests asked him, "How is this time different than the many other times you have completed *Shas*? You have completed *Shas* many times and you never invited us to a meal. Why have you seen fit to depart from your custom this time?"

"Today," the Rav replied, "we are talking about a very special kind of *siyum*. The *Shas* that I am completing today I learned during moments which I managed to steal from my spare time. For example, when forced to stand in lines in various places, I would use the time to learn *Shas*. Each time, I would continue from the place where I had stopped the time before.

"My happiness today, therefore, is especially great. I managed to use time that would otherwise have been lost to learn the entire *Shas*!"

The Businessman's Tefillin

וּקְשַׁרְתָּם לְאוֹת עַל יָדֶךָ וְהָיוּ לְטֹטָפֹת בֵּין עֵינֶיךָ

"Bind them as a sign upon your arm and let them be totafos be-tween your eyes."

(Devarim 6:8)

A few days before he departed this world, R' Chaim ben Attar, the author of *Ohr HaChaim,* summoned his wife and told her that if she found herself in financial difficulties after his death, she had his permission to sell his *tefillin* to a wealthy person who would pay a nice amount for them. But she was to warn the buyer that he must be careful to behave in a very holy manner while wearing the *tefillin*.

In the months following her husband's passing, the poor widow did not have enough money for food. Matters reached such a point that she was forced to sell the *tefillin*.

The man who bought them accepted the condition that the widow had stipulated, according to her late husband's wishes. When he put on the *tefillin,* he sensed himself becoming spiritually elevated. For many years he was careful to keep the promise that he had made to the *Ohr HaChaim's* widow.

One day, one of his clerks came to see him in the *beis midrash* to tell him about an important business proposal. The businessman had to decide about the proposal at once. Because he was still wearing the *Ohr HaChaim's* tefillin, however, he sent the clerk away, signaling him to wait until he had finished *davening*.

The clerk waved his arms urgently, to hint at the urgency of the matter. Enormous sums of money were at stake. The clerk pressed the rich man to stop *davening* for just a few minutes, so that he could listen to the proposal.

At last, the businessman yielded. He listened to the proposal, gave his decision, and returned to his prayers.

From that moment on, the man sensed that his *davening* was not going well. The *tefillin* that had aroused such spiritual sensitivity and enthusiasm in him, now felt as though a wall of steel blocked him from his Father in Heaven. Sorrowfully, he realized that the *tefillin* had been flawed by his actions and by his distraction from his prayers. The rich man took the *tefillin* to a *sofer stam* to be checked.

When the *sofer* opened up the *tefillin* and took out the *parashiyos*, he was greatly taken aback. The parchment was completely blank. The letters had vanished!

Only then did everyone see clearly how far the *Ohr HaChaim's* holiness had reached.

R' Yosef Chaim Sonnenfeld, who later became the Chief Rabbi of Jerusalem, was drafted into the army as a young man. He went to the Sanzer Rebbe, the Divrei Chaim, for a *berachah*.

The Divrei Chaim blessed him as follows: "Young man, do they want to make you a general in the army? You are wanted as a general in Eretz Yisrael!"

Then the Rebbe instructed R' Yosef Chaim to return home and wrap his hand in bandages.

R' Yosef Chaim traveled home. On the way, his left hand swelled up. He appeared before the draft board in this condition. Seeing his swollen and injured hand, they exempted him from army service at once.

By the time R' Yosef Chaim returned to the Pressburg Yeshivah, it was very late at night. Suddenly, his left hand began to ache terribly and to swell up even more. R' Yosef Chaim became worried that he would not be able to put his *tefillin* on that hand the next morning. His anxiety over this made him forget the pain he was suffering in his hand.

Because it was so late at night, he could not go to a doctor. The youth did not know where to turn. In desperation, he began to press the injured place with his good hand. As he did so, the wound burst open and a bloody discharge spurted out. R' Yosef Chaim continued to squeeze the wound until it stopped oozing.

The next day, upon waking, he saw that the wound had disappeared. Nevertheless, R' Yosef Chaim went to see a doctor. The

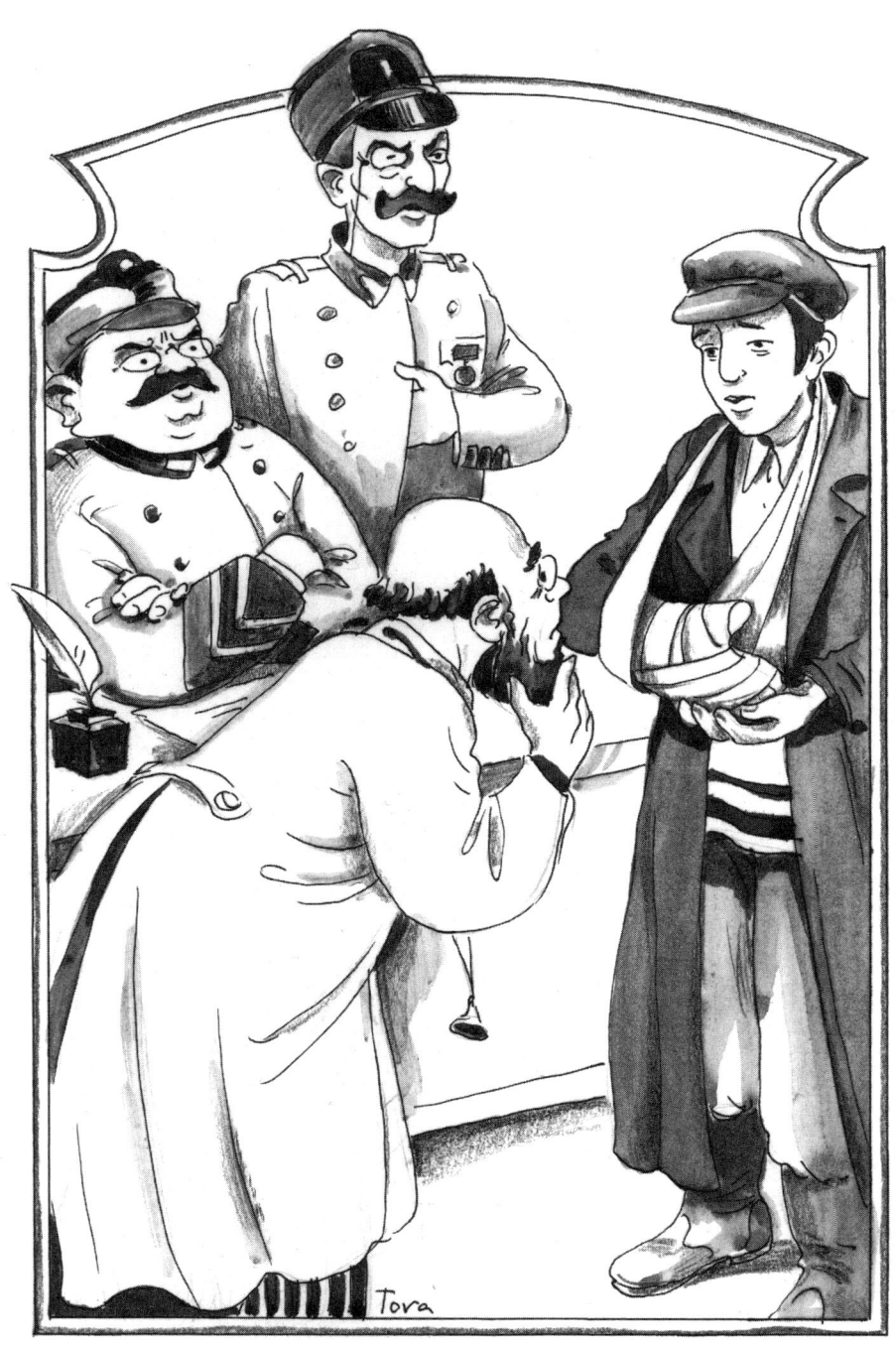

doctor told him that, had he not squeezed out the discharge the night before, the infection might have spread throughout his body. Now, he would be all right.

R' Yosef Chaim understood that his escape from danger had come about because of his concern about the mitzvah of *tefillin*.

The Stolen Wallet

אֶת ד' אֱלֹקֶיךָ תִּירָא וְאֹתוֹ תַעֲבֹד

"Hashem, your G-d, shall you fear, Him shall you serve"

(Devarim 6:13)

When the young Yechezkel Levenstein — later to become the *Mashgiach* of the Ponovizher Yeshivah — turned 13, his father wanted to send him to work in a flower shop, where he would earn money delivering flowers to the homes of the wealthy. But Heaven had decreed that R' Yechezkel would spread a different kind of beauty and bring the fragrance of faith and piety to the hearts of thousands.

Circumstances did force the youth to go to work. For a time he worked at various jobs and earned some money. But one Friday, when he went to bathe in the *mikveh*, his wallet was stolen, and inside it was all the money that he had earned.

R' Yechezkel drew an important lesson from this. "If this is the nature of money, that it can be taken away and stolen from a person at any moment, then it is not something worth losing one's life over!"

In that instant, he decided to devote his life to Torah.

A year later, he traveled to Radin to learn in the Chofetz Chaim's yeshivah. There he met R' Yerucham Levovitz, the *Mashgiach*. The first lecture that R' Yechezkel heard from the *Mashgiach* left a profound impression on him — an impression that was to last his whole life. He felt that it was impossible for him, or for anyone, to live without studying *mussar*.

And this became the direction he took for the rest of his life, as he guided others in the ways of *mussar*, purity and fear of Heaven.

The Oath

אֶת ד' אֱלֹקֶיךָ תִּירָא וְאֹתוֹ תַעֲבֹד וּבִשְׁמוֹ תִּשָּׁבֵעַ

*"Hashem, your G-d, shall you fear, Him shall you serve, and in
His Name shall you swear."*

(Devarim 6:13)

*"If all these traits are present in you, that you fear His Name and
you serve Him, then, 'in His Name you shall swear' — for as a result
of your fearing His Name, you will be careful of your oath."*

(Rashi)

R' Shlomo Zalman Porush was the founder of Jerusalem's large
Chevras Sha'arei Chesed Gemach (free-loan fund). He performed
his job with great dedication and honesty. In those days, the *gemach*
provided loans mainly to *kollels*. The *gemach* held notes in the bor-
rowers' names to guarantee repayment of the loans.

One day, R' Shlomo Zalman Porush visited a representative of a
certain *kollel*. He handed over the notes the *gemach* had been holding in the *kollel's* name, and asked for the money that was owed. But
the *kollel* man mistakenly believed that he had already paid back
the money and was now simply getting the notes back.

"No, it never happened!" R' Shlomo Zalman protested. "I did not
receive payment from you. I have come to collect that now!"

They brought the matter to the *beis din* of R' Shmuel Salant,
Chief Rabbi of Jerusalem. R' Shmuel ruled that R' Shlomo Zalman
must swear that he had not received the money.

When R' Shlomo Zalman heard this, he became very agitated.
"Please don't make me swear," he pleaded, "even though what I say
is true!"

But R' Shmuel Salant summoned R' Shlomo Zalman and decreed
that he must swear an oath. R' Shlomo Zalman still refused — and offered instead to pay the loss to the *gemach* out of his own pocket.

R' Shmuel Salant was not satisfied with this suggestion. "If you
pay back the money," he said, "the public may suspect your honesty. They may suspect that you actually did receive the money
from the *kollel*. Being a man with public responsibility, you are required to safeguard your reputation for honesty." R' Yehoshua Leib
Diskin agreed: R' Shlomo Zalman must swear.

A day was set up and an appointment made for R' Shlomo Zalman to make the oath. The day was a sorrowful one in the Porush home. The entire family fasted and wept bitterly. At last, R' Shlomo Zalman went to the big shul in R' Yehudah HaChassid Square, and swore an oath in the presence of R' Shmuel Salant, Chief Rabbi of Jerusalem.

Only hours later, R' Shlomo Zalman's honesty was proved beyond a shadow of a doubt. In the home of the *kollel* representative, his daughter found a bundle of money hidden in a secret place in the house. It seems that the money had been lost, and the others had mistakenly assumed that it had been paid. This mistake led to the swearing of an oath and a great deal of emotional anguish for R' Shlomo Zalman Porush and his family.

Beyond the Letter of the Law

וְעָשִׂיתָ הַיָּשָׁר וְהַטּוֹב בְּעֵינֵי ד' לְמַעַן יִיטַב לָךְ

"You shall do what is fair and good in the eyes of Hashem, so that it will be good for you"

(Devarim 6:18)

"This is compromise, [and] going to within the line of the law [i.e., going beyond what the law requires]."

(Rashi)

A woman once visited R' Meir of Premishlan to ask that she be blessed with living children. The Rebbe blessed her, saying that Hashem would fulfill her wish.

Some time later, a letter arrived for the Rebbe. Enclosed in the envelope was the sum of 300 *dinar*. The letter, from the woman's husband, said that because his wife had given birth in the merit of the *tzaddik's* blessing, he was sending the money as a token of his gratitude.

R' Meir summoned his sons. "In my opinion, this letter was sent by mistake," he said. "First of all, it uses flowery titles that do not fit me. Secondly, am *I* the one who remembers the barren? I want to send the money back."

His sons protested that their home was destitute. Hashem had sent them this money, they said, in order to buy the things that the household most urgently needed. Why give it up?

But R' Meir was adamant. "I am not permitted to use this money!"

Finally, the father and sons agreed to take the question to a *beis din*. The panel listened to both sides and ruled that it was permissible to use the money without any doubt at all. Even if R' Meir did not hold himself worthy of the titles the letter-writer had used, the man had obviously meant the letter and money for him. The man also believed that the Rebbe's blessing had helped him, and had sent the money as an outright gift.

R' Meir bowed to their judgment, but mentioned that he would still like to consult his wife about the matter. He went home and told her that there was a question about whether or not he was permitted to use a certain sum of money, and that the court had ruled that he was allowed to use it.

"R' Meir!" his wife exclaimed. "I am surprised at you! I know you as a person who takes care never to eat or take pleasure from anything that has any kind of question connected to it. What's the difference between a question about meat or a question about money? How can you think of departing from your custom and taking the money?"

R' Meir listened to his wife, and sent the money back.

R' Shlomo, father of R' Dovid of Lelov, was an extraordinarily honest and spiritually elevated man. He once wanted to sell a pair of oxen. One buyer offered nine gold coins for the pair, but R' Shlomo replied that he wanted fifteen. The man left without buying the oxen.

That night, R' Shlomo thought it over and decided that he would be satisfied with the nine coins.

While he was *davening* the next morning, the same buyer returned and asked, "Will you take twelve gold coins?" Unable to answer because he was in the middle of his prayers, R' Shlomo said nothing.

The buyer then placed fifteen gold coins on the table and said, "Take the amount you want, and give me the oxen!"

R' Shlomo finished *davening*, and said, "Take back six coins, sir. I don't want any more than that. Last night, I decided to accept your lower offer. It was only because I was praying that I didn't answer you at once ... Take back your money and take the oxen!"

Saved From a Fall

וְיָדַעְתָּ כִּי ד' אֱלֹקֶיךָ הוּא הָאֱלֹקִים הָקֵל הַנֶּאֱמָן שֹׁמֵר
הַבְּרִית וְהַחֶסֶד לְאֹהֲבָיו

"You must know that Hashem, your G-d — He is the G-d, the faithful G-d, Who safeguards the covenant and the kindness for those who love Him"

(Devarim 7:9)

There was once a gentile government official who hated Jews, and particularly hated one chassid who used to rise early each morning, summer and winter, wrap himself in his *tallis*, and go to shul to learn and teach.

The official conjured a plot that endangered the chassid's life. One night, he ordered his servants to dig a hole on the very path that the Jew used in the early morning on his way to shul, and to cover the hole lightly. In the darkness, he knew that the chassid would never see the hole.

What did Hashem do? He sent an important guest to visit that chassid. The two sat up talking Torah together until very late that night, so that the chassid did not wake up the next morning until the sun was already shining in the sky. He got out of bed and went to shul as usual. Seeing the newly-dug hole in the daylight, he skirted around it and continued on his way.

Meanwhile, the wicked gentile ran down to the path, believing that the Jew must have fallen into the hole and died. How great was his astonishment to find the chassid walking peacefully along exactly as he did every morning!

"Why are you so late today in going to your house of worship?" the official asked.

The chassid told him that because he had stayed up late the night before discussing Torah topics with his guest, he had gotten up late that morning.

The gentile was forced to give reluctant praise to the G-d of the Jews — the force behind the chassid's timely rescue from disaster.

Speaking of this incident, the Chozeh of Lublin said, "Now we understand the verse, 'Praise Hashem, all nations; praise Him, all the states! For His kindness has overwhelmed us.' The recipient of a miracle does not recognize his own miracle. But the haters of Israel know the extent of the wicked plots they weave — and recognize Hashem's great kindness in saving His nation!"

פרשת עקב

Parashas Eikev

Hidden Miracles

הַמַּסֹת הַגְּדֹלֹת אֲשֶׁר רָאוּ עֵינֶיךָ וְהָאֹתֹת וְהַמֹּפְתִים וְהַיָּד הַחֲזָקָה

"The great tests that your eyes saw, and the signs, the wonders,
the strong hand"

(Devarim 7:19)

R' Shloimele of Bobov heard of a Jew from a distant community who was on his way to Sanz, but had fallen seriously ill. The man was lying in strange lodgings with no one to care for him, and his life was in danger. R' Shloimele hurried to place the man under the care of the city's best doctors. The doctors did their utmost to cure the man, whose illness was affecting his lungs, but their efforts did not help. They despaired of the patient's life.

"He has no lungs left," one of the doctors said. "There is no hope."

Upon hearing this, R' Shloimele went to his grandfather, the Divrei Chaim, crying, "The patient is in very bad shape. The doctors have given up on him. Mercy!"

R' Chaim seized R' Shloimele's coat and said, "Why are you crying to me? The doctors do not decree what *Hakadosh Baruch Hu* does. If the man has no lungs, Hashem can create a new one for him. Go to the patient and wish him a *refuah sheleimah*."

R' Shloimele returned to the sick man and told him what the *tzaddik* had said. The man began to show signs of recovery just a few hours later, until he looked unimaginably healthier that same day. Dr. Wahrman, the physician who had despaired of the patient's life only the day before, was astonished. "Has a miracle really happened to this man? Has he actually grown a new lung? Or was I simply mistaken in my diagnosis?"

R' Shloimele told him that he had asked the holy R' Chaim to intercede with Heaven on the patient's behalf — and that the *tzaddik* had answered that it is within Hashem's power to create a new lung.

Dr. Wahrman, a non-observant Jew, asked, "Can I believe that the Rebbe decreed that this miracle occur, the way you say, 'A *tzaddik* decrees and G-d fulfills'? Can a lame man grow a new leg, or a blind man whose eye has been knocked out grow a new one?"

"If Hashem did that," R' Shloimele replied, "our free will would be completely done away with. Even a man like yourself, Dr. Wahrman, would repent and become a G-d-fearing person. Who can withstand open miracles?

"But an internal organ is hidden. You, the doctor, can still be uncertain whether you made a mistake in your diagnosis, or whether the patient was never really as sick as he seemed to be. Hashem wants us to return to Him out of love. He wants Dr. Wahrman to choose Torah from his own realization, not because of the influence of a stunning incident."

Later, when R' Shloimele related this conversation to his grandfather, R' Chaim nodded his head and said, "You spoke well. You spoke the truth."

Buried Treasure

לֹא תַחְמֹד כֶּסֶף וְזָהָב עֲלֵיהֶם וְלָקַחְתָּ לָךְ

"You shall not covet and take for yourself the silver and gold that is upon them"

(Devarim 7:25)

After his marriage, R' Yissochor Ber of Radoshitz lived in the city of Chamelnik. He was very poor, yet he continued to learn Torah and trust in Hashem for his support.

When hunger and poverty were extreme, R' Yissochor Ber asked Hashem to send him money with which to revive himself and his family. Before he had even finished speaking, a gentile child came up to him in the street and offered to sell him a purse filled with gold. The purse had been hidden in the ground for a long time, and the coins had increased in value. In fact, they were worth a fortune.

The child offered to sell the purse to R' Yissochor Ber for just a few kopeks. R' Yissochor Ber took it, rejoicing that his prayers had been heard.

Immediately, he was struck by another thought. "Berel, from now on you won't need Hashem anymore, *chas v'shalom*. You are a wealthy man now. What will happen to all your prayers, which until today were said with a broken heart? And what about your learning? You will have to devote some of your time to money matters now."

He stood up, picked up the fortune, ran after the gentile boy, and asked him to rescind the deal. The boy refused at first, but R' Yissochor Ber persuaded him to go speak to a certain Jew who lived at the end of the street. "He will certainly agree to do business with you," R' Yissochor Ber said.

That other Jew was indeed very poor, and rejoiced at the fortune that fell into his lap — never knowing that R' Yissochor Ber's hand had been involved in his good luck.

As for R' Yissochor Ber, he was doubly happy: First, because Hashem had listened twice to his prayers, and second, because he himself had withstood the challenge and had not turned to idols of silver and gold.

The Test of Poverty

לְמַעַן עַנֹּתְךָ לְנַסֹּתְךָ לָדַעַת אֶת אֲשֶׁר בִּלְבָבְךָ

"So as to afflict you, to test you, to know what is in your heart"

(Devarim 8:2)

As a young man, the Chofetz Chaim was extremely poor, relates the Ponovizher Rav. His wife would go the baker each day to purchase the cheapest bread available. She did not even have enough money for that, and she would buy it on credit. The Chofetz Chaim would dip the bread in water and eat it, and that was his meal.

Once, when the Rebbetzin arrived at the baker's shop, he refused to sell her any more bread until she paid up the large sum that was owed him. She returned home empty-handed. As she served her husband a cup of coffee without bread, she burst into tears.

The Chofetz Chaim's daughter, who was present at the time, later told the Ponovizher Rav that the Chofetz Chaim was quiet at first. Then he beat his hand twice on the table, and said, "Satan, Satan, I know what you want. You want me to abandon my Gemara.

Well, know this: I will not listen to you!"

As everyone knows today, the Chofetz Chaim did not abandon his Gemara. Had he listened to his *yetzer hara,* there would be no *Mishnah Berurah,* no *Chofetz Chaim,* and no *Likutei Halachos.* There would be no thousands of students who spread Torah.

But no one knew that then. Only the Satan knew — and that was why he did what he did.

Not Really Forgotten

הִשָּׁמֶר לְךָ פֶּן תִּשְׁכַּח אֶת ד' אֱלֹקֶיךָ

"Take care lest you forget Hashem, your G-d"

(Devarim 8:11)

The Rebbe of Peshischa once came to the Rebbe of Lublin and found him sighing grievously.

"Why does the Rebbe sigh like that?" the Pesishcha Rebbe asked.

"I transgressed the prohibition 'Take care lest you forget Hashem, your G-d.' I let myself get distracted and did not devote my entire heart to the reality of Hashem."

The Peshischa Rebbe had comforting words to offer. "The Mishnah (*Pe'ah 6:6*), says, 'An *omer* that consists of two *se'ah* and is forgotten is not really forgotten.' A good thing is not forgotten. If a man forgets, he will remember at once, because 'to forget and immediately remember' is not really forgetting. The Rebbe, too, has not transgressed, because he was bound to remember again at once."

The Rebbe brightened, and exclaimed, "Your words have given me new life!"

An Arrogant Heart

וְרָם לְבָבֶךָ וְשָׁכַחְתָּ אֶת ד' אֱלֹקֶיךָ

*"And your heart will become haughty and you will forget
Hashem"*

(Devarim 8:14)

The Chofetz Chaim was always careful to run away from honor,
like a person fleeing a fire. He would mock the flowery titles that
people used when writing him letters — titles such as *Gaon* and
Tzaddik.

The Chofetz Chaim used to tell the story of a certain villager who
was ignorant and uneducated, but who had studied the Jewish cal-
endar in detail. This villager would answer questions about the
proper times to celebrate Rosh Chodesh and the Jewish festivals.
The other villagers honored him and called him "Rabbi." Gradually,
the simple villager grew used to this title, until he began to believe
that he was a great man of Torah!

One day, the villager chanced to be in Vilna. He went to the Gra's
shul to *daven Minchah,* and between *Minchah* and *Ma'ariv* he sat
and listened to the Torah scholars discussing various ideas in the
Gemara. Needless to say, the villager was downcast. He could not
understand so much as a word of what the others were saying!

"That is how things are in this world," the Chofetz Chaim explained. "Simple folk have become used to being called 'Rabbi' and
'*Gaon,*' until they come to believe that they really deserve those titles! But when they come to the World of Truth — they will be
humiliated as they sit near true Torah giants. They will not understand what those great men are saying! Can *Gehinnom* be any
harsher than that?"

R' Yissochor Ber of Radoshitz once went to see his Rebbe in
Lublin. On his way he lost the little money he had been carrying with
him, and he had nothing with which to buy food for himself. He grew
so weak from hunger that he nearly fainted.

R' Yissochor Ber always accepted with love everything that happened to him. Now, too, he did not grow bitter. He just asked Hashem to help him, and to save his life.

He had just finished *davening* when he caught sight of a gold *dinar* that had rolled away in the dust. The *tzaddik* picked up the coin — and found beside it a leather purse filled with many gold coins!

Holding the purse, R' Yissochor Ber said, "Master of the Universe, I did not ask for anything but some food to keep me alive. I do not need any more than that. I am afraid that a great deal of money will distract me from my Creator, as is written, 'And your heart will become haughty and you will forget Hashem.'"

Then he took out only a single coin, and flung the purse back into the dust where he had found it.

An Obedient Grandson

כִּי הוּא הַנֹּתֵן לְךָ כֹּחַ לַעֲשׂוֹת חָיִל

"That it was He Who gave you strength to make wealth"

(Devarim 8:18)

R' Yehoshua of Belz was very worried about his grandson, Aharon. Aharon, a young child, ate and slept very little, and this was likely to damage his health.

R' Yehoshua told his grandson, "Your tired body needs sleep, my dear boy. Please see to it that you take a nap every afternoon. Rest and recharge your energy to serve Hashem!"

The boy was eager to do his grandfather's bidding. Each and every day, he made sure to rest for a while. How did he go about this?

First he thought, "I am hereby ready to fulfill the command of my grandfather, who has ordered me to rest a little." Then he laid himself down on his bed without removing the blanket, and covered his head with his *tallis katan*. A moment later, he stood up again and went back to serve *Hashem Yisbarach*.

Fasters and Sinners

לֶחֶם לֹא אָכַלְתִּי וּמַיִם לֹא שָׁתִיתִי

"Bread I did not eat, and water I did not drink."

(Devarim 9:9)

"Rebbe," said a disciple to R' Meir Yechiel of Ostrovtza, "you fast very frequently. But *Chazal* have said [*Ta'anis* 11], 'He who sits fasting is called a sinner.'"

"*Chazal* were very careful in the words they chose," the Rebbe replied. "Why didn't they say, 'He who habitually fasts' instead of 'He who sits fasting'? Their meaning is this: A Jew whose strength is diminished by fasting so that he has to sit down — he is called a sinner. For such a man, fasting weakens his body and takes away the energy he needs to serve Hashem and to learn Torah. But I am able to stand on my feet and learn all day. Fasting does not affect my service of Hashem!"

Then the Rebbe added, "A person who is in the category of a 'sitter,' who does not move forward in his service of Hashem, is forbidden to impose fasts upon himself. But someone who is striving to perfect his *avodas Hashem* through fasting is not forbidden at all."

All who saw R' Meir Yechiel of Ostrovtza's continual fasting were astounded at the way his soul remained strong even as his physical self grew weak. His desire to change his physical nature was tremendous. He wanted to reach the point where his body would not demand food at all. Through all his suffering, his eyes shone with happiness.

Those close to him found it hard to watch the Rebbe's suffering. They tried to persuade him to stop fasting so much, but their efforts were in vain.

R' Meir Yechiel once rebuked a Jew whose behavior was leading others to desecrate the Shabbos.

"But the Rebbe also desecrates the Shabbos!" the man protested.

R' Meir Yechiel was taken aback. "How so?"

"The Rebbe fasts on Shabbos!"

The Rebbe smiled. "You are right, my son," he said. "But others will learn from you and follow your example, while they will surely not follow mine."

◈

Like R' Tzaddok, who fasted for forty years before the destruction of the *Beis HaMikdash,* the Ostrovtza Rebbe fasted constantly in the forty years before the coming of the Nazi Holocaust.

Wise chassidim said that the Rebbe's fasts were no simple thing, but were filled with a hidden purpose that came from the highest spheres. The Rebbe once hinted at this when he said, "How good would my lot be, if Heaven would allow me to eat."

The Klausenberger Rebbe, R' Yekusiel Yehudah Halberstam, spent some time in Ostrovtza in order to improve his *middos.* He related that he spoke with the Ostrovtza Rebbe about his fasts, and the Rebbe told him, "If everyone would know what I know about the fate that awaits the Jewish people in the near future, I am certain that no one would eat a morsel."

And the Klausenberger Rebbe added, "That *tzaddik* knew, through secrets that Hashem reveals to those who fear him, what was happening to *Klal Yisrael* in the upper realms and in the lower ones."

All Due Precautions

וְעַתָּה יִשְׂרָאֵל מָה ד' אֱלֹקֶיךָ שֹׁאֵל מֵעִמָּךְ כִּי אִם לְיִרְאָה
אֶת ד' אֱלֹקֶיךָ

"And now, Israel, what does Hashem, your G-d, ask of you, but to fear Hashem, your G-d"

(Devarim 10:12)

R' Yisrael Salanter once came to a village inn.

"Are you by any chance a *shochet*?" the innkeeper asked him. "I have an animal to slaughter, and it's a lot of trouble for me to take it to the next town."

"No," answered R' Yisrael. "I am not a *shochet.*"

A little while later, R' Yisrael asked the innkeeper, "Can you lend me one ruble?"

Astonished, the innkeeper replied, "I'm not acquainted with you at all. How do I know you're honest?"

"Listen to yourself," advised R' Yisrael. "When it comes to money matters, you do not trust my honesty even to the extent of lending me a single ruble. But when it comes to *shechitah,* on which several books of law have been written, I am considered trustworthy enough after a mere 'hello'!"

R' Yoel Brenchik, a disciple of R' Yosef Yoizel, the Alter of Navoradok, related the following incident:

"I once went to the city of Bialystok together with the Alter in order to found a yeshivah there. We walked on foot all through the night. Near the end of our journey, we chanced upon a passing wagon, climbed aboard, and fell asleep.

"When we awoke, the Alter was struck with fear lest we had missed the proper time for saying *Kerias Shema.* He said the *Shema* immediately. When he was done, he fainted!

"A little while later, he regained consciousness. The Alter's first question was, 'Did we pass the *zeman* (proper time)?'

"I answered that, according to the height of the sun, we had not passed the Vilna Gaon's time for saying *Shema.*

"I did not see the Alter for seven years. When we next met, he asked me once again, 'Are you sure we were not late, or did you just say that in order to give me peace of mind?'

"We met again six years after that, and the Alter said, 'I'm worried that we were late saying *Kerias Shema* that time.'

"For thirteen years, the matter — or the fear that he had committed a sin — did not leave his mind!"

The Rebbe Does a Mitzvah

וּמַלְתֶּם אֵת עָרְלַת לְבַבְכֶם וְעָרְפְּכֶם לֹא תַקְשׁוּ עוֹד

*"You shall cut away the barrier of your heart and no longer
stiffen your neck."*

(Devarim 10:16*)*

R' Yisrael of Vizhnitz used to take a walk every evening in the
company of his *gabbai.*

Once, their walk took them to the home of a wealthy man, a local bank manager. This man, who belonged to the Enlightenment
movement, was not one of the Rebbe's chassidim. When the Rebbe
reached the house, he knocked on the door. It was opened by a
maid. R' Yisrael walked in, his *gabbai* on his heels.

The *gabbai* was quite surprised. He could not understand why
the Rebbe had entered the rich man's house, but dared not ask for
an explanation. Their host was a polite and well-mannered man.
Seeing his guests, he hurried forward to greet the Rebbe with all due
respect. He offered the Rebbe a chair. R' Yisrael sat down without
saying a single word. The rich man could not find the courage to ask
the Rebbe why he had come. Instead, he turned to whisper the question to the *gabbai.* The *gabbai* whispered back that he hadn't a clue.

After sitting in silence for some time, the Rebbe stood up, parted
from his host, and went on his way. The wealthy man accompanied
his guests respectfully all the way home. On their arrival at the
Rebbe's house, he was about to turn back when he burst out impul-
sively, "Forgive me, Rebbe. In my own house, I did not think it polite
to ask why the Rebbe honored me with a visit. But now, here, perhaps his honor might explain the purpose of his visit."

The Rebbe replied, "I went to your house in order to fulfill a mitzvah — and I did it, *baruch Hashem!*"

In astonishment, the wealthy man asked, "Which mitzvah?"

"Our Sages say, 'Just as it is a mitzvah to say something that will
be heard, it is also a mitzvah not to say something that will not be
listened to.' If I sit in my house and you sit in your house, what kind
of mitzvah would it be not to say 'something that will not be listened
to'? It is necessary to go to the home of the man who won't listen,
and not tell him anything *there*! That is the only way to fulfill the
mitzvah. And that is what I did!"

"Forgive me, Rebbe," the rich man said. "But perhaps his honor will tell me what he wanted to say. Maybe I *will* listen!"

"No," answered R' Yisrael. "I am certain that you will not listen."

The longer the Rebbe refused to tell him, the stronger the man's curiosity grew. He pleaded with the Rebbe to reveal the 'something that will not be listened to' until, finally, the Rebbe yielded.

"A certain destitute widow owes your honor's bank a sum of money on the mortgage of her home," R' Yisrael said. "In a few days, the bank is going to foreclose on her house and sell it in a public sale. The poor widow will be homeless. I wanted to ask his honor to forgive the woman her debt."

"But such a thing is impossible!" the rich man sputtered. "She doesn't owe the money to me, personally, but to the bank. I am not the bank's owner, only its manager! We're talking about several hundred *reinish*."

"This is exactly what I was talking about," the Rebbe said quietly. "I knew that you would not want to listen. That is why I did not want to tell you my request, because of the 'mitzvah not to say ...'"

With that, the Rebbe went into his house.

The other man also went home. But the Rebbe's words had pierced his heart like an arrow. They gave him no peace — until, at last, he took out his wallet, removed the sum of money that the widow owed the bank, and deposited it in her name.

One day in Elul, as R' Mordechai of Lechovitz was walking down the road, he heard an old farmer instruct a younger one: "Let us work and not be lazy now, because this month holds the rest of the year in balance. If we slacken in our work now, we will be hungry all year long."

R' Mordechai arrived at his home, went into the *beis midrash,* and announced, "*Rabbosai,* this month, Elul, holds the rest of the year in balance. If we slacken in our work now, we will have trouble all year long. The farmers in the field know this, and we do not?

"My brothers, each minute is precious!"

To Gladden a Widow's Heart

עֹשֶׂה מִשְׁפַּט יָתוֹם וְאַלְמָנָה וְאֹהֵב גֵּר לָתֶת לוֹ לֶחֶם וְשִׂמְלָה

"Who carries out the judgment of orphan and widow, and loves
the convert to give him bread and garment."

(Devarim 10:18)

R' Naftali Amsterdam once saw that R' Yisrael Salanter had departed from his normal daily schedule, and was waking up later than usual. R' Naftali asked for an explanation.

"My wife just brought a new maid into the house," R' Yisrael said. "She is a widow. If I get up early in the morning, as usual, and leave the house, the widow will wake up in order to lock the door behind me. Because I'm afraid of violating the prohibition against causing suffering to a widow or orphan, I've changed my schedule."

Then R' Yisrael added, "What would you suggest, R' Naftali? That I dismiss the widow, so that I can leave my house on time? But if that is your suggestion, then it would emerge that it should be forbidden to let a widow or orphan work in a Jewish home, lest they be caused to suffer. And how is it possible to say that?!"

R' Yechezkel Abramsky related the following:

Though R' Chaim was the Rav and *Av Beis Din* of Brisk, he never signed his name "*Av Beis Din* of Brisk." In his humility, he avoided titles — even one that was legitimately his.

When *did* R' Chaim use his title as Rav of Brisk?

He was once told about a certain widow who lived at the outskirts of town and needed support and encouragement. R' Chaim himself hurried over in person. After all, it is a great mitzvah to gladden a widow's heart!

Somebody accompanied R' Chaim. As they came near the widow's house, he asked his companion to go ahead and announce to the widow, "The Brisker Rav is coming!"

That was when the Brisker Rav used his title — to make a widow happy!

R' Yitzchak Shlomo Blau spoke about R' Yosef Chaim Sonnenfeld's younger days.

Whenever the yeshivah boys made their way from the yeshivah to the place where they were to eat on Shabbos, R' Yosef Chaim would disappear for a time, only to slip back into the group a little later.

When his friends noticed this, they became very curious about where he went. One Shabbos, immediately after R' Yosef Chaim vanished, two boys secretly followed. They were astonished to see him slip into one of the side streets that made up the poor neighborhood of Pressburg, go down several steps to a modest basement apartment, and knock on a door there. The door was opened by a widow. Smiling cheerfully, young Yosef Chaim called out, "Good Shabbos!" Then he hurried back to rejoin his friends.

The other students could not contain themselves. "Who is that widow?" they burst out curiously. "Is she your aunt?"

"She is a great woman," R' Yosef Chaim replied, "who merited raising all her children to be *talmidei chachamim*. How can I not make her happy by wishing her a good Shabbos?"

This remained his custom, Shabbos after Shabbos, during all his time in Pressburg.

R' Yitzchak Shlomo Blau added a postscript. "That widow," he said, "was my grandmother. I was only a boy of 6 or 7 then. We would eat at her table on Shabbos night, and I would wait outside in order to announce excitedly, "The *bachur* is coming!"

R' Shlomo Zalman Auerbach was a support and pillar of strength for widows and orphans in Eretz Yisrael and abroad. When they had no food to eat, he would concern himself with their livelihood. More than this — he cared for their emotional and spiritual well-being, giving them the will to go on with courage and good cheer.

A man in another country died at a young age, leaving behind a wife and seven young children. R' Shlomo Zalman, hearing of the widow's plight, called her up to offer words of encouragement.

"You should know," he said, "that a similar thing happened to my sister. By holding on to her *emunah* and *bitachon,* she was able to keep her spirit strong. In this way, she succeeded in raising a generation of wonderful *talmidei chachamim!*

"You, too, have this holy mission — for your own sake and for your children's — to raise them with love of life and a cheerful spirit, with affection and joy!"

Then R' Shlomo Zalman called the children to the telephone, and spoke to each in a similar vein. To one of them, he said, "Tomorrow, when you go to *Talmud Torah,* tell your friends that R' Shlomo Zalman Auerbach from Yerushalayim called you up!"

R' Shlomo Zalman Auerbach heard about a young widow whose husband passed away on the day she gave birth to their son. The woman's anguish was terrible. She was left with a newborn baby who had never even seen his father's face.

R' Shlomo Zalman went to the hospital in person, and sat beside the widow to take away some of her agony and revive her wilting spirit. He infused her with new life.

Before he left the hospital, he asked the new mother to bring her baby to him. To the unfortunate woman's pleasure, R' Shlomo Zalman rejoiced over the newborn as though the baby were his own offspring. Then he recited *Kerias Shema* over the baby and parted warmly from them both.

R' Meir of Premishlan took great care to ensure that the poor Jews of his town had meat for Shabbos. He would begin collecting money for this purpose on Sunday, and continue all week, until he had collected enough.

It once happened that Thursday came and he still did not have the amount he needed. Without stopping long to think, he took his own cow, and in the middle of the night went to a *shochet,* and had it slaughtered. Asking the *shochet* not to reveal this to anyone, he distributed the meat among the town's poor.

In the morning, the Rebbetzin went out as usual to milk the cow — and found it gone. She made a great outcry, searched everywhere, and asked the neighbors if they had seen the cow in the fields outside the town. Finally, she went to her husband and cried that their cow had been lost.

"Do not be alarmed," the Rebbe said. "The cow has not been lost — she's gone to Heaven."

R' Shlomo of Zvil once sent his daughter with money to help support a poor widow and her orphaned children. When she came home, the daughter complained, "Look who you waste your money on, Father. I found the family sitting around a table eating a good meal — while in our own home your own children are hungry!"

"Are you sure you're not exaggerating what you saw?" R' Shlomo asked his daughter. She stood firmly by her story.

"In that case," R' Shlomo said, "they must have been used to eating well before their father died. I sent too little money; from now on I will double it."

A Four-Year-Old "Soldier"

וְאָהַבְתָּ אֵת ד' אֱלֹקֶיךָ וְשָׁמַרְתָּ מִשְׁמַרְתּוֹ וְחֻקֹּתָיו וּמִשְׁפָּטָיו וּמִצְוֹתָיו כָּל הַיָּמִים

"You shall love Hashem, your G-d, and you shall safeguard His charge, His statutes, His ordinances, and His commandments, all the days."

(Devarim 11:1)

"When I was a boy of 4," R' Chaim of Sanz once told his chassidim, "I noticed how careful soldiers were to fill their superiors' orders. I said to myself, 'If they do that, how much more so must we Jews — soldiers of the King of kings — know all of Hashem's laws and mitzvos and be careful to fulfill them!'

"At once, I went and learned all 613 mitzvos according to the Rambam. I reviewed the list so many times that it would even wake me up in the middle of the night. I knew all the positive and negative commandments by heart!"

A Quick Trip

אֶרֶץ אֲשֶׁר ד' אֱלֹקֶיךָ דֹּרֵשׁ אֹתָהּ תָּמִיד עֵינֵי ד' אֱלֹקֶיךָ בָּהּ

"A land that Hashem, your G-d, seeks out; the eyes of Hashem,
your G-d, are always upon it"

(Devarim 11:12)

When R' Yaakov Chaim Sofer, author of the *Kaf HaChaim,* was preparing to publish the first volume of his work, he had no idea how to pay for the cost of printing. He had not so much as a penny in his pocket at the time. His friends advised him to travel abroad in order to raise money.

This was a very hard thing for R' Yaakov Chaim to do. He was always begging Hashem not to ever force him to leave Eretz Yisrael. But in the end, having no choice, he did go — praying that he would not have to stay away for long.

R' Yaakov Chaim took a train to Alexandria, Egypt. When he stepped off the train onto the platform, he ran into one of the wealthiest philanthropists of his time, a man by the name of Yosef Somocha.

Mr. Somocha asked, "To what do we owe the honor of this visit?"

R' Yaakov Chaim explained his purpose in coming. The rich man immediately took 200 lira out of his pocket — the cost of printing the first volume.

That same day, R' Yaakov Chaim boarded a train for the return trip home. It was the same train that had brought him to Alexandria.

His friends back in Jerusalem were surprised to see him back so soon. When R' Yaakov Chaim explained the amazing thing that had happened, they protested, "If you were so successful in raising the money, you should have stayed a few days and raised the amount you'll need for future volumes!"

"No!" R' Yaakov Chaim declared. "I will not remain in a foreign country one minute longer than urgent necessity forces me to stay!"

Wise Words

וְהָיָה אִם שָׁמֹעַ תִּשְׁמְעוּ אֶל מִצְוֹתַי

*"And it will be that if listening, you will listen to My command-
ments"*

(Devarim 11:13)

R' Mordechai, a disciple of the Ba'al Shem Tov, was known as
the "Chazzan of Zlotchov." One of a *chazzan's* duties in those days
was to say *Kerias Shema* with the *cheder* students on the night before a *bris milah*. A friend of R' Mordechai's, R' Pinchas of Koritz,
once asked him what he thought about while reciting the *Kerias
Shema* in the newborn baby's house.

"*Chazal* (*Berachos* 13) ask," R' Mordechai answered, "why the
parashah of *Shema* comes before *V'hayah im shamoa* ('And it will be
that ... you will listen to My commandments')? They explain that it is
so that the people first accept the yoke of Heaven, and then the yoke
of mitzvos.

"In the mitzvah of *bris milah,* which the baby is about to fulfill on
the following day, he will be accepting the yoke of mitzvos. We come
to recite the *Kerias Shema* on the night before, to accept the yoke of
Heaven on his behalf."

R' Pinchas, much moved at this deep insight, praised his friend
greatly.

A Good Question

הִשָּׁמְרוּ לָכֶם פֶּן יִפְתֶּה לְבַבְכֶם וְסַרְתֶּם וַעֲבַדְתֶּם אֱלֹקִים אֲחֵרִים
וְהִשְׁתַּחֲוִיתֶם לָהֶם ... וְעָצַר אֶת הַשָּׁמַיִם וְלֹא יִהְיֶה מָטָר

*"Beware for yourselves, lest your heart be seduced and you will
turn astray and you will serve other gods and prostrate yourselves to
them ... He will restrain the Heavens and there will be no rain"*

(Devarim 11:16-17)

A non-religious Jew once came to the author of the *Chidushei
HaRim* and asked, "It says in *Kerias Shema*: 'Beware for yourselves,

lest your hearts be seduced ... and there will be no rain.' But I see just the opposite happening. The righteous are suffering, while I have every good thing!"

The Chidushei HaRim answered, "Since you asked your question by quoting from the *Shema,* you must have recited the *Shema* at least once in your life."

The man confirmed, "Yes, I have!"

"In that case," the Chidushei HaRim continued, "you should know this. For that one time that you said the *Shema,* you deserve far more than you already have. But *tzaddikim* wait to receive their wonderful reward in the future, while Hashem gives the wicked their reward during their lifetime, so that they get no share in the World To Come."

All but Two

וּקְשַׁרְתֶּם אֹתָם לְאוֹת עַל יֶדְכֶם וְהָיוּ לְטוֹטָפֹת בֵּין עֵינֵיכֶם

"You shall bind them for a sign upon your arm and let them be for tefillin between your eyes."

(Devarim 11:18*)*

The following story is told in the *sefer "Tefillin U'Mezuzos K'Hilchasan"* — a guide for kosher *sifrei Torah, tefillin,* and *mezuzos:*

A holocaust survivor by the name of R' Menachem Binyamin Beinish Frankel managed to put on *tefillin* every single day of the war, except for two!

Not even the horrendous conditions in the ghettos and in the Buchenwald concentration camp had the power to keep him from this precious mitzvah. When dire danger threatened, he clung to the mitzvah even more tightly.

R' Menachem would later express his anguish over the two days that he was forced to forego the mitzvah of *tefillin.* The first time was when a Nazi soldier caught him taking his *tefillin* out of their secret hiding place in the camp. The Nazi attacked him in a fury, grabbing the *tefillin* by the straps, and beating R' Menachem repeatedly on the head with them until R' Menachem fainted. The Nazi, thinking his victim had died, slashed the *tefillin* with his knife before tossing them aside and walking away.

When R' Menachem regained consciousness, he picked up the pieces of *tefillin* and stored them away, crying bitterly. That day, he did not put on *tefillin*.

On the following day, he heard that there was another Jew, in another part of the camp, who owned a pair of *tefillin*. Each day thereafter, R' Menachem would climb the gate separating the two sections of the camp, put on the *tefillin,* and return the same way. Moving from place to place through the camp was a risk that could easily have cost him his life. The Nazis would shoot at anyone they caught climbing the fence. Nevertheless, he persevered.

The second incident occurred after the camp was liberated by the Americans. From sheer exhaustion, R' Menachem fell asleep in a haystack — and continued to sleep soundly for more than thirty hours! This was the second time during all the years of the Holocaust that this remarkable man did not put on *tefillin*.

Brick By Brick

וְלִמַּדְתֶּם אֹתָם אֶת בְּנֵיכֶם לְדַבֵּר בָּם

"You shall teach them to your children to speak in them"
(Devarim 11:19)

During the last years of his life, the Ridvaz — R' Yaakov Dovid Wilovsky — lived in the holy city of Tzefas. Before that, he served as the Rav of Slutzk, Poland. He was considered one of the *geonim* of his time, and wrote a commentary on a portion of the *Talmud Yerushalmi*.

One cold winter afternoon, the Ridvaz came to shul for *Minchah* earlier than his usual time. It was his father's *yahrtzeit*. He walked up to his *shtender,* planted his elbows on it, and stood lost in thought. As he stood there for long moments, musing, his eyes filled with tears.

The other men coming into shul for *Minchah* saw the Ridvaz crying. Knowing that it was his father's *yahrtzeit,* they kept a respectful distance from him. They assumed that their rav was immersed in memories from the past.

One close friend did approach him, however. "Why are you so sad?" he asked. "Your father was 80 years old when he passed away — certainly not a young man. And he died fifty years ago!"

"I will tell you," said the Ridvaz quietly.

Here is the story that the Ridvaz told:

"I've been thinking about the time when I was a young boy, and my father arranged for the best *melamed* in town, R' Chaim Sender, to become my private tutor. R' Chaim's fee was one ruble per month — a very steep price in those days, especially for my father, who was a poor man. It was a struggle to come up with the money each month.

"My father supported us by building ovens. One winter, there was no cement or plaster to be found, so my father could not build any ovens. He could not afford to pay R' Chaim Sender's fee. Three months passed in this way. Finally, I came home one day with a letter from my tutor saying that he would not be able to continue teaching me unless he received his salary by the next morning.

"When my parents read the letter, the world turned black in front of their eyes. For them, my Torah education was everything!

"That evening, my father went to shul as usual. There he heard a certain wealthy man complain that the contractors who were building a house for his son and future daughter-in-law had been unable to get hold of an oven because of the shortage of cement and plaster. The rich man offered six rubles to anyone who could get him an oven. In Russia, an oven was an absolute necessity, used for heating the houses, for cooking, and for baking.

"My father returned home from shul and discussed the matter with my mother. They came to an agreement: My father would dismantle our own oven, brick by brick, and use the materials to build a new one for the rich man's son. Then they would have six rubles for my *melamed*.

"My father put the plan into action at once. He brought the oven to the rich man and received six rubles in return, for me to pay to R' Chaim Sender.

"'Tell the *melamed*,' my father said, 'that three of these rubles are for payment I owe him, and the other three are for the next three months' tuition for my Yankel Dovid!'

"It was a very cold winter, and we continually shivered and froze. And all this, so that I would have the very best teacher and would grow in Torah!

"It was cold outside today," continued the Ridvaz, "and I thought that maybe I would arrange for a *minyan* to come to my house instead of my going out to shul. Then I decided, in my father's honor, that I must make a special effort to go to shul today, and not to *daven* at home.

"When I got here a short while ago, I thought about my family's suffering during that long-ago frigid winter — suffering for me and my Torah. That is why I cried. I recalled my parents' endless love and devotion, all dedicated to making sure that their son would learn the holy Torah!"

A Good Bargain

וּכְתַבְתָּם עַל מְזוּזוֹת בֵּיתֶךָ וּבִשְׁעָרֶיךָ

"And you shall write them on the doorposts of your house and upon your gates."

(Devarim 11:20)

R' Yitzchak Yerucham Diskin related that his father, the Maharil Diskin and founder of the Diskin Orphans' Home, used the institution's money to pay special people to go from house to house and check the *kashrus* of *mezuzos*.

The Maharil Diskin justified using the orphanage's money for this purpose by saying, "Kosher *mezuzos* lead to long lives. If parents live long, then their young children will not become orphans."

In the long run, paying people to check the *mezuzos* was actually saving the orphanage money!

פרשת ראה

Parashas Re'eh

Setting an Example

אַחֲרֵי ד' אֱלֹקֵיכֶם תֵּלֵכוּ

"Hashem, your G-d, shall you follow" (Devarim 13:5)

"Is it possible for a person to follow the Shechinah? Rather, one should imitate Hakadosh Baruch Hu's traits; as he clothes the naked, so you, too, shall clothe the naked; Hakadosh Baruch Hu comforts the bereaved, so you, too, shall comfort the bereaved"

(Rashi)

R' Yosef Chaim Sonnenfeld was truly outstanding when it came to comforting the bereaved. Jerusalem old-timers had many a tale to tell about his behavior at such times.

When he entered the home of a mourner, his voice was filled with compassion and warmth. His whole being was like a healing potion for broken hearts.

There was one family living in Jerusalem's Old City who lost their mother. Not everyone had telephones at that time, and days could sometimes pass before people outside the Old City walls heard news of what went on inside. But the very day after the funeral, R' Yosef Chaim was already on hand to comfort the bereaved family.

"How did the Rav hear the news?" they asked him.

"As I sat in my room at home after midnight," R' Yosef Chaim said, "I heard someone in the family saying *Kaddish* up on *Har HaZeisim* — and I understood that your mother had passed away."

There was once a poor Torah scholar whose fellow townspeople took no notice of his extreme poverty and miserable living conditions, and made no effort to help him.

R' Yisrael Salanter heard about this situation. He knew that the man was an outstanding *talmid chacham*. He got up and traveled to the man's city, where everyone rushed out to greet the illustrious R' Yisrael with great respect.

R' Yisrael asked the town notables where that poor *talmid chacham* lived and went to visit him at home. Together they discussed Torah topics at great length. When the townspeople saw the respect R' Yisrael gave this man, they began to honor him as well. And from then on, they helped support him generously.

When the Chofetz Chaim was a boy, a water-carrier lived in his town. This water-carrier was not very bright, and the children enjoyed poking fun at him and making jokes at his expense. One winter, they thought of a new trick to play on the water-carrier. Each night, when he was done with his day's work, he would leave his empty buckets beside the well. The children filled them with water, which then froze during the night. When the water-carrier returned in the morning, he had to work very hard to break the ice so that he could use his buckets. The children were delighted with their joke.

Young Yisrael Meir could not bear to see the water-carrier's distress. He began to linger secretly by the well each night. After the children filled the buckets with water and ran off, Yisrael Meir would slip quietly back and empty them again.

The Two 'Ki's'

כִּי עַם קָדוֹשׁ אַתָּה לַד' אֱלֹקֶיךָ

"For you are a holy people to Hashem, your G-d"

(Devarim 14:2)

In his younger days, R' Uri of Strelisk lived in great poverty, in the city of Lemberg. Once, when a son was born to him, he invited the Chozeh of Lublin's brother-in-law, R' Leib DiMeimels — a very wealthy gentleman — to be *sandak* at the *bris*. R' Uri had no money with which to provide a *seudas mitzvah* for the assembled guests. He wandered through the crowd, saying to himself, "And because Uri does not have money for a *seudah*, should his son not enter the covenant of Avraham Avinu?" Hearing this, the people collected money and prepared a meal.

After the *bris*, R' Leib asked R' Uri, "How do you support yourself?"

"I have two *'kiyalach*,'" R' Uri replied.

Now, "*kiyalach*" in Yiddish means "cows." R' Leib assumed that R' Uri owned two cows and earned his living by selling their milk. He ordered his household to buy milk only from R' Uri, and to pay him double its worth. But when the maid came to R' Uri's house the next morning looking to buy some milk, the Rebbetzin thought she was joking. "It has been years since the walls of this house have seen any milk," the Rebbetzin told her.

Hearing this, R' Leib asked R' Uri why he had told him that he supported himself from two "*kiyalach*," when he actually owned no cows!

"I did not lie, Heaven forbid," R' Uri replied. "What I meant is that I live on a *pasuk* that mentions the word '*ki*' twice: '*Ki bo yismach libeinu, ki b'shem kodsho batachnu*' ('Because our hearts rejoice in Him, because we trust in His holy Name'). It is from these two '*ki's*' that I support myself."

R' Leib began to understand the elevated spiritual nature of the young R' Uri. From then on, he personally supported R' Uri's household, providing all his family's needs. R' Uri himself knew nothing of this. He once asked his rebbetzin how she found money for their needs, and she told him that R' Leib DiMeimels was supporting them.

"Apparently," R' Uri said, "is has been decreed that our lot be eased. Still, we don't want to depend on a specific person who might be able to influence us." Immediately, he moved to Strelisk. It was there, within a short time, that his light shone forth and beckoned thousands of Jews to flock to him.

Kashrus at Any Price

לֹא תֹאכַל כָּל תּוֹעֵבָה
"You shall not eat any abomination."
(Devarim 14:3)

It was the end of World War II. The Americans entered the concentration camps to liberate them. The starving inmates were stunned, almost unable to grasp the meaning of the word "freedom."

An American army officer told the survivors, "You are now under the protection of the United States Army. Very soon, you will be cared for. You will receive food, sleep securely, and not lack for anything!"

The survivors gazed around in bewilderment, as though they could not understand what was happening. Then the Klausenberger Rebbe, who was among the survivors, stood up and told the American officer, "You should know that some of the people you see here are Jews. In accordance with the laws of their religion, they may eat only kosher food. We will be very grateful to the liberating army if you will see to this."

While everyone else was confused and dazed, the Rebbe's mind was clear as ever. He remembered who his Creator was, and what Hashem demanded of him. *Kashrus* must be observed!

But there were some in the crowd who didn't see eye to eye with the Rebbe.

"Who needs kosher food?" they demanded angrily. "Already he's starting with his crazy ideas!"

Calmly, the Rebbe answered, "The horrors have ended. We are about to rejoin the human race. We are Jews, and each of us must stay away from forbidden foods!"

And to the tiny band of chassidim who had remained with him all through the war, he repeated, "We must remember that we are Jews — and a Jew is obligated to eat kosher!"

In short order, the American soldiers brought food into the camp. The gentile prisoners immediately grabbed all the food, leaving nothing over for the Jewish inmates. Another kitchen was opened a little later, but by this time the Jews were almost too weak to eat. Sunk in apathy, some of them said, "It would have been better to have died before."

The Rebbe, though in the same physical state as the others — nothing but skin and bones — stood up and cried, "We are alive — because we are Jews! Our holy Torah says, 'And you, who cleave to Hashem, are all alive today!'"

Laughter on High

וְשָׂמַחְתָּ אַתָּה וּבֵיתֶךָ
"And you shall rejoice — you and your household."
(Devarim 14:26)

The Ba'al Shem Tov was once sitting at his Shabbos table on a Friday night, surrounded by his chassidim. Suddenly, he let out a great laugh. Everyone was surprised and curious, but none dared ask the Rebbe why he was laughing. When the Ba'al Shem Tov laughed again, the others looked at R' Wolf Kitzis, whose custom it was on *motza'ei Shabbos* to ask the Ba'al Shem Tov about things that had happened on Shabbos.

On *motza'ei Shabbos*, R' Wolf entered the Ba'al Shem Tov's room and asked him to explain the reason for his laughter on Friday night.

"I will show you so that you can see it with your own eyes," the Ba'al Shem Tov said. He ordered his servant, Alexei, to harness the horses. They set out at once for the city of Koznitz, where they stopped at the home of R' Shabsai, the bookbinder.

"Tell us what happened to you last night," the Ba'al Shem Tov ordered R' Shabsai. "Don't leave anything out!

"I had no money in the house to buy the things we needed for Shabbos," R' Shabsai began, "but I did not want to ask any person for help — only *Hakadosh Baruch Hu.*"

His wife agreed to this. On Thursday, as she was cleaning the house, she found an old coat with gold buttons on it. She sold the buttons and used the money to prepare for Shabbos. Meanwhile, R' Shabsai — convinced that there was nothing at all for Shabbos at home — remained fasting in the *beis midrash* and did return to his house.

On Friday night, after *davening*, he finally went home. Seeing the lit candles, he began to fear that his wife had gone against his wishes and asked their neighbors for help in preparing for Shabbos. As he walked in, his wife told him about the coat she had found — a gift from Hashem to give them pleasure on Shabbos. At once, R' Shabsai broke into a joyous dance around his wife, because she had not undermined the promise he had made to himself, and because Hashem had taken pity on him and allowed him to have a Shabbos without taking anything from anybody.

When the bookbinder finished his story, the Ba'al Shem Tov turned to R' Wolf and said, "When R' Shabsai broke into a dance from sheer joy, there was joy in Heaven as well. That is why I laughed." Then the Ba'al Shem Tov blessed the couple: A son would be born to them who would light up the nation, and whom they would name after him.

A son was indeed born to the good couple in their old age, after they received the Ba'al Shem Tov's blessing. He later became the Maggid of Koznitz.

A Widow's Livelihood

וְהַגֵּר וְהַיָּתוֹם וְהָאַלְמָנָה אֲשֶׁר בִּשְׁעָרֶיךָ וְאָכְלוּ וְשָׂבֵעוּ לְמַעַן יְבָרֶכְךָ ד' אֱלֹקֶיךָ בְּכָל מַעֲשֵׂה יָדֶךָ אֲשֶׁר תַּעֲשֶׂה

"And the convert, and the orphan, and the widow who are in your cities, and they shall eat and be satisfied, in order that Hashem, your G-d, will bless you in all your handiwork that you may under-take."

(Devarim 14:29)

One day, a poor widow came to see the Malbim in the city of Mohilov. There were tears in her eyes.

"Rebbe!" she cried. "How will I support my young children?"

The Malbim thought for a few moments, then asked, "Tell me, is there any sort of work you know how to do?"

Now it was the widow's turn to think. Suddenly, she brightened. "I know how to make *latkes* that have the taste of *Gan Eden*!"

"Very good," said the Malbim. "In that case, let us be partners. I will invest 100 rubles, and you will open a *latke* store!"

As a fresh bout of tears welled in the widow's eyes, the Malbim added, "The *Shechinah* must preside over everything a person does — and the *Shechinah* is not present unless one is happy. If you cry, you may cause the *Shechinah* to leave, Heaven forbid!"

The widow conquered her tears, accepted the money from the Malbim, and went out to buy the ingredients she needed to make her *latkes*.

In due time she opened her store. It was not long before her name was known throughout Mohilov. Customers eagerly bought her *latkes* as fast as she could make them, calling them "the Malbim's *latkes*." Her profits grew from day to day, and the widow's home was comfortable again.

Little by little, she saved money out of the profits with which to pay the Malbim his share. When she had the full amount, she went to his house.

"Rebbe! There are no words to express my gratitude over the *chesed* you did for me. *Baruch Hashem*, my business is so successful that I managed, in just a few weeks, to make a very respectable profit. The Rebbe's share of the profits come to 50 rubles!"

She took out a bundle of notes and held them out happily to the Malbim. But her hand remained hanging in the air; the Malbim did not extend his own hand to take the money.

"You know," he said, "that when a business is successful, it is not a good idea to take out the profits. I prefer to reinvest my share of the profits in the business. Don't bother taking the trouble to come to me again with my money. Just keep writing down my share in your ledger, and if I ever want my money, I'll come and get it from you."

For years afterward, the widow kept a careful accounting of the Malbim's share in her store's profits. The amount grew and grew, but the Malbim never came to get his money.

R' Eliezer Lipa Negotiates

כִּי יִהְיֶה בְךָ אֶבְיוֹן מֵאַחַד אַחֶיךָ בְּאַחַד שְׁעָרֶיךָ בְּאַרְצְךָ אֲשֶׁר ד'
אֱלֹקֶיךָ נֹתֵן לָךְ לֹא תְאַמֵּץ אֶת לְבָבְךָ וְלֹא תִקְפֹּץ אֶת יָדְךָ
מֵאָחִיךָ הָאֶבְיוֹן

*"If there shall be a destitute person among you, of one of your
brothers in any of your cities, in your land that Hashem, your G-d,
gives you, you shall not harden your heart nor shall you close your
hand against your destitute brother."*

(Devarim 15:7)

R' Eliezer Lipa, father of the holy brothers, R' Elimelech of
Lizhensk and R' Zusha of Hanipoli, gave a great deal of *tzedakah*,
both by bringing poor people into his home and through secret gifts.

Once, R' Eliezer Lipa traveled by wagon from his own village to
the city of Lvov. On the road, he met a poor man making his way on
foot. R' Eliezer Lipa got down and asked the poor man to travel
along with him — but the man refused.

"When I go on foot, I stop at every village and collect alms," the
poor man explained.

"How much do you make?" asked R' Eliezer Lipa.

"About twenty gold coins."

R' Eliezer Lipa wanted to give him the money at once, on the
condition that the man come up on his wagon — but again the poor
man declined the offer. "The village Jews are used to giving me a
regular sum of money each year. If I don't visit them this year, who
knows if I'll get anything from them next year!"

But R' Eliezer Lipa would not give up. "Let us say that you are
right, and it's not a good idea to ruin a longstanding routine. But
what about your heavy backpack? Give it to me, and I'll return it to
you at the next village! Why carry it yourself?"

Again, the poor man shook his head in refusal. "A man who goes
from door to door collecting without something on his back gets less
money!" he maintained.

"How much would you lose?"

"Perhaps five gold coins."

R' Eliezer Lipa paid the poor man five gold coins and lifted the
heavy backpack onto his wagon.

The Unasked Question

לֹא תְאַמֵּץ אֶת לְבָבְךָ וְלֹא תִקְפֹּץ אֶת יָדְךָ מֵאָחִיךָ הָאֶבְיוֹן כִּי פָתֹחַ
תִּפְתַּח אֶת יָדְךָ לוֹ וְהַעֲבֵט תַּעֲבִיטֶנּוּ דֵּי מַחְסֹרוֹ אֲשֶׁר יֶחְסַר לוֹ

*"You shall not harden your heart nor shall you close your hand
against your destitute brother. Rather, opening, you shall open your
hand to him, and grant him enough for his lack which is lacking for
him."*

(Devarim 15:7-8)

The year was 5683 (1923). The Chofetz Chaim came to the city
of Vienna to take part in the first large gathering of Agudas Yisrael.

The Chofetz Chaim stayed at the home of R' Akiva Schreiber, a
noted Jewish citizen in Vienna. As usual, many people streamed to
the house to see the Chofetz Chaim, though only a select few actually got to enter and talk with him.

A well-known Jewish activist from England asked R' Akiva
Schreiber for permission to talk with the Chofetz Chaim for just a few
minutes. He had something to speak about that was very important
to him. In fact, his entire future depended on it.

As he respected the man and his activities, R' Akiva agreed to
this request. He brought the man to the table where the Chofetz
Chaim was eating, with a promise to introduce him right after
bentching.

In the middle of the meal, the Chofetz Chaim began to recite
"*Mizmor l'David, Hashem ro'i lo echsar,*" as he always did at meal-
times. When he had finished saying the final words, "*Ach tov
vachesed yirdefuni kol yemei chayai*" ("Only goodness and kindness will pursue me all the days of my life"), he turned to his guest
— a man he had never seen before — and said, "It is astounding that
David HaMelech says that goodness and kindness will pursue him.
Is it possible that these two good things have turned into hunters?
Murder and robbery hunt down a man — but goodness and kindness?"

The Chofetz Chaim paused, then continued. "It seems to me that
we learn from this that acts of goodness and *chesed* can appear to
harass a person, stealing away his precious time, disturbing his work
and causing him losses, affecting the peace of his home and the like.

The *yetzer hara* urges him to abandon his acts of goodness and kindness. What must a man do in such a case?

"David HaMelech has this piece of advice: Listen, my son. Even if you feel that goodness and kind deeds are harassing you in earnest — do not abandon them. *Daven* instead to Hashem that 'Goodness and kindness will pursue me all the days of my life.' May only these things 'harass' you, and no others, Heaven forbid, for there are other things ... From these things, no harm will befall a righteous person. He will only see the fulfillment of the words, 'And I will sit in Hashem's house for long years.'"

When the Chofetz Chaim finished speaking, the guest stood up, deeply moved. He turned to his host to take his leave.

R' Akiva Schreiber looked at the man in astonishment. With permission in hand to speak to the Chofetz Chaim about an important question, he had suddenly seen no need to ask the question, and was about to go away!

"It's very simple," the guest said, laughing. "The Chofetz Chaim has already answered my question, even before I presented it to him." And he went on to explain.

The man had established a Talmud Torah and a free-loan fund in his city, and he managed both of them personally. With Hashem's help both institutions had flourished, and the work they entailed stole most of the man's time. He was forced to neglect his business affairs, which had suffered as a result. His wife had begun to complain. She wanted him to hand over management of the institutions to other people.

"I myself do not want to abandon 'goodness and kindness,'" he said. "But for the sake of *shalom bayis* I came to an agreement with my wife: We would bring the question to the Chofetz Chaim. Whatever he says, that is what we will do."

He had received his answer, loud and clear. Now he was going to hurry home to his wife, to share the answer with her.

A Long Memory

כִּי פָתֹחַ תִּפְתַּח אֶת יָדְךָ לוֹ

"Rather, opening, you shall open your hand to him"

(Devarim 15:8)

R' Isser Zalman Meltzer was once walking down a Jerusalem street together with his visiting son-in-law, R' Aharon Kotler. R' Aharon noticed a poor man on the street. R' Aharon told his father-in-law, "On my last visit to Eretz Yisrael, a few years ago, this same poor man was standing together with some others, and I gave each of them a donation. But when I came to this particular fellow, I realized that I had no money left. I studied his face intently and decided that, if I ever met him again, I would make it up to him.

"Now I see him, right there, opposite us! I must hurry over and do as I promised myself I would."

And R' Aharon ran over to the poor man and gave him a generous donation.

R' Isser Zalman, watching his son-in-law, said with satisfaction, "Such an action stems not only from R' Aharon's phenomenal memory, but from his pure and profound *yiras Shamayim*!"

On *Shabbos HaGadol*, R' Menachem Mendel of Linsk rose to the *bimah* in shul and announced, "It is the custom for the Rav to deliver a sermon on this Shabbos, and to try to reconcile a difficult Rambam. I, too, will try my hand at this.

"The Rambam rules that even the poorest of the poor must eat matzah on the *Seder* night. In another place, the Rambam rules that there is no justification for stealing. This is difficult: What will the poor man do if he cannot buy matzah legally, and stealing matzah is forbidden him?

"We can solve the problem as follows: The rich must supply the needs of the poor. They must give *maos chitim* generously — and thereby reconcile the difficult Rambam!"

Not a Word

הִשָּׁמֶר לְךָ פֶּן יִהְיֶה דָבָר עִם לְבָבְךָ בְלִיַּעַל

"Beware lest there be a lawless thought in your heart"

(Devarim 15:9)

One day, young Meir Alter, oldest son of R' Avraham Mordechai, the Gerrer Rebbe, stormed out of his house in a rage. Meeting a friend in the street outside, he said, "Let me tell you what I just heard from my father."

The boy went on to tell his companion about a certain man who always acted as if he were the Rebbe's friend, but who secretly plotted against him. This man once wrote a letter bringing false accusations against the Rebbe, which he intended to send to the authorities in Petersburg. At the same time, he prepared a second, glowingly commending letter to send to the Rebbe himself, presenting it as a copy of what he had written to the authorities. Heaven decreed that the letters become switched. The accusing letter came to the Rebbe's hands instead of going to Petersburg.

"Had that letter reached the authorities," Meir Alter fumed, "my father would have been arrested at once. My father showed me the letter, and it spoke for itself. It is clear that a miracle happened to him then.

"And yet, in all the years since, that man continues to live among us as though nothing happened. My father has never said a word to him about the letter. And not only that, my father has continued to act especially friendly toward that man.

"I've always wondered what lay behind this extraordinary warmth my father showed him. Now I know."

Tzedakah: For the Giver's Benefit

וְלֹא יֵרַע לְבָבְךָ בְּתִתְּךָ לוֹ כִּי בִּגְלַל הַדָּבָר הַזֶּה יְבָרֶכְךָ ד' אֱלֹקֶיךָ
בְּכָל מַעֲשֶׂךָ וּבְכֹל מִשְׁלַח יָדֶךָ

*"And let your heart not feel bad when you give him, for because
of this matter, Hashem, your G-d, will bless you in all your deeds
and in your every undertaking."*

(Devarim 15:10)

R' Shmelke of Nikolsburg was very active in the mitzvah of
tzedakah. Not only did he give of his own meager salary, but he took
the trouble to collect money from rich people, urging them to give
according to their ability. In every way he could, he gathered a great
deal of money for charity.

Before Pesach, he used to collect "*maos chitim*" for poor people.
He once came to a rich man's house for this purpose. The man welcomed him with honor and offered drinks and cakes. R' Shmelke
asked for a large donation for *tzedakah,* but the man said that his financial situation was not as good as it had once been and he was
losing money. Therefore, he said, he was unable to give a large
amount and wished to donate a small one instead. But the Rebbe refused to take this small amount from him. He got up to go.

The rich man was very embarrassed that the Rebbe did not want
to take anything from him. He was forced to give the full amount that
R' Shmelke had requested. The Rebbe blessed him that Hashem
would supply what he lacked and give him ever greater success.

"I have a question," the rich man said. "But please, let the Rebbe
not become angry with me."

"I will not," R' Shmelke replied.

"What is the difference between being forced to give money to
an armed robber so that he will not harm you — and being forced to
give a large amount of money to the Rebbe so that he will not become angry with you?"

"I will tell you a parable that is similar to this situation," the
Rebbe answered. "The king had a son who was very ill. It reached
the point where the doctors despaired of the prince's life. The sickness grew so severe that the prince could not put anything into his
mouth. Then a new doctor came and said that he had a wonderful

medicine that could cure the prince — but the prince was unable to even open his mouth to take the medicine. So the doctor ordered an incision to be made in the prince's cheek, and poured the medicine directly into the hole, and thus into the patient's mouth.

"The prince's health began to improve until he had recovered completely. The king and the entire kingdom rejoiced. Then the son said to his father, 'That man is a murderer! He cut my face — he deserves to die!'

"'My dear son,' the king said, 'that man saved your life. You owe him a thousand thanks. What he did was done for your benefit, so that you could take in the medicine you needed and be cured.'"

The Rebbe concluded, "You should know this. By taking your money for *tzedakah,* I have sweetened all the judgments that stood against you up Above. Otherwise, you would have sunk lower and lower."

Then the rich man understood that the Rebbe had actually done him a great service. As R' Shmelke had promised, the man returned to his former riches and his wealth grew in leaps and bounds.

R' Yisrael Joins the "Guests"

כִּי לֹא יֶחְדַּל אֶבְיוֹן מִקֶּרֶב הָאָרֶץ
"For destitute people will not cease to exist within the land"
(Devarim 15:11)

Kovno's "guest house" was a dismal and neglected building. In those days, such a house was known as a "*hekdesh,*" and the poor people who spent the night there had to sleep on cold and dirty floors. The community's wealthier members did not trouble themselves about conditions in the *hekdesh,* and those people who would have wanted to improve matters found Kovno's coffers generally empty. And even if some money happened to be available, no one saw improving the uncomfortable guest house as an urgent matter.

R' Yisrael Salanter lived in Kovno at that time. When he heard about the way matters stood in the *hekdesh,* he decided to become active in changing the situation at once.

That evening, instead of going home to eat and sleep, R' Yisrael went to the guest house. He joined the group of poor men who were

staying in the *hekdesh* at the time, ate a meager meal with them, and then found a corner of the cold floor on which to sleep until morning.

Just before dawn, the superintendent of the building walked in and noticed, among the huddled poor, a most unusual guest. The newcomer's radiant face testified to the fact that he was on a different level than the others. The superintendent came closer — and gasped. The man sleeping peacefully in the cold, hard corner was none other than R' Yisrael Salanter himself!

Shaken to the core, the superintendent begged R' Yisrael to go home — but R' Yisrael firmly refused to go. After *Shacharis*, R' Yisrael picked up his *sefarim* and sat and learned in the central room of the *hekdesh*.

Word of these unusual goings-on soon spread through the town. All of Kovno was talking about it. Community leaders came to the *hekdesh* and pleaded with R' Yisrael to learn in his own *beis midrash* — but he was adamant. "I will stay here with all the poor men! I will not budge until I am promised that everything that needs to be repaired will be repaired this very week!"

The community leaders had no choice. On the spot, they announced a special campaign to raise funds for improving the *hekdesh*. Only then did R' Yisrael agree to leave.

The Man Who Vanished

פָּתֹחַ תִּפְתַּח אֶת יָדְךָ לְאָחִיךָ לַעֲנִיֶּךָ וּלְאֶבְיֹנְךָ בְּאַרְצֶךָ

"Opening, you shall open your hand to your brother, to your
poor one, and to your destitute in your land."
(Devarim 15:11*)*

Someone knocked on the door of the Brisker Rav's home. As was his habit, the Rav, R' Chaim Soloveitchik got up personally to open the door. He found a poor man standing on his doorstep, hoping for a donation. R' Chaim searched his pockets but did not find so much as a single coin.

"Wait here a minute," he told the poor man. "I'll get some money from my desk and give it to you."

R' Chaim hurried into an inner room, took money from the drawer, and returned to the front door. To his shock, the poor man had not waited. The man had disappeared!

R' Chaim's face grew pale, and he began to tremble. His family, seeing how frightened he was, became afraid, too. They ran to find the poor man in order to give him the donation.

Having formed an intention of giving the man money, R' Chaim felt it was a form of *neder*, or vow. In addition, he was afraid of transgressing the mitzvah of "You shall open your hand to your brother, to your poor one." Is it any wonder that he trembled when he saw that the man had vanished?

Each According to His Level

לֹא תֹאכַל עָלָיו חָמֵץ
"You shall not eat leavened bread with it"
(Devarim 16:3)

R' Yechezkel of Kozmir was very scrupulous with regard to the laws of Pesach. He kept many stringencies. Before Pesach, he would prepare water for all the days of the festival and keep it in large barrels. This water was brought in from a certain spring outside the city, and R' Yechezkel personally rode along with the wagons to supervise the drawing of the water.

R' Yechezkel did not permit any Pesach items to rest on the floor, not even a bottle of wine. If a bottle did happen to be placed on the floor, he would not drink from it, even though he was careful to clean out all the cracks between the wooden floorboards before Pesach.

Once, as he was wearing his *kittel* on Yom Kippur, someone gave him a chair on which to sit. Before sitting down, R' Yechezkel checked the chair to make sure it contained no crumbs of *chametz*, as he would wear the same *kittel* on Pesach night.

His guarded wheat was in a sack, and the sack was placed inside a barrel, which R' Yechezkel placed, in turn, inside another strong sack which he hung from the ceiling rafters. When it was time to send the sack of wheat to the millers to grind into flour, the sack had to be cut down from the rafters. One year, someone took out a *chametzdike* knife to cut down the sack.

"*Chas v'chalilah!*" R' Yechezkel cried, aghast. "Bring a *Pesachdike* knife!"

Turning, he noticed another man standing by, wearing a puzzled expression. The man was clearly bewildered at all this scrupulousness. R' Yechezkel said, "*Chametz* on Pesach is for each person according to his level." That was why he, personally, took such precautions to stay away from even the slightest hint of *chametz*.

An Unforgettable Moment

לְמַעַן תִּזְכֹּר אֶת יוֹם צֵאתְךָ מֵאֶרֶץ מִצְרַיִם כֹּל יְמֵי חַיֶּיךָ

"So that you will remember the day of your departure from the land of Egypt all the days of your life."

(Devarim 16:3)

R' Chaim Shmulevitz, *rosh yeshivah* of the Mirrer Yeshivah, had a heart that was always filled with profound feeling. He would examine every aspect of his life from a Torah perspective, and bring parallels from the Torah to explain everyday things. Here is what he said about *yetzias Mitzrayim*:

"There are moments that a person remembers very well. These are times when he feels the moment's significance to its fullest. Something that you hear at such a moment is not easily forgotten. It is guarded and remembered.

"The day the Jewish people left Egypt was such a moment. The Jewish nation felt the full significance of the exodus from slavery to freedom. There was no better time for them to receive the commandment about freeing slaves.

"There have been big moments in my own life, some of them happier and others less happy. But there are moments that are just unforgettable. During the World War, when we left the port at Vladivostok, Russia, on board ship, we were still not certain whether freedom had really come. Russian war boats escorted us until we left Russia's territorial waters. There were Russians accompanying us on our own boat. We sat silent, afraid ... Each man looked at his neighbor, wondering if it was safe to express our joy, or if we would regret it later.

"When we left Russian territorial waters, our Russian companions transferred to the war boats that had been escorting us. The boats began to move away.

"When we realized the significance of this, all our tension and fear fell away. A great song burst from our throats, and our feet began to dance enthusiastically of their own accord! A mighty joy exploded in every heart.

"There have been many big moments — but that is one that I can never forget."

The Widow's Daughter

וְשָׂמַחְתָּ לִפְנֵי ד' אֱלֹקֶיךָ אַתָּה וּבִנְךָ וּבִתֶּךָ ... וְהָאַלְמָנָה אֲשֶׁר בְּקִרְבֶּךָ

"You shall rejoice before Hashem, your G-d — you, your son, your daughter ... and the widow who is among you"

(Devarim 16:11)

At long last, happiness reigned in the home of the widow Berachah. It had been a long time since she had last smiled. Now, thanks to Hashem's merciful help, she had merited finding a proper husband for her good daughter. The engagement party was to be held shortly.

All the money that she had managed to save by the sweat of her brow had been promised to the young man as his bride's dowry. The widow was left without even enough money to prepare a *seudas mitzvah*. Still, she did not allow these worried thoughts to interfere with the joy of the occasion.

The engagement was fixed for the lucky day of Tuesday. The widow Berachah hurried to the home of the Rav, R' Chaim Chizkiyahu Medini, author of the *Sdei Chemed*, to invite him to the festivities.

In happy times and in sorrowful ones, the Sdei Chemed was like a father who shared in his people's lives. R' Chaim Chizkiyahu greeted the widow and asked after her health and that of her family.

"*Baruch Hashem*, we are all well," she answered. "And now I have come to invite the Rav to my daughter's engagement."

"Mazal tov, mazal tov — in a fortunate hour! And where will you make the party?"

"In my house," she replied simply.

R' Chaim Chizkiyahu knew where the widow lived. He remembered the tiny hovel that could scarcely be called a "house." One small bedroom, a tiny kitchen, and a foyer — that was the entire place.

"Do you have enough room in your house for all the guests?" he asked.

With a sigh, the widow said, "And who will come to join in a widow's *simchah*? There is enough room in my house for my few friends."

The Rav did not want pain and hardship to overshadow the woman's happiness. Compassionately, he said, "It's possible that many people in the city will want to join in the *simchah*. Your daughter is known as a modest and G-d-fearing young woman, and the *chasan* is well respected for his learning. Please G-d, we will hold the celebration here, in my home, for all who wish to attend!"

The widow, taken aback, did not know how to answer. But R' Chaim Chizkiyahu quickly called in his rebbetzin, who persuaded the widow Berachah to accept the plan.

"Your *simchah* is our own," the Rebbetzin told her. "We will hold the party here and take care of everything. You just come with your family at the appointed time."

With words of thanks on her lips, the widow left the *Sdei Chemed* and his wife and hurried home to her miserable hovel to share the good news with her daughter.

The day of the engagement arrived. The widow and her family were the first to arrive at the Rav's home. By the time the *chasan* arrived with his family, the guests had begun to stream into the house. The tables were set with all kinds of good things. There were scrumptious baked goods, many different drinks, and other foods to satisfy a large crowd.

When the people of the city had heard that the engagement party was to take place at the Rav's house, all hurried to take part in the *simchah* — though they had had no thought, originally, of marking the occasion at the widow's home.

In short order, nearly all the townspeople were present and the party was at its height. The widow Berachah and her daughter were aglow with joy. They had never dreamed of such an honor. Their personal *simchah* had become the whole city's!

The sound of song echoed from afar. As they said in Chevron long afterwards, whoever did not participate in the *simchah* of that engagement has never seen a real *simchah* in his life!

R' Aharon Cohen, a rebbe in the Chevron Yeshivah, once traveled to Bnei Brak and went to stay in a hotel there. On his arrival, he heard loud music coming from a wedding hall nearby. He was told that an orphan was getting married there that night.

Immediately, R' Aharon put down his bags, and without stopping to rest from his journey, went at once to the wedding hall. He went over to the *chasan*, shook his hand warmly, and wished him a hearty "Mazal tov!" Then he began to dance vigorously with the *chasan*, as though the young man were his only son!

When asked whether he knew the *chasan*, R' Aharon replied that he did not. Seeing the questioner's surprise, he said, "Is rejoicing with a *chasan* and *kallah* a small thing in your eyes — and especially when the *chasan* is also an orphan?!"

An orphan who was a student at his yeshivah came to R' Aharon Cohen with the news that he had just become engaged. After wishing him a "Mazal tov," R' Aharon — who knew that the young man was financially hard-pressed — asked him, "Have you bought your *kallah* an engagement gift yet?"

The young man replied in the negative.

"Go to the jewelry store," R' Aharon told him, "and pick out a gold watch for your *kallah*. You give it to her, and I will take care of the payment."

Afterwards, the orphan would say, "At that moment, I felt that I still had a father."

פרשת שופטים

Parashas Shoftim

The Rebbe Arranges Matters

שֹׁפְטִים וְשֹׁטְרִים תִּתֶּן לְךָ

"Judges and officers shall you appoint"

(Devarim 16:18)

A stranger once came to see R' Baruch of Vizhnitz with a problem. He was a visitor from Poland who had traveled to the area on business, and had found lodgings with a householder in the town of Kotzman for a few days. As he prepared to depart, he went into his room and reached under his pillow for the wallet he had kept there. To his shock, the wallet wasn't there!

The businessman went to the owner of the lodgings and explained what had happened, but the owner claimed to know nothing about the wallet. He claimed that no one had entered the man's room. In fact, he accused the traveler of making up the whole story in order to get out of paying his bill.

R' Baruch listened to the story, and then said, "Be patient. Please go wait in the next room." Then he summoned the owner of the lodgings. When the man came in, the Rebbe began to discuss various public matters with him.

In the midst of the conversation, the Rebbe suddenly got up and left the room. A few moments later, when he came back in, he asked the man, "Please lend me your gold watch." With the watch in hand, R' Baruch left the room a second time.

He told his assistant, "Hurry to the wife of the man who is sitting in my room and tell her as follows: 'Your husband sent me to ask you for the wallet that is under his pillow. He gave me this gold watch as a sign that the message is indeed from him.'"

R' Baruch returned to his room and continued to converse with the man. His wife accepted the tale she was told and it wasn't long before the Rebbe's assistant returned with the wallet. Hearing his asistant's footsteps in the corridor, R' Baruch hurried out, took the watch and wallet from him, and returned to the room, where he gave the watch back to its owner. The talk wound to a close, and the man took his leave.

He had no clue as to what had happened until he got home and learned the whole story.

The Insult

לֹא תַכִּיר פָּנִים

"You shall not take notice of [someone's] presence"

(Devarim 16:19)

R' Dovid of Lelov and the Rebbe of Peshischa once went together to collect *tzedakah*. They visited a rich man, a tax collector by profession, who gave a donation to R' Dovid but refused to give one to the Peshischer Rebbe. Insolently, he said, "I have a shrewd eye and I know a thing or two. This old man is genuinely collecting for charity, but *you* are only out to gain for yourself. I won't give you a penny!"

R' Dovid returned the donation he had received, and the two left the man's house.

Before long, the tax collector learned the identity of his two visitors. He tracked them down, and apologized profusely to the Pesishcher Rebbe. "I didn't recognize you. I didn't mean to talk to you that way. Please forgive me!"

"I forgive you for the slight to my honor," the Rebbe said. "After all, you did not intend to insult me. You intended to insult some anonymous poor man, as I appeared to be in your eyes. But I have no right to forgive the slight to *his* honor!"

Then the Rebbe added, "I have one suggestion for you. From now on, whenever a poor man comes to you, don't let him leave you empty-handed. And make sure to ask each one to forgive you for the insults you said about the poor that day."

An Innocent Man

כִּי הַשֹּׁחַד יְעַוֵּר עֵינֵי חֲכָמִים

"For the bribe will blind the eyes of the wise."

(Devarim 16:19)

R' Chaim Kafusi was one of Egypt's foremost rabbis. Well versed in Torah and Kabbalah, he was very close to R' Yosef Bagiliar. This friendship linked R' Chaim with those who followed the ways of the Arizal, and he was counted among them

R' Chaim Kafusi was known as the "*Ba'al HaNes*" ("Master of the Miracle") because of an incident that happened to him while serving as a *dayan* (judge) in Egypt. In one particular *din Torah*, he ruled in favor of one of the litigants. This ruling surprised the community, who were convinced that it was a mistake. They began to voice a suspicion that R' Chaim had accepted a bribe. Not long afterwards, R' Chaim lost his eyesight — which only served to make his detractors more certain. As it says, "for the bribe will blind the eyes of the wise ..."

Brokenhearted, R' Chaim prayed to Hashem to remove the taint of suspicion from him. He himself was certain that he had committed no sin. In front of the entire community, he declared that the tales told about him were lies.

"If it is true that I took a bribe, Heaven forbid," R' Chaim cried, "then let my blindness last all the rest of my life! But if it is a false accusation — let my vision be restored!"

To the shock of all those present, the *dayan's* eyesight returned and he was able to see again! Stunned and shaken, the community regretted their suspicions of this *tzaddik,* and streamed toward him to receive his blessing.

The Chidah, in his book *Shem HaGedolim,* writes that he saw R' Chaim's signature on a ruling after this incident. It said, "Hashem is my Rescuer — Chaim Kafusi."

Repairing an Oversight

צֶדֶק צֶדֶק תִּרְדֹּף

"Righteousness, righteousness shall you pursue"

(Devarim 16:20*)*

In his later years, R' Isser Zalman Meltzer once returned from the *mikveh,* accompanied by a student who lived with him. A few minutes afterwards, R' Isser Zalman suddenly remembered something. "I must return to the bathhouse at once!" As he spoke, he put on his hat and coat, picked up his stick, and turned to go.

"But what is it that you have just remembered?" his student asked.

"When I took off my clothes at the *mikveh,* I put them in a cubicle and placed my hat in the adjoining cubicle. But I only paid for one cubicle! I must go back and pay for the cubicle that held my hat."

His student tried to persuade R' Isser Zalman that the bathhouse attendant had not suffered any loss because of this oversight. "I saw that there were other empty cubicles," he said. "You didn't take anyone's place." This was a case of one person benefiting and the other not losing out.

But all his words were in vain. His rebbe was determined to go.

Seeing this, the student said, "If the Rebbe has already decided that he has to pay for the additional cubicle, let *me* go and pay! Why should His Honor trouble himself?"

R' Isser Zalman shook his head. "By using the additional cubicle without paying," he said, "I transgressed the prohibition against theft. As you know, there is a rule that a thief must compensate the person from whom he stole. Therefore, I must go personally to pay for the second cubicle — to compensate the bathhouse attendant and beg his forgiveness!"

Despite his fatigue and weakness, R' Isser Zalman returned at once to the bathhouse, asked the attendant to forgive him, and paid him for the second cubicle he had used.

The Elusive Saying

וְכָתַב לוֹ אֶת מִשְׁנֵה הַתּוֹרָה הַזֹּאת עַל סֵפֶר ... וְקָרָא בוֹ כָּל יְמֵי חַיָּיו

*"He shall write for himself two copies of this Torah in a scroll...
and he shall read from it all the days of his life"*

(Devarim 17:18-19)

R' Shneur Zalman of Lublin, author of the *Toras Chesed*, was blessed with a phenomenal memory. It was said that he knew both the entire *Talmud Bavli* and *Talmud Yerushalmi* by heart.

It once happened that two scholars were arguing about a certain saying. One of them said that *Chazal* had originally come up with the saying, while the other claimed that the saying appeared nowhere in *Chazal*.

As they were unable to come to an agreement, they decided to take the question to R' Shneur Zalman. R' Shneur Zalman listened, and then — without a moment's hesitation — answered, "The saying does not appear anywhere in the *Talmud Bavli* or the *Talmud Yerushalmi*, nor does it appear in *Midrashei Chazal*. It appears in the *sefer Tzenah Urenah* (a Yiddish-language *sefer* usually read by women). I've remembered the saying ever since I first heard it from my mother. She was reading the *Tzenah Urenah* while rocking the cradle in which I lay."

Total Concentration

וְהָיְתָה עִמּוֹ וְקָרָא בוֹ כָּל יְמֵי חַיָּיו לְמַעַן יִלְמַד לְיִרְאָה אֶת ד' אֱלֹקָיו

"It shall be with him, and he shall read from it all the days of his life, so that he will learn to fear Hashem, his G-d"

(Devarim 17:19)

R' Zelmaleh, brother of R' Chaim of Volozhin, came to Volozhin to participate in his nephew's wedding. R' Chaim, the father of the *chasan*, wanted to make his brother happy. "I will send musicians to play before you!" he declared.

When the musicians entered R' Zelmaleh's room, they saw him sitting in his chair as though waiting for them. They began to tune their instruments and then burst into a lively melody — one man playing the drum, the second a fiddle, a third a trumpet, and the fourth clashing cymbals. As they played, R' Zelmaleh's lips moved continuously, learning Torah.

When the musicians had finished their performance, they turned and left the room.

R' Chaim entered immediately afterward. His brother glanced at him and remarked, "I thought you said you were going to send me musicians. Where are they?"

R' Shraga Feivel Mendelovitz told his students how moved and inspired he had been by the way R' Aharon Kotler used his time. As the two men left a public meeting and walked toward the elevator, R' Shraga Feivel heard R' Aharon murmur to himself, "Now I understand R' Akiva Eiger's question ..."

"I was extremely moved," R' Shraga Feivel said later, "at the *rosh yeshivah's* ability to dive to the depths of a *sugya* in the blink of an eye — without wasting a second. Just a minute before, literally, he had been completely absorbed in the public matter about which we had been meeting."

R' Raphael Baruch Toledano, one of Morocco's Torah giants, made the arduous trip from Meknes to Ushda in order to spread the word of Torah.

It was at the height of World War II. The roads were clogged with army units. The weather was unpredictable. R' Raphael Baruch's health was poor. But the news reached R' Raphael Baruch that the children's Talmud Torah was being shut down in Ushda. And despite all the barriers, he made an instant decision: He would not wait even a day, but would leave at once for Ushda in the middle of a storm.

He made his way to the train station, accompanied by R' Yitzchak Ochana. All the cars were filled to capacity. The Arab passengers beamed hatred at the Jewish "Rabbino" and insolently spat in his face. With great difficulty, R' Raphael Baruch managed to get a seat on the steps of the railway car, exposed to the elements and in real danger of toppling off the train at any moment. After a harrowing journey, he arrived at long last, exhausted and shivering, at Ushda. But even then, he refused to rest.

Quickly, R' Raphael Baruch called a meeting of the community leaders and tried to persuade them to reopen the Talmud Torah immediately. Otherwise, he said, their very existence during this critical time stood in danger. As it says in *Tehillim*: "Out of the mouths of youngsters and sucklings You have founded strength against Your enemies, to subdue the enemy and take revenge."

But Ushda's leading members refused to heed the Rabbi's advice. They had no plan to reopen the Talmud Torah.

In front of all the onlookers, R' Raphael Baruch burst into a storm of tears. The crowd was moved and uneasy. Someone begged his pardon, and others pleaded with him to calm himself.

But R' Raphael Baruch could not be calm. "Do you think I am crying for you? I am crying for myself! Our Sages, may their memory be blessed, have said, 'Whoever has fear of Heaven, his words will be heeded.' Here I've stood, talking and talking to you — and no one is listening! It's a sign that I do not have fear of Heaven. It is my fault."

He spoke with honest simplicity, and the words, which emerged from his heart, came to rest on his listeners' hearts. Ushda's leaders bowed to his will, and R' Raphael Baruch left victorious. That same day, the Talmud Torah of Ushda was reopened for the community's precious children.

Rules of the Game

לְמַעַן יִלְמַד לְיִרְאָה אֶת ד' אֱלֹקָיו

"So that he will learn to fear Hashem, his G-d"

(Devarim 17:19)

One Chanukah night, R' Yisrael of Ruzhin entered the *beis midrash* and saw his chassidim playing checkers. Sensing their rebbe's presence, they became very embarrassed.

The Rebbe told them, "Learn and remember the rules of the game, for they are rules for life:

"You give one piece in order to take two; two men cannot move at the same time; you must move forward and never, ever move backward; and when you reach the highest level, then you are able to go in any direction you want, right or left, up or down, with each step carefully thought out — *Sof ma'aseh b'machshavah techilah.* Not everyone wins. And the most important rule of all: The best defense is a good offense, as *Chazal* have said: 'A man should always make his *yetzer tov* angry at his *yetzer hara.*'"

As a youth, R' Yechiel Meir of Gostynin wanted to learn how to play chess. But when he was told that one of the rules was that a player could never take back a move, he declined to learn anything further about the game, saying, "It is forbidden for me, as a Jew, to know something that has no room for remorse and repentance."

Amazing Humility

לְבִלְתִּי רוּם לְבָבוֹ מֵאֶחָיו

"So that his heart does not become haughty over his brothers"

(Devarim 17:20)

"We are warned here to remove the trait of haughtiness from our hearts, and that the great shall not feel superior to the small, but shall be humble"

(Sha'arei Teshuvah, Sha'ar Gimmel, 34)

R' Avraham Abish, Chief Rabbi of Frankfurt, would often raise money for various charities. Once, during the month of Elul, he approached a businessman from another city and asked for a donation. The visitor had no idea who was standing before him, and thought R' Avraham Abish a simple fund-raiser. Being occupied with business matters at the moment, he snapped, "Get out of here — I have no time for you now!"

Quietly, without answering the man or revealing who he was, R' Avraham Abish left.

After the Rav had gone, the businessman began to search for his walking stick. "That collector must have stolen my stick!" Running after R' Avraham Abish, he began to berate him furiously: "Thief! Return my stick at once! If I was asked for a donation to *tzedakah* and didn't give it, does that give you permission to steal my stick?"

"Heaven forbid," the Rav replied. "I did not touch your stick."

But the businessman did not believe him. He began to beat R' Avraham Abish — who bore the beating silently, still not revealing who he was.

On *Shabbos Shuvah*, the Rav delivered a sermon in shul, as is customary in many countries. Every Jew in the city came to hear him speak — including the visiting businessman. The shul was packed from end to end, and it was only with difficulty that the businessman managed to get inside. He finally lifted his head — and the world turned black in front of his eyes. The Rav was the very same "collector" that he had beaten.

The businessman crumpled and fainted.

After the others revived him and heard his story, they urged him to beg the Rav's forgiveness. "He will certainly not hold a grudge. He'll forgive you."

He waited until the Rav's talk was over. Many people crowded around R' Avraham Abish to thank him, and the businessman was among them, hoping to be forgiven. Seeing him, the Rav thought, "Here comes that man again about the stick." He went forward to meet the visitor. Before the latter could say a word, R' Avraham Abish said apologetically, "I testify here, in this holy place, that I did not take your stick!"

When R' Shlomo left his city, Zvil, for Eretz Yisrael, many of his fellow townspeople accompanied him. On his arrival in the Holy Land, however, he decided to conceal his identity from his new countrymen.

While still on board the ship at the port of Yaffo, the Rebbe called his grandson, one of those who had traveled with him, and said, "We are throwing the mantle of leadership into the sea." And he ordered his grandson not to reveal his identity to a soul.

For three full years, R' Shlomo lived in poverty, learning Torah as one of the students in Yeshivas Chayei Olam in Jerusalem. No one knew who he was. All they knew was that he was a quiet Jew from Zvil who sat learning diligently in a corner of the *beis midrash* every day. During this period, R' Yosef Chaim Sonnenfeld received a sum of money to be passed on to the Rebbe of Zvil — who, he was told, was living somewhere in Jerusalem. Since no one knew the Rebbe's identity, R' Yosef Chaim had no idea who he was.

A traveler from Zvil arrived in Jerusalem one day. Visiting Yeshivas Chayei Olam, he asked someone, "Who is that man learning in the corner?" He was told simply that the man was "a Jew from Zvil."

The tourist looked more closely at the man from his hometown — and realized that the face was familiar to him. In fact, it was his rebbe's face!

"It's the Rebbe of Zvil! It's R' Shloimele!" he cried in astonishment.

The other students, alerted by his shouts, were amazed to hear that the man who had sat learning among them for three years was none other than the famous and holy Rebbe of Zvil.

R' Shlomo's secret was out. Once again, he was forced to take up the mantle of leadership. His home, in the Beis Yisrael neighborhood, became a center of Torah. People came to him from all over the country, for advice or a blessing. He became like a father to the many who needed a loving, encouraging, and compassionate guide.

Wondrous Bitachon

תָּמִים תִּהְיֶה עִם ד' אֱלֹקֶיךָ

"You shall be wholehearted with Hashem, your G-d"

(Devarim 18:13)

"Walk with Him with wholeheartedness. Look ahead to Him [i.e., trust in what He has in store for you] and do not delve into the future. But rather, whatever comes upon you accept with wholeheartedness"

(Rashi)

R' Yosef Zundel attained the highest levels of faith and trust in Hashem. Wondrous tales are told of his *bitachon* (trust), which amazed all who knew him.

R' Yosef Zundel would say, "Whoever sits and learns Torah and does not concern himself with earning a living, but rather trusts in his Creator to support him, is guaranteed support — even to the point of having gold coins fall from the walls of his house."

When R' Yosef Zundel's second daughter reached marriageable age, her father sought a suitable husband for her in Jerusalem — but did not find one. "I am certain," he said, "that the first ship to come from abroad will bring a *chasan* for my daughter. I will give my daughter as a wife to the first young man I meet among the new immigrants coming off the ship."

When the next boatload arrived in Eretz Yisrael from Lithuania, R' Yosef Zundel — along with many others from Jerusalem — traveled to Kfar Motza to greet the newcomers. Among them was a young man named Nosson Nata Naskin. He was dressed in simple workingman's clothes and gave the impression of being a common man. R' Yosef Zundel began to question him about his character and family tree, but the young man avoided answering.

"Perhaps you will agree to marry my daughter?" R' Yosef Zundel asked.

"Yes," the youth replied with bashful innocence.

The *tena'im* (engagement contract) was written up that very day, and a wedding date was set.

A few days before the wedding, a number of Torah scholars sat in the Churvah shul, learning Torah. Among them was R' Shmuel Salant, R' Yosef Zundel's first son-in-law. At a difficult point in the Gemara, they ran into a thorny problem. Though the scholars questioned and groped for answers, they were not able to reach a satisfactory conclusion.

The *chasan*, Nosson Nota, entered the shul and sat down, off to one side. No one paid him any attention. He listened to the debate among the *talmidei chachamim*, tearing up mountains with their questions, but not agreeing on the answers. Finally, he was unable to contain himself. Standing up, he approached the table and said, "My grandfather, the Sha'agas Aryeh, explained this *sugya* in a completely different way."

And he launched into the Sha'agas Aryeh's interpretation with an amazing depth and sweep of knowledge, explaining the problem away with crystal clarity.

Word of this incident spread among Jerusalem's scholars, who marveled at the *chasan's* wisdom. As for R' Shmuel Salant, he ran to his father-in-law's house to bring R' Yosef Zundel the news that his future son-in-law, Nosson Nota, was a Torah luminary and grandson of the Sha'agas Aryeh!

Sweetening the Decree

וְעָמְדוּ שְׁנֵי הָאֲנָשִׁים אֲשֶׁר לָהֶם הָרִיב

"Then the two men [and those] who have the dispute shall stand"

(Devarim 19:17*)*

While still a boy, R' Yitzchak of Vorka left his parents' home and went to live nearby with R' Dovid of Lelov. R' Dovid guided him and supervised his learning, and he took the boy with him when he went to see his own rebbe, the Chozeh of Lublin.

One Rosh Hashanah, when R' Dovid was in Lublin with his young ward, the Chozeh was late in coming to shul for the shofar blowing. The congregation waited impatiently, but still the Rebbe did not come.

R' Dovid, as one of the elder chassidim, gathered the courage to enter the Rebbe's inner room to learn the reason for the delay. Young R' Yitzchak went with him. The Chozeh explained to R' Dovid that he saw a stern prosecutor speaking against *Klal Yisrael* in Heaven, and he did not know how to sweeten the decree against his people.

As they talked together, the Chozeh noticed the boy standing nearby and asked R' Dovid about him. Then he called R' Yitzchak over and asked him what he was learning just then.

"I am learning the laws of *eidus* (legal testimony by witnesses)," the boy replied.

"And what do you find difficult?"

"I don't understand the law that says a person's relative is disqualified to act as a witness, whether he is coming to testify for or against him. I can see why he would be disqualified if he came to testify *for* his relative, as one can assume he would want to benefit a family member. But if he comes to testify *against* his relative, why isn't his testimony acceptable?"

"*Nu?*" prompted the Chozeh. "What is your answer to this question?"

R' Yitzchak replied, "It says in the Torah, 'Then the two men shall stand.' The two must fall into the category of 'men.' Someone who comes forward to testify against his own relative in a way that could cause him harm or even the death penalty — such a person is not a 'man,' and therefore his testimony is disqualified."

The Chozeh was happy with this explanation. "This is how we will sweeten the decree!" he cried. "*Hakadosh Baruch Hu* is our father, and we are His children. He can't see His own children as guilty parties."

And with that, he got up and went into the shul to hear the blowing of the shofar.

The Alter Stands Firm

וְרָאִיתָ סוּס וָרֶכֶב עַם רַב מִמְּךָ לֹא תִירָא מֵהֶם כִּי ד' אֱלֹקֶיךָ עִמָּךְ

"And you see horse and chariot — a people more numerous than you — you shall not fear them, for Hashem, your G-d, is with you"

(Devarim 20:1)

The book *Meoros HaGedolim* describes R' Yosef Yoizel, the Alter of Navoradok, as a man of tremendous faith and trust in Hashem — a faith that stood by him during times of direst danger.

During the last year of his life, war broke out with a fury. Russian citizens fought bitterly against the invading Bolsheviks. Once, on a *Motza'ei Shabbos*, R' Yosef Yoizel was standing with the *Havdalah* cup in his hand, about to begin reciting the *Havdalah*, when a group of wild men burst into town and started shooting in the streets. The mob kept advancing, nearing the Alter's house. Bullets flew into his yard. Everyone ran to hide from the flying bullets.

But R' Yosef Yoizel continued to stand where he was, filled with trust in Hashem. As his students watched in awestruck admiration, he made *Havdalah* calmly. His voice did not change in the least — nor did he spill so much as a drop of wine from his cup.

The Fruit of the Tree

כִּי הָאָדָם עֵץ הַשָּׂדֶה

"Is, then, the tree of the field a man"

(Devarim 20:19*)*

A respected Jew fell victim to the spirit of the times and sent his sons to a *gymnasium* (public high school) to acquire some "practical" education. His rebbe rebuked him, demanding that he remove his sons from the school — but the man refused. Angered, the Rebbe declared that the man could not return to see him until he had done as the Rebbe had ordered.

"I'll go to Vizhnitz," the man thought. "The Rebbe there loves all Jews. He won't rebuke me."

He put his plan into action, and the Vizhnitzer Rebbe received him kindly. Someone told the Rebbe that the man had been banished from his own rebbe's sphere because of the education he was providing his children, but the Rebbe did not change his manner toward the visitor. On the contrary — he invited the man to join him on his daily walk.

They strolled along a broad avenue. The Rebbe pointed at the trees and said, "When I was a child I learned in *cheder*. As Pesach drew near, my teacher's wife asked us to learn outside in the yard, as she needed to clean the house. We went outside, and naturally our attention was distracted from our studies. A bird chirped here, a butterfly flew there, and a horse-drawn wagon rolled by. Seeing this, our teacher decided to grab our attention with a host of facts about the trees around us, which had just begun to burst into leaf after the snowy winter.

"'You can tell which kind of tree it is by the shape of its trunk and its leaves,' he told us. 'See, these leaves belong to an apple tree. These belong to a plum tree ...' But we paid scant attention. His words went in one ear and out the other.

"But," concluded the Rebbe, "we all knew which tree was which when the fruit came out. Then we knew that a tree that grows apples is an apple tree. A tree that grows plums is a plum tree ..."

The chassid listened, and understood. On his return home, he took his sons out of the *gymnasium* and placed them in yeshivahs instead.

She Cut the Challah

וְאַל תִּתֵּן דָּם נָקִי בְּקֶרֶב עַמְּךָ יִשְׂרָאֵל

"Do not place innocent blood in the midst of Your people Israel!"

(Devarim 21:8)

R' Yitzchak of Kalisch, brother of R' Meir of Premishlan, kept an open house for any traveler. Once, a gentile man came in and asked for a piece of bread. The Rebbetzin had only whole challahs in the house at that moment — challahs that she had just baked in honor of the Shabbos. She did not want to cut into one of these challahs, but R' Yitzchak urged, "Cut the challah, blood won't come from it."

The Rebbetzin did as her husband asked, and gave the gentile as much bread as he needed to satisfy his hunger.

Some time later, R' Yitzchak traveled to Hungary by way of the Carpathian Mountains. Suddenly, he was seized by a gang of robbers who took away everything he had. Then they marched him to their leader, who would decide whether or not to kill him.

The leader of that gang of robbers turned out to be the very same man to whom the Rebbetzin had fed her challah! He recognized R' Yitzchak at once, and told his men, "This Jew kept me alive. Do not kill him — and return everything that you have taken from him!"

The robbers did as they were ordered, and R' Yitzchak was allowed to leave in peace.

On his return home, he turned to his wife and said, "As I told you: 'Cut the challah, blood won't come from it.'"

פרשת כי תצא

Parashas Ki Seitzei

The Long-Lost Brush

הָשֵׁב תְּשִׁיבֵם לְאָחִיךָ

"You shall surely return them to your brother."

(Devarim 22:1)

R' Yosef Yoizel Hurwitz, known as the Alter of Novaradok, once stayed at an inn where a man from Moscow happened to be a guest at the same time. On *erev Shabbos,* R' Yosef Yoizel asked that man if he could borrow a brush with which to clean his clothes in honor of the Shabbos. Before he had the chance to return the brush, the man from Moscow had already left for shul.

On *Motza'ei Shabbos*, when R' Yosef Yoizel returned to the inn after shul, he was told that the other man had already departed. The brush remained in R' Yosef Yoizel's possession. He was very distressed about this, and was always trying to figure out ways to locate its owner.

Seven years later, R' Yosef Yoizel was traveling on a train when he fell into conversation with a fellow passenger.

"Where are you from?" R' Yosef Yoizel asked.

"I am from Moscow," the other man replied.

R' Yosef Yoizel mentioned the name of the brush's owner and asked if his fellow passenger knew him. It turned out that the two men lived in the same neighborhood! R' Yosef Yoizel rejoiced greatly — and gave the man the brush so that it might be restored to its rightful owner.

Once, when visiting the Beis HaTalmud in Kelm, a man accidentally left behind his walking stick. Thirteen years later he returned for another visit — to find the stick hanging in the exact spot where he had left it all those years before!

Similarly, a man once placed a coin on a windowsill in the Beis

HaTalmud. The coin remained in the same spot for many years. No one moved it an inch!

A red handkerchief belonging to R' Eliezer Shulevitz was once mistakenly exchanged for a similar handkerchief that belonged to R' Naftali Zilberberg of Warsaw. R' Eliezer intended to return R' Naftali's handkerchief to him, but World War I broke out unexpectedly and he was unable to do so.

When he left Poland, R' Eliezer took the handkerchief with him. He kept it through all his wanderings during the years of the war.

Seven years later, when he at last returned to Poland, he brought along the handkerchief — and sent it at once to R' Naftali in Warsaw.

R' Meir Michel Rabinowitz, the Rav of Shat and author of the *HaMeir LaOlam*, once stayed in the city of Liboi. One day, he was seen standing in his room vigorously shaking out an old *sefer Tehillim* and a *tallis katan*.

Twenty years earlier, during a fire in his town, the *Tehillim* and *tallis katan* were found in the street with no sign of their owner. The finder handed them to R' Meir Michel, the town's Rav, to keep until the owner came to claim them.

According to Jewish law, a *sefer* or article of clothing that is found must be shaken out every thirty days. R' Meir Michel had brought the things with him to Liboi in order to shake them out, as his visit there fell on the thirtieth day.

Why R' Nosson Danced

לֹא תַחֲרשׁ בְּשׁוֹר וּבַחֲמֹר יַחְדָּו

"You shall not plow with an ox and a donkey together."

(Devarim 22:10)

R' Nosson Adler was traveling together with his student, the Chasam Sofer, when they were caught in a snowstorm. The wagon

driver tried with all his might to move forward so that they might reach the next town, but his efforts were in vain. To add to their predicament, one of the horses collapsed and died.

With no other choice, the driver was forced to walk to town on foot to fetch a new horse and free his wagon from the snow.

Some time later, the driver returned ... pulling a donkey after him.

When R' Nosson set eyes on the donkey, he climbed off the wagon and began to dance. The Chasam Sofer stared at him in amazement. Why was his rebbe so happy?

R' Nosson explained. "Don't you see that the driver has brought a donkey instead of a horse? I have merited a rare mitzvah! At home in Frankfurt, I never believed I could personally fulfill the mitzvah of 'Lo sacharosh b'shor u'vachamor' — the prohibiting against plowing using two types of animals together (or hitching them together to do any work). And now — I have merited that mitzvah!"

Then, at R' Nosson's request, the driver returned to the town and brought back a horse for his wagon.

Knocking on Doors

עַל דְּבַר אֲשֶׁר לֹא קִדְּמוּ אֶתְכֶם בַּלֶּחֶם וּבַמַּיִם

"Because of the fact that they did not greet you with bread and water"

(Devarim 23:5)

The government once issued a law evicting all Jews from their towns and villages. R' Naftali of Ropshitz sensed that this terrible edict was the result of a Heavenly decree against the Jews for some wrong they had done. So, on a cold, snowy night, he traveled from town to town, knocking on doors, but no one would allow him in. Finally he came to the home of a Jewish villager and knocked on his door as well. "I went to several gentile homes before I came here," he explained, "but no one wanted to let me in."

The Jewish villager shook the snow off R' Naftali's coat and gave him food and drink and a bed for the night. In this way, the Heavenly decree — and ultimately the goverment's law — was annulled. Jews would be permitted to remain in their towns and villages, for the gentiles would not offer hospitality to travelers.

The Chofetz Chaim Hosts Soldiers

וְהָיָה מַחֲנֶיךָ קָדוֹשׁ
"So your camp shall be holy"
(Devarim 23:15)

Not far from Radin, in the town of Lida, was an army camp. Each year, the platoon passed through Radin on its way to the place where it carried out its yearly maneuvers. There was a tradition among the Jewish soldiers to stop at the home of the Chofetz Chaim, where a table laden with delicious food would be waiting to refresh them. In his warm and affectionate way, the Chofetz Chaim would sit and chat with each soldier individually and with all of them as a group. This conversation would put new heart into the men, as well as instill in them the determination to guard their Jewish identity despite all the hardship they faced.

In order to make it easier for such soldiers to obtain kosher food, the Chofetz Chaim urged Jewish communities throughout Russia to make sure there were kosher kitchens operating near each army base. Sometimes he would travel personally to cities that boasted a military camp, in order to encourage the Jewish community there to provide the service for their brethren who were serving in the Russian army.

A Permanent Sale?

לֹא תַשִּׁיךְ לְאָחִיךָ נֶשֶׁךְ כֶּסֶף נֶשֶׁךְ אֹכֶל נֶשֶׁךְ כָּל דָּבָר אֲשֶׁר יִשָּׁךְ
"You shall not cause your brother to take interest, interest of money or interest of food, interest of anything that he may take as interest."
(Devarim 23:20)

One day, a wealthy man died in the city of Pozen. During his lifetime, he had lent out money for interest. The members of the

Chevrah Kaddisha refused to bury him unless they were paid an enormous sum of money.

The dead man's heirs were furious. They turned to the nobleman who owned the town and complained about the "exaggerated and unlawful" demand of the *Chevrah Kaddisha*. The nobleman, in turn, went to R' Akiva Eiger, who was responsible for the *Chevrah Kaddisha* in this community.

The wise R' Akiva Eiger gave the nobleman an answer that he could accept.

"We Jews believe in *techiyas hameisim* — the resurrection of the dead. Therefore, we sell burial grounds cheaply. After all, it's only a temporary sale, until the dead will rise again.

"But we also have a tradition that a Jew who lends money for interest will not be resurrected. His heirs, therefore, are buying his plot permanently. It is only right that they should be charged much more for it!"

Even for a Year

מוֹצָא שְׂפָתֶיךָ תִּשְׁמֹר וְעָשִׂיתָ

"You shall keep what emerges from your lips and do [it]"

(Devarim 23:24)

As a young man, some time after his engagement, R' Isser Zalman Meltzer fell ill with tuberculosis. His life was in danger. He was forced to leave yeshivah and return to his parents' home in the city of Mir.

A fire broke out in Mir and many houses were consumed. R' Isser Zalman had to leave his home. Some compassionate people rented a room for him in a farmer's house in the woodlands outside Mir, and made sure that he had milk to drink every day.

The fresh air of the woods was healthful, as was the milk he drank daily. His illness, which had been growing worse until then, began to stabilize. His relative, R' Yom Tov Lipman HaCohen Boslavski, the Rav of Mir, sent Mirrer Yeshivah boys to visit R' Isser Zalman. They spoke words of encouragement and discussed Torah with him.

When the young *chasan* realized how serious his illness was, it went against his conscience to ask his *kallah* to remain engaged to him. He wrote to her family, informing them of his condition and making it clear that they were free to break off the match. If they did so, he would have no hard feelings against them.

When the girl's family received the letter, they wrote back at once asking him to rent a wagon and come to stay with them in Kovno, a city that boasted renowned doctors. Maybe these doctors would be able to find a cure for his serious and dangerous illness.

After examining him, the doctors ordered complete rest and various medical treatments for R' Isser Zalman. The *kallah's* family, the Franks, sent him, at their own expense, to a health spa in the forest. At the same time, they began to try to persuade the *kallah*, Baila Hinda, to break off the *shidduch*. But Baila Hinda was a wise young woman who had inherited her father's love of Torah and respect for Torah scholars. She refused to break the engagement.

The pressure increased. The family tried in every way they could to impress upon Baila Hinda that they thought she was making a grave mistake. Finally, she went to the doctor and asked him about her *chasan's* prospects for recovery.

"In light of his condition," the doctor replied, "he won't live more than a year."

"To live with such a *talmid chacham* — a man of such fine character who is already among the top students in the Volozhin Yeshivah — is a special privilege, even if only for a year," Baila Hinda thought to herself. "I will not break off the match. Besides, with my devoted care he will live, please G-d, for many years!"

As her family continued to pressure her to break the engagement, Baila Hinda went to see the Chofetz Chaim to ask his advice.

"What do the doctors say?" he asked.

"They tell me he can live only another year, at most," she answered.

The Chofetz Chaim thought a moment, then said, "There are healthy people, and there are people who live long lives."

Hearing this answer from the holy *tzaddik* and Torah leader, Baila Hinda returned home more resolved than ever to marry R' Isser Zalman despite her family's objections.

True to the Chofetz Chaim's prediction, R' Isser Zalman went on to live for many long years. He passed from this world in Jerusalem in the year 5714 (1954), at the age of 84.

The Rebbe Stays for Shabbos

כִּי יִקַּח אִישׁ אִשָּׁה

"If a man marries a woman"

(Devarim 24:1)

R' Yechezkel of Shinov had tremendous respect for every person, even the simplest ones. The Rebbe once stayed in a small town for several days during the week. On Thursday, the townspeople came to ask him whether he planned to stay with them over Shabbos, so that they might make suitable preparations.

"What difference does it make whether I am here for Shabbos or not? What sort of preparations do you have to make for me?" And he would not add another word.

The townspeople did not know whether or not the Rebbe was planning to stay for Shabbos. But when Friday morning came and he showed no sign of traveling on, they understood that he meant to stay and they made preparations in his honor.

On Shabbos morning, before *davening*, R' Yechezkel asked, "Where does the tailor live — the one whose son is about to be married, and who is being called up to the Torah today?"

Surprised at this question, they pointed out the tailor's home to the Rebbe. He went there together with a *minyan* of men and a *sefer Torah*, to hold Shabbos morning services in the tailor's home. (Like most small villages, this one had an *eruv* that allowed carrying on Shabbos.) When the reading of the Torah portion was concluded and the *chasan* was called up to the Torah for *maftir*, the Rebbe began to bang the table with his hand. He kept up this noise until the *chasan* had finished reading the *haftarah* and its concluding *berachos*.

The people did not understand the meaning of all this. They assumed that the Rebbe had his reasons.

As, indeed, he had. Before Shabbos, the tailor's son had come to see him.

"I never learned in my life," he said, "and I don't know how to read the *haftarah* properly. I'm terrified about getting up in front of the whole congregation to read. Please, Rebbe, what shall I do?"

"I'll give you my advice on Shabbos," the Rebbe had answered.

And what R' Yechezkel did had been his "advice" — to remain in town for Shabbos for the sake of that young *chasan,* to bring a *minyan* to *daven* in the *chasan's* own home, and to bang on the table as the young man read, in order to save him from the others' mockery and laughter.

For One Jewish Daughter

וְכָתַב לָה סֵפֶר כְּרִיתֻת וְנָתַן בְּיָדָהּ וְשִׁלְחָהּ מִבֵּיתוֹ וְיָצְאָה מִבֵּיתוֹ
וְהָלְכָה וְהָיְתָה לְאִישׁ אַחֵר

*"And he wrote her a bill of divorce and presented it into her
hand, and sent her from his house, and she left his house and went
and married another man."*
(Devarim 24:1-2)

R' Yechezkel Abramsky's son related an incident that happened to his father during World War II, when R' Abramsky served as *Av Beis Din* in London.

It was one of the nights when the Germans bombed London. Thousands of bombs fell on the city during the course of the night. When R' Abramsky heard that the *beis din* building had been burned, he pleaded with his sons to travel with him to the spot at once, as the safe in the building contained a *get* (divorce document) that a Jewish soldier had left with him before leaving with his army platoon. The *get* had not yet been delivered to the wife.

When they arrived at the *beis din* building, they saw that the staircase had been destroyed. All they could do was climb a ladder to the second floor and look among the ruins. R' Abramsky began to climb up, while his sons prayed silently below that he return safely to them.

When R' Abramsky climbed down again, his face was radiant with joy. He had saved the soldier's wife from falling into the category of an *agunah* (a woman who is married but whose husband is missing). This great man had risked his life on behalf of one daughter of Israel.

The Silver Spoon

וְאִם אִישׁ עָנִי הוּא
"If he is a poor man"
(Devarim 24:12*)*

A poor man walked out of R' Nachum of Chernobyl's room in good spirits. The Rebbe had given him a nice sum of money. On his way out, he spied a silver spoon, which he took and hid among his own belongings.

When the family noticed that the spoon was missing, they suspected the poor man and seized and searched him. The spoon was found on him. They decided to take the thief to the Rebbe, so that he might see just whom he was wasting his money on. But the poor man began to shout, "I didn't steal! The Rebbe gave me the spoon as a gift."

In order not to embarrass the man, R' Nachum confirmed this, saying that he had indeed given the spoon to the man as a gift. The poor man, encouraged by this, said, "Because they embarrassed me, according to the law I have to be compensated."

Even now the Rebbe agreed. On the spot, he took an additional sum of money out of his pocket and gave it to the poor man, asking only that he forgive those who had caused him embarrassment.

His Life Force

וְלֹךְ תִּהְיֶה צְדָקָה לִפְנֵי ד' אֱלֹקֶיךָ
"And for you it will be an act of righteousness before Hashem,
your G-d."
(Devarim 24:13*)*

Although he and his family lived in poverty, R' Shlomo of Karlin was extremely generous to all. One *erev Shabbos,* while he still did not have the money he needed to prepare for Shabbos, a man walked in with a respectable sum of money for him. At the same time, a poor man walked in asking for help. Without hesitation, R' Shlomo handed the poor man the money he had just received.

After the man had left, the Rebbe's assistant came to ask for money with which to buy what was needed for Shabbos. The Rebbe told him that he had nothing. The assistant ran after the man who had just left, and explained that a mistake had been made. "The Rebbe only meant to give you part of that money."

The poor man returned the rest of the money. When the assistant went back and told the Rebbe what he had done, the Rebbe fainted! It was only with difficulty that they managed to revive him.

At the Rebbe's insistence, they ran after the poor man and gave him all the money back.

"You have touched the innermost part of my heart. My whole life flows from the mitzvah of *tzedakah* that I have merited to do. And you are asking to steal away my very life force?"

Their Day's Wages

לֹא תַעֲשֹׁק שָׂכִיר עָנִי וְאֶבְיוֹן מֵאַחֶיךָ

"You shall not cheat a poor or destitute hired person from among your brothers"
(Devarim 24:14)

The narrow street in the Jewish Quarter of Jerusalem's Old City was deserted, except for one elderly Jew, walking slowly. Presently a young man appeared, hurrying home. He had just passed the old man when the latter suddenly slipped and fell, landing heavily on the ground in a near-faint.

The young man, R' Menachem, was startled. He quickly recovered and went over to try and lift the fallen man. But he proved too heavy for R' Menachem.

"I will go to Chaim, the porter," R' Menachem decided. "He has strong arms and muscles."

Fast as lightning, he ran to the marketplace where the porters sat around waiting for customers. Before many minutes had passed, the narrow street was filled with three burly porters. All of them had broad shoulders with which they earned their living, and were experienced in carrying heavy loads. Carefully, they lifted the old man and brought him to the Misgav Ladach Hospital in the Old City.

Evening fell. There was a knock at R' Menachem's door. He opened it — to find the three porters standing on his doorstep.

"We finished the job," they said, "but you haven't paid us yet!"

"What?" R' Menachem asked, bewildered.

"We did as you told us. We carried the old man to the hospital. Now we want our pay!"

"What do you mean? You did a mitzvah! You are as obligated to do this kind of mitzvah as I am!"

Had R' Menachem been more comfortable financially, he would have taken a coin or two out of his wallet and paid the men. But he barely managed to put bread on the table for his growing family, and he simply had no money to spare.

"No," he declared firmly. "I do not owe you a thing!"

The porters did not know what to do. Taking care of the old man had stolen hours away from their workday, and they did not have their usual day's wages to take home. They, too, had families that needed to be fed and clothed. Angrily, they turned and left R' Menachem's house.

The story found its way to R' Yehoshua Leib Diskin. He listened carefully, checked out the details, then summoned R' Menachem to come to see him.

"You are obligated to pay the porters' wages this very day," he ruled.

"But I have no money!" R' Menachem protested, explaining his conduct.

"Even if it seems to you that you are not obligated to pay them, there is room here for being extra strict," the Rabbi said. He went over to a drawer and took out a large sum of money, which he handed to R' Menachem.

"This is for their wages and to appease them," R' Yehoshua Leib said.

R' Menachem left the house with a big job still ahead of him: to find out where each of the three porters lived and to bring each one his wages.

"How marvelous are the ways of R' Yehoshua Leib!" he thought in admiration. "How deep is his understanding — the true wisdom of Torah!"

Stand in His Shoes

לֹא תַטֶּה מִשְׁפַּט גֵּר יָתוֹם

"You shall not pervert the judgment of a convert [or] an orphan"

(Devarim 24:17)

R' Pinchas of Piltz was very compassionate to orphans and poor people, even if they had stumbled or gone astray. Once, he traveled to Dubno and noticed a commotion in the street.

"What's happening here?" he asked.

The Rebbe was told that a certain orphan had regularly stolen money from the shul's *tzedakah* box, and used the money to buy himself liquor. The townspeople had decided to chase him out of their town after a sound beating, but the young man, lame and slow-witted, refused to go. He simply would not budge.

The Rebbe hurried over and asked the leader of the group, "Were you ever a young orphan?"

"I? No!" answered the other man.

"Have you ever been lame?"

"No."

"Hungry for bread?"

"No."

"Have you ever found yourself with no education and no home?"

"No."

"In that case," the Rebbe cried, "how dare you judge him? *Chazal* have said, 'Do not judge your fellow man until you stand in his place'!"

The Unintentional Mitzvah

וְשָׁכַחְתָּ עֹמֶר

"And you forget a bundle"

(Devarim 24:19)

A group of *tamidei chachamim* were once sitting with R' Shlomo Zalman, brother of R' Chaim of Volozhin.

"I once heard," one of the men said, "that there is one mitzvah in the Torah that is most unusual. The more a person tries to fulfill it, the more it eludes him. But when he distracts his mind from it — then he might merit fulfilling it. Years have passed since I heard about this, but I have still not found the solution to this riddle. What is the mitzvah?"

R' Shlomo Zalman replied, "It is the mitzvah of *shich'chah* (forgeting a bundle in the field). There is a clear *Tosefta* in *Maseches Pe'ah*. A story is told of a certain chassid who forgot a bundle of grain while gathering the crop from his field. He rejoiced and told his son, 'Go and sacrifice a cow for me as a *korban olah*, and another as a *korban shelamim'* (to thank Hashem for letting him have the privilege of fulfilling this mitzvah).

"'But father, why are you more happy about doing the mitzvah of *shich'chah* more than you are about doing other mitzvos?'

"'All the other mitzvos,' the father answered, 'are ones that Hashem gave us to fulfill intentionally (that is, if we make the effort to do them, we can merit doing the mitzvah). But this one is not intentional. If we do this mitzvah with forethought, we are *not* fulfilling it at all — as it says, "When you reap your harvest in your field, and you forget a bundle in the field, you shall not go back to take it ... so that Hashem, your G-d, will bless you in all your handiwork."'

"The *Tosefta* clearly explains: A person who makes an effort to fulfill the mitzvah of *shich'chah* will not succeed. But someone who removes his mind from it and happens to leave a bundle behind by accident — this is not intentional *shich'chah*, but the actual mitzvah!"

The Rebbe's Coat

וְשָׁלְחָה יָדָהּ וְהֶחֱזִיקָה בִּמְבֻשָׁיו וְקַצֹּתָה אֶת כַּפָּהּ לֹא תָחוֹס עֵינֶךְ

"And she stretches out her palm and grasps his embarrassing place, you shall cut off her palm; your eye shall not show pity."

(Devarim 25:11-12)

"Money — the value of his embarrassment. It is all according to the one who embarrasses and the one who is embarrassed."

(Rashi)

One night, when R' Nachum of Horodna was already an elderly man, someone knocked at his door. When R' Nachum opened it, he saw a poor man standing in the doorway, dressed in tattered clothes. His teeth were chattering from the cold. R' Nachum invited him inside to sleep in his house.

The poor man rose before daylight, threw on the Rebbe's warm coat — a gift to R' Nachum from the *Chevras Shas* — and vanished.

When R' Nachum came to shul wearing an old, tattered coat, everyone was surprised. Then somebody said, "I saw the Rebbe's coat on a poor man."

The group wanted to run after the man to take back the coat. But R' Nachum asked, "Does the coat fit the poor man?"

"It fits him exactly!" answered the one who had seen him wearing it.

"In that case," the Rebbe said, "let him have it. He is destitute, weak, and liable to catch cold. Hashem will get me another coat!"

R' Sholom Schwadron told the following tale.

In Jerusalem's Sha'arei Chesed neighborhood there lived a world-class *gaon* by the name of R' Yosef Shimshelevitz.

The *gabbai* in shul once gave a young yeshivah man the honor of leading the *davening* for the Shabbos *Mussaf* service. The young man took a little too long singing the *Kedushah*. R' Yosef Shimshelevitz, a member of that morning's *minyan*, grew impatient. Time was short, there was much to learn that day, and here was the *shaliach tzibbur* taking his time. R' Yosef tapped the young man on the shoulder and sighed, "Nu …"

The *chazzan* understood that R' Yosef was displeased. He hurried through the rest of the service, and everyone left the shul.

A short time later, when the young man was at home, he suddenly saw the aged R' Yosef approaching his house with two *gabbaim* supporting him. R' Yosef reached the steps of the house, climbed them with difficulty, and called loudly in the doorway, "R' Mordechai, help! Forgive me!"

R' Yosef was deathly afraid that he had, Heaven forbid, embarrassed the young *shaliach tzibbur*. What a powerful lesson for all of us to remember!

When R' Meir Chodosh, *mashgiach* of the Chevron Yeshivah, was hospitalized, a doctor entered his room in order to attach an I.V. to his arm. R' Meir asked the students who were standing in the room to leave.

On their return, they asked him why he had requested that they leave the room.

"The doctor was young," R' Meir explained, "and young doctors sometimes have a hard time finding the vein. He might have been embarrassed by your presence."

The Scales Are Witness

לֹא יִהְיֶה לְךָ בְּכִיסְךָ אֶבֶן וָאָבֶן גְּדוֹלָה וּקְטַנָּה

"You shall not have in your pouch a stone and a stone — a large one and a small one."

(*Devarim* 25:13)

The *Me'am Lo'ez* showers honor on honest shopkeepers who take care never to cheat their customers with false weights.

A fast was decreed in a certain town because no rain had fallen for a long time. But even with the whole town fasting, no rain fell. That night, the town's Rav had a dream in which he was told that Heaven would answer the prayers for rain if a certain shopkeeper would *daven* for the *tzibbur* in shul. This seemed surprising to the Rav, as that shopkeeper was not considered in any way a Torah scholar. However, when the dream repeated itself several more times, the Rav summoned his congregation to shul and — to everyone's astonishment — asked the shopkeeper to serve as *shaliach tzibbur*.

The shopkeeper declined at first, saying that he was a simple, uneducated man and not worthy of the honor. When the Rav insisted, the shopkeeper finally rose, left the shul, and went to his shop. He returned a few minutes later, carrying his weights and scales.

Standing in front of the *bimah*, the shopkeeper said, "Master of the Universe, the two sides of this scale stand for the two letters *hei* that are in Your holy Name. The pole in the center is for the *vav*, and the handle by which one holds the scales stands for the letter *yud*. Master of the Universe, be my witness: If I have committed a sin with this scale, if I have measured less than accurately and harmed Your holy Name, then let a fire come down from the sky to consume me. But if I have not sinned, I implore You to shower down blessed rain in the merit of these scales!"

Then the sky filled with clouds, and a plentiful, blessed rain began to fall.

Every *erev Rosh Chodesh*, R' Mendel of Rimanov or his assistant would visit the local Jewish shops in town to check the weights and scales. Much use and handling could make the weights inaccurate, causing the shopkeeper to transgress the Torah's prohibition: "Stone and stone, measure and measure ..."

Once, one of R' Mendel's people found that a certain shopkeeper's liquid measure was flawed. He warned the man that he must get rid of that vessel, but the shopkeeper said, "I don't use it anyway, so it doesn't matter if it stays in the store."

The Rebbe's assistant insisted, "According to Jewish law, you are forbidden to keep this vessel in your shop. You must throw it away."

"And since when has a *shamash* become such an expert on Jewish law?" the shopkeeper asked mockingly.

The assistant grew angry. He seized the flawed vessel and crushed it beneath his feet. On his return, he told R' Mendel nothing about what had happened.

But the Rebbe heard about it indirectly, from another source. At once, he ordered another of his assistants to go around to all the stores in town and rap on their doors with a wooden stick, a sign that the shopkeepers were being summoned to an urgent meeting in the shul.

When all the shopkeepers were gathered together, the Rebbe mounted the podium and delivered a forceful lecture on the topic of keeping accurate weights and measures. He spoke of the enormous sin of transgressing these laws, and praised all those who were careful with them. The Rebbe made no mention of the shopkeeper who had mocked and laughed at his messenger.

Nevertheless, the shopkeeper sensed that the Rebbe was addressing him, and he was ashamed of himself. As soon as R' Mendel finished speaking, the shopkeeper went up to him and confessed his bad behavior.

"Please forgive me, Rebbe," the man said humbly. "From now on, I am going to be very careful with weights and measures, and I will welcome the Rebbe's messengers pleasantly."

A Table and a Ruler

אֶבֶן שְׁלֵמָה וָצֶדֶק יִהְיֶה לָךְ אֵיפָה שְׁלֵמָה וָצֶדֶק יִהְיֶה לָךְ לְמַעַן יַאֲרִיכוּ יָמֶיךָ עַל הָאֲדָמָה

"A perfect and honest stone shall you have, a perfect and honest measure shall you have, so that your days shall be lengthened on the land"

(Devarim 25:15)

R' Tzvi Hirsch Keindenover, in his *Kav HaYashar*, relates the following episode.

"I once saw a Jew who worked as a tailor, toiling with his hands to earn a livelihood. Before his death, he ordered the members of the *Chevrah Kaddisha* to fashion his coffin out of the boards of the table on which he had worked, and to bury him with the ruler he had used to measure fabric in his hand.

"The *Chevrah Kaddisha* was surprised by these instructions. The tailor explained, 'The table and ruler will be two witnesses in my defense, to testify in the Heavenly Court that I did not take so much as a centimeter of cloth from the customers who asked me to sew their clothes, and that I served them faithfully and honestly!'"

Feather Quills

זָכוֹר אֵת אֲשֶׁר עָשָׂה לְךָ עֲמָלֵק

"Remember what Amalek did to you"

(Devarim 25:17)

The Sfas Emes would write with a feather quill dipped in ink. Every time he took a new feather, he would check to see if it was fit for use, or too thick to produce neat, thin letters.

He had a special sheet of paper for this purpose. Apparently, the Sfas Emes used this paper for many years. He would check each quill by writing the word "Amalek" on the paper, and then he would cross it out. That sheet of paper — which still exists today — has the word "Amalek" written thousands of times, and then crossed out.

פרשת כי תבוא

Parashas Ki Savo

The Imam's Letter

וַנִּצְעַק אֶל ד׳ אֱלֹהֵי אֲבֹתֵינוּ וַיִּשְׁמַע ד׳ אֶת קֹלֵנוּ וַיַּרְא אֶת עָנְיֵנוּ

"Then we cried out to Hashem, the G-d of our forefathers, and Hashem heard our voice and saw our affliction"

(Devarim 26:7)

A group of Jewish men were learning in R' Yichyeh Yitzchak HaLevi's *beis midrash* in Yemen in the year 5684 (1924) when a police officer suddenly burst into the room. In his hand was a letter from the local Imam. The letter said that the Imam's fellow Arabs had prayed in vain for rain to fall. Now he was asking the Jews to do their share in begging the Creator for rain. The Yemenite ruler ended his letter with the words, "The danger is great and the hour is urgent!"

The message was clear: If no rain fell, the Jews would be held to blame.

R' Yitzchak lifted his eyes and sighed deeply. "Am I or my congregation responsible for stopping the rain?" he murmured sadly.

There was no time to be lost. That same day, a messenger from the city's *beis din* went around calling for a public prayer rally the next morning in the community's two largest shuls. The announcer added that anyone who did not join with the others in their time of distress would not merit being part of the salvation.

The Jews came out in droves. Under the shadow of the Imam's threat and encouraged by R' Yitzchak HaLevi, the two shuls overflowed with people who had answered the summons. Together, their prayers rose to the Heavens.

That very afternoon, Hashem sanctified His Name by opening the skies and letting the much-needed rain fall on the land.

In Russia under the Bolshevik government, R' Yechezkel Abramsky was arrested and sent to Siberia. As soon as he arrived

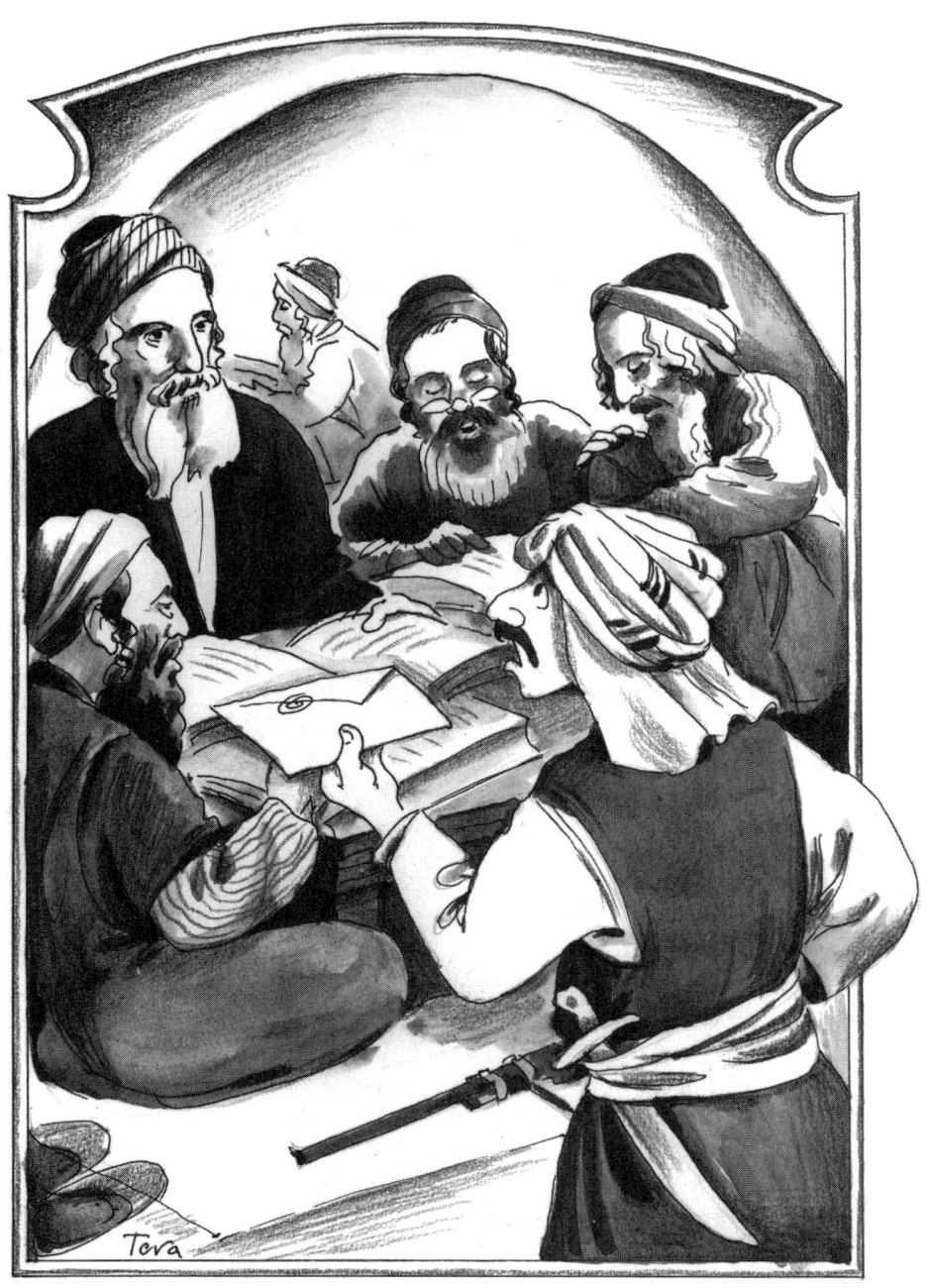

there, he was treated the way all other Siberian prisoners were treated: His shoes and socks were taken away, and he was forced to run barefoot across the frozen tundra. Most of the prisoners became ill with pneumonia from these cruel measures, and some of them died, but R' Yechezkel never forgot that he had a Father in Heaven — a loving and benevolent Father to Whom he could pray. And this was R' Yechezkel's prayer:

"Father, it says in Your holy Gemara: 'Everything is in Heaven's hands except for *tzinim u'pachim* — Everything is in Your hands except for colds and fevers,' things which it is possible for a person to protect himself against. Under normal circumstances, I would take care of my health and not expose myself to such freezing weather. But this time, despite the harsh climate, I can't do a thing. I am in Your hands! Please, Father, protect me!"

And, indeed, during his entire stay in Siberia, despite the inhuman conditions, R' Yechezkel did not fall sick even once!

A Joyous Life

וְשָׂמַחְתָּ בְכָל הַטוֹב אֲשֶׁר נָתַן לְךָ ד'

"You shall rejoice with all the goodness that Hashem, your G-d, has given to you"

(Devarim 26:11)

The following is told about R' Meir Feist:

At the age of 14, R' Meir fell sick, and both of his legs became completely paralyzed. From that day on, he was unable to take a single step and was confined to a wheelchair. In addition, R' Meir suffered from other health problems. He was alone, with no parents and no family.

For decades, doctors were astonished at the way R' Meir continued to live. One of them stated flatly that, from a medical perspective, there was no way that R' Meir could live past the age of 40. But R' Meir lived about twenty-eight years longer than that, passing from this world at the age of 68 and from an illness that had nothing to do with his general condition.

A man in his situation would very likely become bitter and depressed. He would be filled with despair, and would envy others who were healthier than he. Certainly he would not have much desire to live. But R' Meir was just the opposite: He was filled with the joy in living, he was patient and content, hopeful and encouraging, as joyous in another's good fortune as in his own. R' Meir's desire for life was enormous!

His face always radiated happiness and contentment, no matter what the circumstance. How did he achieve this remarkable state?

It says in *Tehillim* (84:11): "One day in Your domain is better than a thousand." Rashi explains, "It is better to spend one day in your domain and die the next (day), than to live a thousand years anywhere else." R' Meir learned Torah and lived with joy and blessing all his life. Each day of his life was equivalent to more than a thousand years to someone who was not a *ben Torah*. That was his secret.

Is there any joy equal to that of casting all worldly cares away and devoting oneself to Torah and prayer day and night? Such a life is a *Gan Eden* here on earth! As R' Meir once remarked, "I can't imagine a *Gan Eden* greater than learning here in Lakewood."

A holy and righteous friend of R' Avraham of Chechnov once asked him the following question: "We have both learned great things in Torah together. Like you, I have taught Torah, and like you, I have done good deeds. Why, then, do they call you 'Rebbe' and not me?"

The Chechnover Rebbe replied, "Tell me, my friend, have you ever felt such a great joy that it was simply indescribable?"

"Yes, once," his friend said. "When I made a profit of 10,000 rubles all at one time."

"Know this, my dear friend," the Rebbe said. "When I reach out my hand for my *tefillin*, before I even put them on ... when I simply think about being prepared to put on my *tefillin* as my Creator commanded me to do ... I feel a joy thousands of times greater than you felt when you made your 10,000 rubles."

The other *tzaddik* began to weep. "In that case, the world is not mistaken. You are the one who deserves to be called 'Rebbe.'"

Like His Own Children

וְנָתַתָּה לַלֵּוִי לַגֵּר לַיָּתוֹם וְלָאַלְמָנָה וְאָכְלוּ בִשְׁעָרֶיךָ וְשָׂבֵעוּ

"And you will have given to the Levite, to the convert, to the orphan, and to the widow, and they will have eaten in your cities and will have been satisfied"

(Devarim 26:12)

One year, three young orphans came to Mesivta Torah Vodaath in New York. They had lost their father, and their mother had sent them to the yeshivah from the distant town in which they lived. After a few days of dormitory living, the brothers left the yeshivah and went back to their home.

Hearing this, R' Shraga Feivel Mendlowitz, principal of the Mesivta, called up the boys' mother.

"Please," he pleaded, "let the boys come back to learn Torah. If they don't like living in the dormitory, I am prepared to take them into my own home as though they were my own children!"

The boys returned, and for a considerable period of time lived as R' Shraga Feivel's personal guests. Devotedly, he attended to their needs, dedicating much time and effort to making life pleasant for the boys. Always, he related to them with wonderful compassion and affection.

After a while, the boys mainstreamed into yeshivah life in every way, and grew into outstanding *bnei Torah*.

The Scent of a Mitzvah

כְּכָל מִצְוָתְךָ אֲשֶׁר צִוִּיתָנִי

"According to the entire commandment that You commanded me"

(Devarim 26:13)

Even in a generation of great men who served Hashem with devotion, R' Levi Yitzchak of Berditchev was unusual. His love and desire for Hashem's mitzvos were legendary.

Each week, on *Motza'ei Shabbos*, he would wait impatiently for the dawn, when he would be permitted to put on his *tefillin*. He would say that his hand and arm burned with desire for the mitzvah of *tefillin*.

One *Motza'ei Yom Kippur*, R' Levi Yitzchak fainted from the hard work he had put into the long day's services. His disciples, who knew their rebbe's nature, quickly brought an *esrog* that had been bought for Sukkos, and held it to his nose. R' Levi Yitzchak returned to consciousness at once. The scent of a mitzvah was guaranteed to revive him!

R' Nachum Disappears

אֶת ד' הֶאֱמַרְתָּ הַיּוֹם לִהְיוֹת לְךָ לֵאלֹקִים ... וַד' הֶאֱמִירְךָ הַיּוֹם לִהְיוֹת לוֹ לְעַם סְגֻלָּה

"You have distinguished Hashem today to be a G-d for you ... And Hashem has distinguished you today to be for Him a treasured people"
(Devarim 26:17-18)

The Chofetz Chaim told his students that, at the age of 15, he went to learn from R' Nachum of Horodna. R' Nachum would sometimes disappear at night, and no one knew to where. Finally, some of his disciples followed him, and discovered that the Rebbe always went to an empty shul.

One night the Chofetz Chaim went to *daven Ma'ariv* in that same shul. After the service, he went into the *ezras nashim* (women's section) and hid under one of the benches. The *shamash*, who made the rounds before closing up the shul, did not notice him hiding, and locked the doors.

Later, the Chofetz Chaim described what he saw that night.

"At exactly midnight, I heard the door opening. I began to shake all over. R' Nachum came in, climbed onto the *bimah*, and reached for one of the boxes that stood there. It was a *genizah*, containing *sheimos* (remnants of holy books) and *talleisim*. R' Nachum pulled out a *sefer* and began to learn from it. Apparently, it was a *sefer* of Kabbalah.

"Suddenly, I saw a fire surrounding him. I began to tremble and wanted to shout out loud, but sensed at once that this was no ordinary fire. I closed my lips and did not utter a sound. Still, the trembling continued, until I felt as though my soul was about to burst out of me!

"R' Nachum stood and learned this way for an hour. When he was done, he closed the *sefer*, replaced it in its box, and the fire subsided. R' Nachum left.

"As soon as he was gone, I began to feel better. I stayed where I was until morning, still trembling. Just before it was time to *daven Shacharis* at the yeshivah, I finally stood up and left the shul."

How the Kosover Rebbe Prayed

וְעָנוּ הַלְוִיִּם וְאָמְרוּ אֶל כָּל אִישׁ יִשְׂרָאֵל קוֹל רָם

"The Levites shall speak up and say to every man of Israel, in a loud voice"

(Devarim 27:14)

The Chozeh of Lublin's son once went to visit R' Menachem Mendel of Kosov, the Ahavas Shalom. On his return, he told his father, "All the things that the Kosover Rebbe does in his service to Hashem are things that I've seen you do as well — except for his devotion when he says '*Mizmor l'David havu l'Hashem bnei elim.*'

"When I *davened* behind the *mechitzah* that separates the Kosover from the other men in shul and heard the seven '*kolos*' said with unusual energy, I stood up on a bench and peeked over the *mechitzah*. I saw the Rebbe fall backward onto the ground as he pronounced those seven '*kolos*' with holiness and purity."

It is said that the gentile shepherds tending their flocks on the hills surrounding Kosov would ascertain the time by the Rebbe's *tefillos*. When the Rebbe said the seven "*kolos*" of "*Mizmor l'David havu l'Hashem*," they knew that it was time to go home. They would tell one another, "The Rebbe has already said '*kol*.'"

The Ahavas Shalom once went to visit his brother-in-law, the Strelisker Rebbe, who asked him to lead the *davening* of *Kabbalas Shabbos*. Here was a chance to see the Kosover Rebbe at his holy work without a *mechitzah* in the way.

The Strelisker whispered to his illustrious disciple, R' Yehudah Tzvi of Stretin, "Look at the Kosover Rebbe and take note of his prayer. His *Kabbalas Shabbos* is like our *Kol Nidrei*!"

The Short Shabbos Meal

אָרוּר מַטֶּה מִשְׁפַּט גֵּר יָתוֹם וְאַלְמָנָה

"Accursed is one who perverts a judgment of a convert, orphan, or widow."

(Devarim 27:19)

A disciple of R' Yisrael of Salant once invited his rebbe to spend Shabbos in his home. Knowing how careful R' Yisrael Salanter was in every detail, and how reluctant he was to stay as a guest in just any home, the disciple described the way he ran his household.

He bought his meat, he said, from a G-d-fearing butcher. His cook was the widow of a Torah scholar who observed every stringency. And the Shabbos meals in his home were conducted properly, with *divrei Torah* said at each course and Shabbos *zemiros* lending an atmosphere of holiness. It was no wonder, the disciple concluded, that the Friday night meal at his home ended at a very late hour of the night.

"I accept your invitation," R' Yisrael said, "but only on the condition that you shorten the length of the Friday night meal by two hours."

Eager to host his rebbe, the disciple quickly agreed.

That Friday night, the Shabbos meal was rushed. The courses followed each other rapidly, without the usual lengthy break in between. It was not so very long after they had washed their hands for the meal that the *mayim acharonim* was already being brought to the table.

Just before they *bentched*, the disciple turned to R' Yisrael and said, "Forgive me, Rebbe, but I must ask a question. What fault did the Rebbe find in the way I conduct my Shabbos table, that led him to shorten the meal time by two hours?"

Instead of answering, R' Yisrael asked his host to invite the cook into the room. When she entered, he told her, "Please forgive me for making you tired this evening, and causing the courses to be served so quickly tonight."

To everyone's surprise, the cook exclaimed, "May the Rebbe be blessed with every blessing! If only he was a guest here every Shabbos! The meal always lasts far into the night, after a day I've spent working very hard to prepare everything. By the time the meal is over, I can hardly lift my feet from exhaustion. But tonight, because you finished the meal early, I can go home and rest!"

R' Yisrael turned to his disciple and said, "Here is the answer to your question. Indeed, the way you conduct your Shabbos table is very nice. But when it harms another person, it becomes something not so nice at all!"

R' Yisrael Salanter was very careful about the quality of his *shemurah matzos* for Pesach. His students undertook to do the job for him. Before setting out for the bakery, they asked, "Rebbe, to what should we pay special attention?"

"Be especially careful," R' Yisrael replied, "not to distress the woman who kneads the dough. She is a widow, and if you pressure her while she works you will be doing the sin of *lo sa'anun*!"

R' Yehoshua Leib (the "Maharil") Diskin used to leave the special flour for his Pesach matzos with his loyal student, R' Eliezer Dan Ralbag.

When R' Eliezer Dan passed away, the Maharil Diskin decided to send another student, R' Tzvi Michel Shapiro, to fetch the flour from R' Eliezer Dan's widow. The Maharil Diskin was afraid that she might not guard the flour properly.

R' Tzvi Michel had an objection. "It's possible that the widow will be distressed if the flour is taken away from her during the year. She may feel that her own worth has become diminished since her husband died. This has the ring of 'Do not distress a widow or an orphan'!"

R' Yehoshua Leib Diskin realized that his student was right. The flour stayed with the widow until it was time to bake the matzos for Pesach.

The Man Who Stayed Home

וּבָאוּ עָלֶיךָ כָּל הַבְּרָכוֹת הָאֵלֶּה וְהִשִּׂיגֻךָ

"All these blessings will come upon you and overtake you"

(Devarim 28:2)

One Purim, the residents of Bendin were busy doing the mitzvos of the day: sending *mishloach manos* to each other and giving money to the poor. The chassidim danced enthusiastically at the feasts that marked the day.

Only one man stayed home and learned Torah with great devotion that Purim. This was R' Ze'ev Nachum Borenstein. R' Ze'ev Nachum was an outstanding Torah scholar whose learning was steeped in holiness and purity. He was an important disciple of R' Menachem Mendel of Kotzk.

There was a commotion in the Heavenly Court that day. If not for R' Ze'ev Nachum's learning, the world would have been empty of Torah learning, Heaven forbid.

The Kotzker Rebbe would tell this story, adding, "Because of this, Heaven decided to reward R' Ze'ev Nachum with a great treasure. His son grew to become R' Avraham of Sochatchov — author of the *Iglei Tal* and the *Avnei Nezer* — a prince of Torah, a son who would light up the world with his Torah and his holy service, and who would reveal deep and wonderful truths."

Sudden Panic

יִתֵּן ד' אֶת אֹיְבֶיךָ הַקָּמִים עָלֶיךָ נִגָּפִים לְפָנֶיךָ בְּדֶרֶךְ אֶחָד יֵצְאוּ
אֵלֶיךָ וּבְשִׁבְעָה דְרָכִים יָנוּסוּ לְפָנֶיךָ

"Hashem shall cause your enemies who rise up against you to be struck down before you; on one road will they go out toward you and on seven roads shall they flee before you."

(Devarim 28:7)

At 6 a.m. on *erev Pesach,* 5663 (1903), the gates of the Jewish ghetto in Morocco were closed suddenly. Word went around that a

large and frenzied Arab mob was headed that way. The Arabs were armed with swords and scimitars, metal bars, and other weapons.

With blood-curdling screams, the mob fell on the gates and began beating them with their weapons. Inside, the Jews assembled hastily in the street, young and old alike, to raise a cry to Heaven. Among them was the *tzaddik,* R' Chaim Mashash. The venerable Rabbi fell face-down on the ground so that his long white beard became stained with dust. With anguished cries he beseeched the crowd to do complete *teshuvah.* Then, in a loud voice, he shouted a *Shema Yisrael* that pierced Heaven's gates.

"*Ya'ancha Hashem b'yom tzarah* — Hashem will respond on your day of trouble," R' Chaim called, and the assembled crowd repeated the words after him with tears and pleading.

All the while, the air resounded with the terrible noise that the Arab mob was making with its wild screams and battering weapons. Balls of lead went whirling over the Jews' heads. The weeping inside the ghetto intensified.

And then the miracle happened.

Running figures appeared suddenly in the ghetto street. The Jewish crowd froze in terror. Then, turning fearfully toward the figures, they saw that they were none other than the men who stood watch on the ghetto walls. And their shouts were shouts of joy!

Breathless and excited, the watchers told what they had seen from the walls. In the midst of their frenzied battering of the gates, the Arab mob had suddenly turned and fled! With wild cries, they scattered in every direction.

Hakadosh Baruch Hu had heeded R' Chaim Mashash's prayers, and those of his brethren, in their time of peril. Miraculously, a terrible fear had overtaken the enemy.

R' Raphael Baruch Toledano later wrote about the miracle: "We know that it was in the merit of our holy rebbe, R' Chaim, that we were saved. Not long afterwards, he fell sick. His illness lasted until Hashem's holy ark was taken away and he passed away from this earth ... and redeemed the generation."

No Effort Spared

יְקִימְךָ ד' לוֹ לְעַם קָדוֹשׁ

"Hashem will confirm you for Himself as a holy people"

(Devarim 28:9)

A great fire broke out in Radin in the year 5687 (1927). Nearly every house was burned to the ground. The fire was finally stopped very near the Chofetz Chaim's home and the yeshivah buildings, which survived along with about twenty other houses farther up the street.

Most of the townspeople lost everything. The situation was terrible. The Chofetz Chaim stopped learning and threw himself into the task of helping the victims of the fire. First of all, he secured a loan to help them survive the first few weeks after the inferno. Then he picked up his stick and began to make the rounds of all the large cities nearby: Vilna, Kovno, Minsk, and others. He succeeded in collecting large sums of money for the victims of Radin's fire. In addition, he wrote hundreds of letters asking for help, which he sent to all the Jewish communities in the world.

Everyone who received the Chofetz Chaim's request for help responded generously. Some 10,000 rubles were collected, in addition to clothing, food, and other necessities. He also turned to the government for assistance, basing his request on a special law that had been in effect since the days of Czar Nikolai the First. About a year later, he received 25,000 rubles from this source, which he divided among the fire's victims.

Aiding R' Yisrael Meir in his campaign were his entire household and all the city's other Rabbis. In an amazingly short period of time, the city was rebuilt and its citizens restored to their homes.

Not long afterwards, another fire broke out in the city. This time, it was the twenty homes that had been spared in the first blaze — including that of the Chofetz Chaim — that were burned to the ground. The Chofetz Chaim's concern for himself and his family who were left homeless did not deter him from caring about the other victims. He persuaded the victims of the first fire to separate one-tenth of the government money that they had received, and use it to help the victims of the second fire. In this way, the Chofetz Chaim made it possible for the new victims, too, to rebuild the homes they had lost in the flames.

Word of the Chofetz Chaim's remarkable efforts on behalf of all the victims spread throughout the countryside. Everyone spoke of his love for his fellow man and the good he did for others. Even the non-Jews of Radin who had lost their homes in the fire, and who had received money from the government thanks to the Chofetz Chaim's efforts, were lavish in their praise of him. As a sign of their appreciation, some of them offered to let him use their land for free to plant his crops. They also offered to give R' Yisrael Meir and his family a public parcel of land on which to build a new home.

The treasury minister who brought the government money to Radin to help the victims of the fire also expressed his admiration for R' Yisrael Meir, who had struggled valiantly to help others even while he himself was in distress. His own difficult personal situation did not deter him for a single moment from reaching out a helping hand to his fellow townsmen.

Walking in His Ways

וְהָלַכְתָּ בִּדְרָכָיו

"And you go in His ways."

(Devarim 28:9)

"As He is merciful, so you shall be merciful. As He is compassionate, so you shall be compassionate."

A woman once entered the "Churvah" courtyard in Jerusalem's Old City, in search of the water-carrier who lived there. The water-carrier was not at home. Seeing R' Yosef Zundel of Salant walking down the street wearing the clothes of a poor man, the woman — not recognizing him — asked him to draw five buckets of water for her in exchange for a small sum of money.

R' Yosef Zundel did the job joyously, but declined to take the money. "You can pay me another time, when I happen to draw water for you again."

Some time later, the woman returned to the Churvah and began asking people the name of the man who had drawn water for her, and to whom she owed money. To her shock, she learned that the "water-carrier" had been none other than the *tzaddik,* R' Yosef Zundel! Abashed, the woman hurried to R' Yosef Zundel's house to beg his forgiveness.

Laughing, R' Yosef Zundel waved away her apologies. "Thank you!" he said. "You allowed me to merit such a nice act of *chesed!*"

In the same way that the Chazon Ish took pleasure in taking pains with the details and refinements of mitzvos between man and his Creator, so, too, did he enjoy dealing with the finer points of mitzvos between a person and his fellow man.

He once wrote, "One must be careful not to cause another person distress by his speech for even a moment, because there is a prohibition against it in the Torah."

A man who once walked down the street in the company of the Chazon Ish related a poignant episode. The Chazon Ish was walking slowly, his companion at his side. Suddenly, the Chazon Ish slowed down even more. The other man was surprised — until the Chazon Ish explained.

"There is a man in front of us who has a limp. It isn't nice to pass him with the quick, confident stride of a healthy person!"

A woman once came to R' Moshe Feinstein's door and asked to speak with him.

"The *rosh yeshivah* is busy," she was told.

"But I must speak with him," the woman insisted. "He has to translate this letter that my sister sent me from Russia!"

"Translate a letter?" The men at the door were outraged. "The *rosh yeshivah* is very busy. He mustn't be disturbed for things like that."

"What do you mean?" the woman demanded. "He's been translating my sister's letters for me these past twenty years!"

There was another woman who had the habit of phoning R' Moshe Feinstein several times a day with very simple halachic questions. She frequently called two or three times about the same question, in order to make sure she had understood the answer correctly.

One of R' Moshe's assistants was about to take the phone and explain to the caller that she was wasting the *rosh yeshivah's* valuable time — but R' Moshe stopped him.

"No!" R' Moshe said. "She is afraid. She is incapable of acting in any other way."

All in the Head

וְרָאוּ כָּל עַמֵּי הָאָרֶץ כִּי שֵׁם ד' נִקְרָא עָלֶיךָ וְיָרְאוּ מִמֶּךָ

"Then all the peoples of the earth will see that the Name of Hashem is proclaimed over you, and they will revere you."

(Devarim 28:10)

While R' Aryeh Leib, the "Sha'agas Aryeh," was serving as Chief Rabbi of Volozhin, he once traveled to another city in a covered wagon. R' Aryeh Leib sat beneath the wagon's awning, wrapped in his *tallis* and *tefillin* and learning Torah. The driver, too, wore his *tefillin* and *davened*.

As they passed a forest, a band of five robbers burst through the trees, weapons in hand. They stopped the horses and shouted at the driver, "Give us all the money you have!"

The Sha'agas Aryeh, immersed in his learning, saw and heard nothing until the wagon driver screamed, "*Oy*, Rebbe, we are in great danger!"

The Sha'agas Aryeh poked his head out from under the awning and looked at the robbers. When they saw him, a great fear fell upon them, and they fled back into the forest.

As soon as they were out of danger, the wagon driver turned to the Sha'agas Aryeh and asked, "Rebbe, tell me, why were the robbers more afraid of you than of me? They could clearly see that I am younger and stronger than you are!"

R' Aryeh Leib replied, "They did not run away because of my physical strength, but because of the *tefillin* on my head. Our Sages, may their memory be blessed, said (*Berachos* 6): 'From where do we know that *tefillin* are a source of strength for Israel? As it says, "And all the nations of the earth will see that Hashem's Name is proclaimed over you, and they will revere you." The great R' Eliezer said: "This is the *tefillin* that is in the head."' Therefore, when those men saw the light of my holy *tefillin,* they fled."

"But, Rebbe," protested the driver, "I was also wearing *tefillin* on my head. Why were they not afraid of my *tefillin?*"

The Sha'agas Aryeh had an answer for this, too. "Our Sages said: 'The *tefillin* that is *in* the head.' They did not say, '*Tefillin* that is *on* the head.' The holiness of the mitzvah of *tefillin* must come from inside the head. A man must put on his *tefillin* according to the law and with the proper intentions.

"You were wearing *tefillin on* your head by habit, without the proper intention of performing a mitzvah. That is why the robbers were not afraid of you!"

A student of the Baranovitch Yeshivah was walking down the street one Shushan Purim night, when he met a group of irreligious youth who were behaving improperly. When the yeshivah student scolded them for their behavior, the irreligious youths were insulted. They told their friends that a yeshivah boy had tried to hurt them. The friends blazed into quick anger. The next day, at noon, they marched over to the yeshivah to avenge the insult on their friends.

A few tough youths entered the *beis midrash* during learning hours and began to wander insolently among the benches — apparently in search of the youth who had insulted them. There were about 300 students in the yeshivah at that time, young men who had never lifted a hand against anyone. There was mounting tension in the air.

Suddenly, R' Elchonon Wasserman walked into the *beis midrash*. Seeing the tough youths, he remained calm. Bravely, he went over and tried to send them out. One of the intruders tried to push the *rosh yeshivah* away, drawling mockingly, "No hands!"

R' Elchonon answered coldly, "You have no hands!"

As he stared at the youths with his penetrating eyes, they began to retreat. In a twinkling, they had left the yeshivah.

Before many minutes had passed, a commotion arose in the town — news that electrified all who heard it. The boy who had spoken insolently to the *rosh yeshivah* had become paralyzed in both hands!

That day, everyone saw that the Name of Hashem was indeed proclaimed over R' Elchonon, and both Hashem's Name and His Torah rose to new heights of renown.

False Pretenses

וְהוֹתִרְךָ ד' לְטוֹבָה

"Hashem shall give you bountiful goodness"

(Devarim 28:11*)*

A man from Lvov once came to see R' Meir of Premishlan. This man was a *maskil*, a proponent of the Enlightenment. He entered under false pretenses, offering a *kvittel* and a donation just like all the others who came to see the Rebbe. R' Meir blessed him, and the man left.

The moment the man was gone, the Rebbe asked for his pipe. He took the money that the *maskil* had given him, set it on fire at a candle, and placed the paper bill in his pipe to ignite the tobacco inside. His *gabbai* was shocked.

"I didn't see the government seal on it," the Rebbe explained. "It looked like smooth paper to me."

A short time later, government officials burst into the house to conduct a search for counterfeit money. They checked every nook and cranny, but found nothing. Later, it was discovered that the *maskil* had visited the Rebbe with a counterfeit bill in hand, planning to bring about the Rebbe's arrest. Immediately after leaving the Rebbe's house, he had run to the authorities to accuse R' Meir of using counterfeit money. He was certain that they would find the bill he had planted there that very day. But the Rebbe had been more clever than the *maskil,* and had burned the counterfeit bill to a crisp!

Confusion

עַד רֶדֶת חֹמֹתֶיךָ הַגְּבֹהֹת וְהַבְּצֻרוֹת אֲשֶׁר אַתָּה בֹּטֵחַ בָּהֵן בְּכָל אַרְצֶךָ

"Until the conquest of your high and fortified walls in which you trusted throughout your land"

(Devarim 28:52)

When R' Yechezkel of Shinov was about to depart for Eretz Yisrael, one of his chassidim gave him a check for a few thousand rubles, saying, "Rebbe will doubtless need money in Eretz Yisrael. He will be able to cash the check in a bank in Constantinople on his way to Eretz Yisrael."

On his arrival in Constantinople, R' Yechezkel sensed that he was unable to *daven* properly. He blamed the check for confusing his thoughts. At once he stood up, took out the check and tore it up — so that he would not be tempted to place his trust in any human being.

On the boat to Eretz Yisrael, a wealthy Jew wanted to help R' Yechezkel as well. He handed the Rebbe his calling card, on the back of which he had written a list of important ministry officials in Eretz Yisrael who would be able to assist R' Yechezkel with various matters. But the moment he took the card, the Rebbe sensed the same kind of confusion as he had had with the check. As long as the card was in his pocket, he was unable to concentrate properly. So he took the card and hurled it into the sea — and his confusion disappeared.

True Fear of Sin

לְיִרְאָה אֶת הַשֵּׁם הַנִּכְבָּד וְהַנּוֹרָא הַזֶּה אֵת ד' אֱלֹקֶיךָ

"To fear this honored and awesome Name: Hashem, your G-d"

(Devarim 28:58)

R' Yitzchak Ze'ev HaLevi Soloveitchik, the Brisker Rav, was always afraid of stumbling into sin, Heaven forbid, or of there being some lack in a mitzvah he performed. This fear made him very careful in everything he did. The special care he took when baking his Pesach matzos was well known, as well as the care he took in choosing the *arba minim* (four species) for Sukkos.

When he moved from Brisk to Eretz Yisrael, he had a halachic doubt about the need to tear his clothes each time he would see the Old City of Jerusalem. Therefore, he was always careful not to come within sight of the Old City walls.

Once, when returning from Rechov Shmuel HaNavi by bus, he looked out the window and realized that the bus was heading in the direction of the Old City. He turned at once to the *rosh yeshivah* of Yeshivas Be'er Yaakov, who was seated beside him, and said, "Please go over to the driver and ask him if he's going to pass by the Old City."

R' Moshe Shmuel Shapiro went up to the driver and was told that the bus was following a different route.

Still, as the ride continued, doubt remained in the Brisker Rav's heart. He requested that R' Moshe Shmuel ask the driver again whether the bus would pass close by the Old City walls. His companion did as he was asked, and returned once again with the same negative answer. Nevertheless, the Brisker Rav was not calmed.

R' Moshe Shmuel later said, "Whoever did not see the Rav's face then, as he looked from side to side, afraid and shaken as though he stood at the brink of danger, has not seen true fear of a halachic question!"

Only when the bus arrived at Rechov Yaffo and the Brisker Rav recognized the street did he relax. Even so, for an hour afterwards the lingering signs of anxiety remained stamped on his face.

R' Yechezkel of Shinov served Hashem with a fiery devotion. When he prayed, his face would glow as though on fire, and all his limbs would tremble. He would beat his head against the wall with such energy that the sound was like hammer blows. As he pronounced the word "*V'hanora*" in *Shemoneh Esrei*, his entire body would shake with an awesome fear.

R' Benzion of Bobov related that a Jewish villager once came to see R' Yechezkel with his sick cow. The Rebbe was repeating the *Shemoneh Esrei* aloud for the congregation when the villager came. When he said the word "*V'hanora*," a shudder passed through all who heard him — among them, the village Jew. He was moved to his depths.

The villager forgot all about his ailing cow and everything else. He remained in Shinov for two weeks, and ended up becoming one of the Rebbe's chassidim!

Davening in the Death Camp

וְהָיוּ חַיֶּיךָ תְּלֻאִים לְךָ מִנֶּגֶד וּפָחַדְתָּ לַיְלָה וְיוֹמָם

"Your life will hang opposite you, and you will be frightened night and day"

(Devarim 28:66)

A Holocaust survivor described the Klausenberger Rebbe's behavior in the death camps:

One morning, the Nazis decided to conduct a "selection, to separate out the weak and the inefficient," as those wicked men put it. All the inmates were lined up in long rows. Like beasts of prey, the Nazis walked among the rows, pointing at people who would be sent to the gas chambers.

"I was a young boy at the time," the survivor relates, "without a relative or protector. I tried to find a place to squeeze in so that I would not attract attention, because anything out of the ordinary was liable to send a person out of the line.

"And then, in one of the rows beside me, I saw the Rebbe standing with a stooped posture — contrary to the safety rules during a 'selection.' On his lips was a heartbroken prayer: 'Avinu Malkeinu, kera ro'a gezar dineinu!' ('Our Father, our King, tear up our evil decree!') The men standing near him repeated the words after him. The Rebbe continued, 'Avinu Malkeinu, nekom nikmas dam avadecha hashafuch!' ('Our Father, our King, avenge your servants' spilled blood!'), ... 'Asei l'ma'an rachamecha harabim.' ('Act for the sake of Your bountiful mercy'). And the others repeated every word after him."

The survivor continued: "If I hadn't known that we were standing in a death camp, I would not have believed it. In the midst of the terror of the selection, the Rebbe was publicly announcing that it was

Hakadosh Baruch Hu, Himself, Who would decide our fate. Deep sighs burst from the Rebbe's heart, and tears welled from his eyes. For a moment, it was possible to believe that we were standing in a shul in some town.

"The Rebbe was right. When the selection was completed, every person who had *davened* alongside the Rebbe, and had recited *Avinu Malkeinu* with him, was left among the living."

פרשת נצבים

Parashas Nitzavim

Know Before Whom You Stand

אַתֶּם נִצָּבִים הַיּוֹם כֻּלְּכֶם לִפְנֵי ד' אֱלֹקֵיכֶם

"You are standing today, all of you, before Hashem, your G-d"

(Devarim 29:9)

R' Mendel of Rimanov and the Apter Rebbe (the "Oheiv Yisrael") once came to visit the Chozeh of Lublin when he lived in the city of Lantzut. That Shabbos, thousands of people flocked to Lantzut to bask in the glow of these three *tzaddikim.*

This situation did not please the *maskilim* (proponents of the Enlightenment) in the area. One of them went to the local government with a false accusation against the three *tzaddikim.* He said that the Rebbes were inciting the people against the government.

As the three Rebbes sat at their *melaveh malkah* meal on *Motza'ei Shabbos,* a group of gendarmes appeared at the door.

"You are under arrest!" barked the officer in charge.

The *tzaddikim* were taken to the city of Raisha and thrown into jail.

The Jews in the area were shocked and panicked. They tried various ways to get the government to let the prisoners go, but without any success. On Sunday, the gentiles' day of rest, it was hard to find anyone with the authority to set the Rebbes free. The three *tzaddikim* were forced to remain in prison until at least Monday morning.

On Monday morning, the Rebbes were taken to court to face the judge. R' Mendel of Rimanov, being fluent in German, was spokesman for the three prisoners.

"What is your source of employment?" the judge asked.

"We are employed in serving the Holy One, Blessed be He, with pure thought and complete devotion," R' Mendel replied.

"And what is your purpose in coming to Lantzut?"

"We came to learn from our old friend, R' Yaakov Yitzchak Hurvitz, who is more knowledgeable than we are in this holy service."

"And why are you wearing white clothes?" the judge demanded.

"And why are you wearing black clothes?" countered R' Mendel.

The judge became furious. "Don't you know before whom you are standing?" he thundered. "Answer my questions!"

"We know the precise meaning of the expression, 'Know before Whom you are standing," R' Mendel answered calmly. "And if the judge speaks to us in anger, we will refuse to answer."

As he said those words, the Rimanover Rebbe removed the *shtreimel* from his head. The radiance of his face filled all who saw him with a mighty awe.

The judge was consumed with sudden terror. He began to tremble all over. With difficulty, he managed to stammer, "You're ... free. Go home ... all three of you! I don't want any dealings with people like this."

The Servant and the Minister

אַתֶּם נִצָּבִים הַיּוֹם כֻּלְּכֶם לִפְנֵי יְהוָה אֱלֹהֵיכֶם רָאשֵׁיכֶם שִׁבְטֵיכֶם
זִקְנֵיכֶם וְשֹׁטְרֵיכֶם כֹּל אִישׁ יִשְׂרָאֵל

*"You are standing today, all of you, before Hashem, your G-d:
your heads, your tribes, your elders, and your officers, all the men of
Israel."*

(Devarim 29:9)

When R' Yechezkel Halberstam of Shinov was just 7 years old, a miracle happened to him.

As little Yechezkel was walking down the street, absorbed in his holy thoughts, he did not notice a horse-driven wagon coming down the street toward him. The wagon driver could not stop the horses in time, and the wagon rolled right over the boy!

Critically injured, little Yechezkel was rushed to a doctor, but he had no idea how to save the boy's life. The injury was very severe.

"The child has only a few hours left to live," the doctor said gravely.

There is no describing the weeping and wailing that filled Yechezkel's home. His father, the Sanzer Rebbe, and the entire household fasted and prayed. The Rebbe, realizing the danger his son was in, went into his room and poured out his heart to Hashem, pleading with Him to spare his son.

His prayers were answered. The boy survived, and went on to live a long life.

R' Chaim of Sanz related the tale of the miracle years afterward, when one of the children born to him later in life became very ill. His rebbetzin came to him as he sat at the table with his chassidim. She was weeping. "Please do something for our son," she begged through her tears.

The Rebbe immediately ordered the others to *bentch*, then asked his chassidim to enter the *beis midrash* and recite *Tehillim* for his son's health. The Rebbe said *Tehillim* along with them. Then he told his chassidim, "When I was young, my oldest son, Yechezkel, 7 years old at the time, was run over by a wagon. The doctor despaired of his life, and the uproar at home was great. What did I do? I stood and cried and *davened* to *Hakadosh Baruch Hu*, and with His help the boy survived and grew well again.

"I was young then. I was like a simple servant of Hashem, a servant who throws himself on the ground and begs for salvation. But now I am old, and I am no longer like a simple servant. Now I am like a minister to the King and a minister may not enter the King's chamber at any moment for his own purposes. The minister's job is to concern himself with the public welfare, not to bother the King about his own personal problems.

"But you," the Rebbe concluded, "are like the soldiers of the King of kings. You can pray before Him at any time, and beg Him to have mercy on my sick son."

It was the third day of Elul, 5683 (1923). Dazzling chandeliers lit up the Vienna auditorium where a large group had gathered *l'shem Shamayim* — for the sake of Heaven. On the dais stood a *gaon* whose electrifying presence raised the audience to new heights. The speaker had a proposal to lay before them.

"If every Jew, in every location, will learn the same *daf* of Gemara every day, could there be a more concrete expression of the eternal unity between *Hakadosh Baruch Hu* and his people?"

That was the question that R' Meir Shapiro posed to his rapt listeners. He went on to enthrall the audience with a vivid description of his brilliant new concept: *daf yomi*.

"How marvelous it is! A Jewish man takes a trip by boat, a *Maseches Berachos* tucked under his arm. He travels for two weeks, all the way from Eretz Yisrael to America. Every day, he opens his

Gemara and learns the day's *daf.* On his arrival in America, he walks into a *beis midrash* in New York and finds, to his amazement, that the Jews there are learning the same *daf* that he had studied that very morning! He joins in, discussing the *daf* with them in perfect harmony. What a way to sanctify and glorify *shem Shamayim!*"

His audience sighed rapturously as they pictured the scene. Into the hush, R' Meir Shapiro continued.

"And a Jew from the United States who travels to Brazil in South America, or to Japan in Asia? The first thing he does is enter a *beis midrash* to find everyone there learning the same *daf* that he is learning! Is there a better way to unite our hearts? And not only that: Until now, there have been complete tractates hardly ever learned by the general public. These tractates have been like orphans, with only a few individuals poring over them. The *daf yomi* will correct all that! And here's another benefit: Our youth — the future of our people — will be the ones called upon to begin this mitzvah!"

The great hall erupted in thunderous applause. R' Meir Shapiro's proposal was accepted by all with tremendous enthusiasm. It symbolized a renewal of the three-part bond that exists between Hashem, His Torah, and *Bnei Yisrael.* Orthodox Jewry the world over took upon itself to learn the same page of Gemara each day, beginning with *Maseches Berachos* on Rosh Hashanah, 5684 (1923)!

On that day, the wonderful vision became a reality. There were many who still hesitated. But when the Gerrer Rebbe said, after the Rosh Hashanah *Ma'ariv,* "I'm going to learn the *daf yomi,*" word spread with the speed and energy of an electric current. Everyone ran to find a *Maseches Berachos.*

After that fateful Rosh Hashanah, R' Meir Shapiro related, he received a letter from his only sister who lived in a remote area near Bukavina. She wrote:

"On Rosh Hashanah night I had a dream: I saw you, my dear brother, up in *Shamayim,* surrounded by a great throng of shining *tzaddikim.* And you, my brother, stood at the center of them all, your face glowing like the sun at noon, and everyone smiled at you and thanked you, and rejoiced in you greatly. Tell me please, brother, the meaning of my dream!"

Jews everywhere began to learn the *daf yomi* that night. In every city and every town, groups and classes were formed for the purpose of learning the page of the day together. Jewish newspapers and documents began to mark down the *daf* alongside the date.

When two Jewish men met, they had an immediate topic in common in the *sugyos* of that day's *daf*. R' Meir Shapiro distributed tens of thousands of *daf yomi* calendars and created a special monthly collection of original Torah thoughts based on the *daf yomi*. The monthly magazine "Yavneh," published in Lvov, added a special section for this purpose, and the periodical "Eshkol" devoted a column to it as well. To aid *daf yomi* learners, R' Baruch Gelbart of Lodz created an index for *Chazal's* sayings based on the order of the *daf yomi* tractates of the Gemara. R' Meir Shapiro gave this index his enthusiastic endorsement: "This will light up the eyes of those who learn *daf yomi*. May Hashem be with him."

R' Meir Shapiro would say, "When the idea of *daf yomi* came into my mind, I wanted to propose it to the assembly as something that would be suitable for youngsters. I never dreamed that the group would accept the proposal for the generation's elders as well. But when I began to explain the benefits of learning the *daf yomi* — because I believe that there is a tremendous benefit in tens of thousands of Jews learning one page of Gemara each day — I had a terrific surprise. Everyone agreed, unanimously, that the idea was a good one for *every* Jewish man!"

And he added, "Happy is the generation when the great listen to the small."

It is said that the Pittsburgh Rebbe, R' Avraham Abba Leifer, devoted tremendous energy to his *davening*. With a holy fervor he would pray out loud, accompanying the words with eager gestures.

One day, the Rebbe reflected that his manner of *davening* might bring him to the brink of arrogance. He decided to serve Hashem more simply and modestly. From that day on, his great enthusiasm was no longer visible. The Rebbe kept all his devotion inside, praying silently like a child confessing his sins to his father. The tears flowed copiously as he *davened*; he could not conceal from his Father the intense longing in his heart.

The Rebbe was once forced to *daven Shacharis* alone at home, as no young men came from the yeshivah to join him in forming a *minyan*. His prayers lasted a long time. Two hours later, the Rebbe's assistant opened the door and peeked into the room. The Rebbe was still absorbed in prayer, eyes closed and face aglow. The assistant quietly closed the door.

Half an hour later, he opened it again, certain that the Rebbe must have finished. But the Rebbe was still *davening*. Another half-hour passed. Fearing for the Rebbe's health, the assistant opened the door once more and tried to get the Rebbe's attention. "The Rebbe has not yet eaten breakfast."

But the Rebbe did not lift his eyes from his *siddur*. He had not heard the other man speak at all.

Four full hours after he had begun, the Rebbe finally finished *davening*. He folded his *tallis* and turned to leave the room.

"Why did the Rebbe's *davening* take so long today?" the assistant ventured to ask. "When the Rebbe *davens* in shul, it takes far less time."

Humbly, the Rebbe apologized. "When I am alone with my Creator, it takes a little longer."

Suffering in Silence

וְאָמַר הַדּוֹר הָאַחֲרוֹן בְּנֵיכֶם אֲשֶׁר יָקוּמוּ מֵאַחֲרֵיכֶם ... וְרָאוּ אֶת מַכּוֹת
הָאָרֶץ הַהִוא

"The later generation will say — your children who will arise after you ... when they will see the plagues of that land"

(Devarim 29:21)

R' Moshe Leib of Sassov liked to learn something about serving Hashem from everyone. He once claimed that he learned from a robber how to cope with the sufferings of *galus*. This is the story he told:

R' Moshe Leib was walking from town to town collecting money for *hachnasas kallah*, when a band of robbers attacked him in the woods. The robbers surrounded him on all sides and were about to kill him, when their leader suddenly recognized R' Moshe Leib.

"This is the holy Rabbi from Sassov!" he exclaimed. "I won't let anyone harm him!"

That same robber had once been a beggar. Together with a group of other poor men, he had come one day to the marketplace in the city of Brod. He was very hungry but had no idea how to find something to eat. Then one of his companions told him that R' Moshe Leib gave out bread and borscht for free. The entire group went to the Rebbe's house, and R' Moshe Leib lovingly doled out food and drink to each one, offering words of comfort to the poor people and refusing to take a penny from them. The one who later "rose" to become leader of a band of robbers remembered R' Moshe Leib and the good deed he had done.

The robbers behaved respectfully toward R' Moshe Leib. "We have a Jewish boy with us who once learned Torah but is now a member of our gang," they told him. "Test him and see whether he remembers what he learned."

R' Moshe Leib asked the youth a question on Gemara, but the young robber could not answer. Then the Rebbe asked a question on *Chumash*, but he could not answer that, either. When the robbers saw that their companion was failing his test, they condemned him to a hundred lashes, "just for fun."

R' Moshe Leib saw that the beating was nearly killing the silent youth. He begged the robbers to have mercy. The lashes stopped.

The robbers agreed to let the youth accompany R' Moshe Leib to the next town. As they walked, R' Moshe Leib tried to persuade the young man to turn his life around, and he succeeded in convincing him.

"Tell me," said R' Moshe Leib presently, "how did you bear all those lashings without saying a word? Where did you find the strength to bear such suffering in silence?"

The young man answered, "We robbers are used to this. We beat each other cruelly in order to build up our strength so that, if we are ever caught by the police and tortured to reveal our secrets, we will be able to endure the pain in silence."

"And where does this strength come from?" R' Moshe Leib persisted.

"I keep thinking that each lash is the last, and that after it will come relief. After all, a beating doesn't last forever!"

Later, when Jews would come to R' Moshe Leib pouring out their troubles, he would tell them, "Just imagine that your portion of suffering is full, and that tomorrow you will be free of it. After all, 'a beating doesn't last forever'!"

The Candle Burns

וְשַׁבְתָ עַד ד' אֱלֹקֶיךָ וְשָׁמַעְתָ בְקֹלוֹ

"And you will return to Hashem, your G-d, and listen to His voice"

(Devarim 30:2)

One night, R' Yisrael Salanter walked from his home to the *beis midrash* to learn Torah. As he passed the shoemaker's window, he saw a small flickering light. R' Yisrael was surprised that the shoemaker was working such late hours. He entered the shop and found the shoemaker sitting on his bench fixing a pair of shoes by candlelight.

R' Yisrael greeted him, then asked, "Tell me, why are you sitting and fixing shoes so late at night?"

"Rebbe," the shoemaker answered simply, "as long as the candle burns, one can still make repairs."

R' Yisrael was moved to the depths of his soul. In the shoemaker's words he found a deep and wonderful idea, a tremendous piece of *mussar*. Shlomo HaMelech said in *Sefer Mishlei*: "*Ner Hashem nishmas adam* — A person's soul is Hashem's candle." A soul is compared to a candle. As long as the soul resides inside a person, he can still work to repair his character and his behavior.

For days afterwards, R' Yisrael could be heard pacing his room, repeating to himself with great feeling, "As long as the candle burns, one can still make repairs."

An elderly Jew walked into the Petach Tikvah shul that is named after R' Chaim Ozer Grodzinski. When it came time to read the Torah portion, he was given the honor of being called up to the Torah. But instead of the usual *berachah*, bitter sobs burst from the old man's lips.

It was a few minutes before he was calm enough to go on. Afterwards, he had this story to tell.

"I am 83 years old today. The last time I stepped into a shul was when I became a bar mitzvah ... seventy years ago! I went to shul with my father. We went to the *gaon* R' Chaim Ozer's shul, where I was called up to the Torah.

"The *gaon* didn't recognize my father, who came to shul only on Shabbos.

"'Where does the boy go to school?'" R' Chaim Ozer asked my father after *davening*.

"'He goes to *gymnasia* (public high school),' my father answered.

"Hearing this, R' Chaim Ozer said, 'Know this, my friend. If you continue to send your son to the *gymnasia*, the years of a generation (seventy) will pass before your son will hear the Torah read again.'

"My father did not heed his warning. I continued at the *gymnasia*. And it's been seventy years from that Shabbos when I last heard the Torah read."

The man's voice shook as he spoke, and it was difficult indeed to comfort him.

When the Klausenberger Rebbe was a child in the city of Rudnik, a certain Jew, who had thrown off the yoke of Torah, lived there This man would be awakened in the middle of the night by the sound of crying coming from the *beis midrash* next door.

One night, the man gathered his courage and went to see where the sobs and sighs were coming from. He was amazed to see the future Rebbe, then just a child of 4, weeping bitterly near the open *aron kodesh*. The little boy was bemoaning his sins and pleading to Hashem, "Light up our eyes with Your Torah and let our hearts cling to Your mitzvos."

The child cried for two hours and conducted a *tikkun chatzos* at midnight before starting for home. He didn't want anyone in his family to notice that he had been gone.

The non-religious neighbor was shaken to the depths of his being at the sight of a pure and innocent child crying and pleading for his life, while he himself, a hardened sinner, walked around carefree without thinking about his soul at all. From that night on he began to repent, and became a G-d-fearing Jew.

From the Ends of the Earth

אִם יִהְיֶה נִדַּחֲךָ בִּקְצֵה הַשָּׁמָיִם מִשָּׁם יְקַבֶּצְךָ ד' אֱלֹקֶיךָ וּמִשָּׁם יִקָּחֶךָ

"If your dispersed will be at the ends of the heavens, from there Hashem, your G-d, will gather you in"

(Devarim 30:4)

Fleeing from Nazi persecution, a group of Jewish youngsters was sent from Germany to England. When the Second World War broke out, the group was sent to Australia together with thousands of other German citizens, because the English suspected them of being spies. The refugees made the long trip to Australia on a small, ancient ship under very difficult and crowded conditions.

As if they didn't have problems enough, the refugees aboard the ship had another worry: The English had sent convicted criminals along with them to serve as guards.

These criminals searched through the other passengers' belongings and stole anything of value that they could find. The rest of the belongings were tossed into the sea, in order to cover their tracks.

One morning, a German submarine caught sight of the English ship and began torpedoing it. The first salvo missed the ship. The second, better aimed, headed straight for the walls of the ship. Suddenly, a huge wave lifted the ship, and with Hashem's mercy the torpedo passed beneath the ship without touching it!

The refugees shivered with joy at their miraculous rescue, but also with fear of what was still to come. But to their amazement, the torpedoing stopped completely, and the submarine disappeared from sight.

Some forty years later, the German submarine commander published his memoirs. In his book, he described his amazement when his torpedo had missed the refugee ship. Then he went on to relate that, while shooting at the ship, his crew suddenly noticed some strange-looking objects floating on the water. Obviously, they had been tossed from the ship. The commander immediately gave the order to his men to go out and gather up the objects — which turned out to be the passengers' suitcases.

A search of the suitcases revealed letters written in German, the language used by the Jewish youths who had been born in Germany. It was then that the submarine commander realized that the ship was carrying German refugees and he ordered the attack to stop!

Talking To Himself?

וְאַתָּה תָשׁוּב וְשָׁמַעְתָּ בְּקוֹל ד'

"You shall return and listen to the voice of Hashem"

(Devarim 30:8)

R' Nota Weiss would deliver a *derashah* each Shabbos in one of the shuls in Jerusalem's Old City.

One summer Shabbos, the heat was intense. No one stepped outdoors unless absolutely necessary. R' Nota came to shul at the appointed hour, to deliver his talk, but the shul was empty.

R' Nota thought to himself, "I have a regular custom of delivering a *derashah* on Shabbos. In that case, even if no one is here to hear me, I must say it anyway."

He climbed the steps to the *aron kodesh*, put on a *tallis,* and began his *derashah*. For two solid hours he stood there and spoke to the empty shul.

He concluded his talk. Suddenly, a youth ran out of the women's section, crying, "Rebbe, I am going to do *teshuvah!*"

It seems that the boy had been walking outdoors when, finding the heat unbearable, he caught a glimpse of the open shul door and slipped inside to escape the sun. He lay down on a bench in the women's section and fell asleep. At the sound of someone's voice, he had awoken with a start. Unable to fall back to sleep, he listened to the entire *derashah*.

And the moment R' Nota finished speaking, the unseen listener rushed out, emotionally announcing his intention to improve his behavior and change his entire lifestyle.

Someone once asked R' Yissochor Ber of Radoshitz how much regret a person needs to feel in order to do *teshuvah* to atone for a sin.

R' Yissochor Ber answered with a story.

"A merchant came to market day in Leipzig, bringing with him several wagonloads of merchandise. Customers thronged around him, eager to buy. Seeing so much interest in his goods, the merchant put the customers aside with various excuses. Word spread through the marketplace that there was a great demand for what he was selling.

"What did the other merchants do? They filled wagons with the same merchandise and brought it to the marketplace — which immediately brought down the price. The first merchant now could not find a customer who would pay him even half the amount he had been offered before.

"How strong do you think that merchant's regret was?

"*That,*" concluded R' Yissochor Ber, "is the amount of regret that a sinner is required to feel in order to achieve the level of genuine *teshuvah.*"

From the Mouth to the Heart

כִּי קָרוֹב אֵלֶיךָ הַדָּבָר מְאֹד בְּפִיךָ וּבִלְבָבְךָ לַעֲשׂתוֹ

"Rather, the matter is very near to you, in your mouth and in your heart, to perform it."

(Devarim 30:14)

A storekeeper came to see R' Moshe of Kobrin with a complaint. "Though I sit in my store all day long, it is only with difficulty that I manage to support my family. But the store at the end of the block is always full. That man's shop carries the same merchandise as mine and my prices are no higher than his. But he is earning a good livelihood, while I only manage to scrape by. How can this be?"

The Rebbe answered, "I assure you, you will also earn a good living and not suffer any lack — on one condition. You must not begrudge your neighbor his good fortune. When you see him succeeding in his business and being rewarded for his efforts, give thanks to *Hakadosh Baruch Hu* and say, '*Baruch Hashem* who gives every Jew a plentiful livelihood.'

"It will be hard for you to say this at first. But once you make it a habit, the words will penetrate your heart as well, until you'll be saying them wholeheartedly. As it says in the *pasuk,* 'in your mouth and in your heart.' First it is in your mouth, and afterwards it is in your heart. The things you say will enter your heart!"

Things turned out exactly as the Rebbe had predicted. With time, the storekeeper was able to look upon his fellow man with a benevolent eye and also saw his own efforts crowned with success.

R' Simchah Bunim of Peshischa told a story about a man from Cracow named R' Isaac, who dreamed several times that it would be worth his while to travel to Prague. In Prague, R' Isaac was told in the dream, he was to find the king's palace and dig beneath the bridge that led to it. There he would find a great treasure and become a wealthy man.

R' Isaac traveled to Prague. On his arrival, he went straight to the bridge near the king's palace. As he came closer, he saw that the spot was well guarded by soldiers who stood watch there day and night. No one could come near the bridge without being seen.

R' Isaac was downcast. He had traveled such a long distance for nothing. Now he would have to return home empty-handed. In his distress, he wandered about near the bridge all that day, brooding about the dream he had had and the treasure he was supposed to find. As darkness fell, he found an inn and went to sleep, only to return once again in the morning to the bridge that had held all his hopes. This routine continued for several days.

An army officer noticed the Jew who kept showing up near the bridge and walking around with a troubled face, as he gazed sadly at the bridge and at the soldiers guarding it. The officer decided to investigate. He called out to R' Isaac, "Tell me, Jew, what are you looking for here, and who have you been waiting for these past few days?"

R' Isaac told the officer all about his dream of buried treasure beneath the bridge — treasure that he had traveled so far to find.

The officer burst out laughing. "You based such a long trip, all the way to Prague, on insubstantial dreams? A man like yourself should not believe in dreams. I also had a dream, in which I was told to travel to Cracow and find a Jew named R' Isaac. In his house, beneath the stove, I would find a great treasure. Now, do you imagine I would actually get up and go to Cracow because of some silly dream?"

R' Isaac's heart began to pound wildly. Now he understood that the purpose of his trip to Prague had been to hear this soldier's story. The treasure was not in Prague, it was in Cracow, in his very own house!

R' Isaac returned home at once, dug beneath the stove, and found the treasure that was waiting there for him. He became a rich man. R' Isaac used some of his newfound wealth to build a shul that is called by his name to this very day.

R' Simchah Bunim concluded, "When a man goes to visit a rebbe or *tzaddik,* he must know that the main purpose of his visit is to discover that he will not find treasure in the Rebbe's house, but rather in his own. When he goes home after seeing the Rebbe, he must dig deep into his own soul to find the treasure within. He will search and he will find when he believes the *pasuk,* 'The matter is very near to you, in your mouth and in your heart, to perform it.'"

Question and Answer

לְאַהֲבָה אֶת ד' אֱלֹקֶיךָ לָלֶכֶת בִּדְרָכָיו וְלִשְׁמֹר מִצְוֹתָיו וְחֻקֹּתָיו וּמִשְׁפָּטָיו

"To love Hashem, your G-d, to walk in His ways, and to keep His commandments, His statutes, and His ordinances"

(Devarim 30:16)

One day, R' Boruch Ber traveled to Slutzk and posed a difficult question to the Ridvaz on a topic in *Maseches Berachos.* R' Yaakov Dovid (the Ridvaz) served as Rabbi of Slutzk while R' Boruch Ber Leibowitz was rabbi in nearby Kaminetz.

"I will think about the question," the Ridvaz said. "When I find the answer, with Hashem's help, I will let you know."

R' Boruch Ber parted from his friend and returned to his own town.

Towards evening, the sky filled with dark, heavy clouds and a snowstorm began to rage. The wind howled in the bare trees while the steadily falling snow covered everything. The townspeople shut themselves up in their homes. To step outdoors into that storm was to risk one's life.

Night fell. In the town, everyone slept. In the Rav's home all were asleep as well, except for R' Boruch Ber, still poring over his Gemara. Suddenly, he heard the sound of someone approaching his house. He felt a pang of fear: Who would be walking outside on such a night? The footsteps continued to come closer, crunching over the sheet of solid ice that covered the path. R' Boruch Ber murmured *Tehillim* … Then came a light knock on the door.

"Who can that be?" R' Boruch Ber wondered, shivering with apprehension. He was quiet. The knocking sounded again, and then a third time. R' Boruch Ber sat frozen in his place and did not say a word.

"R' Boruch Ber! R' Boruch Ber!" he heard suddenly, in a familiar voice. "I have the answer!"

R' Boruch Ber leaped out of his chair and ran to the door. There, on his doorstep, stood the Ridvaz, covered with snow from head to foot.

R' Boruch Ber brought his friend inside, gave him dry clothes and a hot cup of tea. Then the Ridvaz said, "At last, after thinking a long time, I succeeded this afternoon in finding an answer to your question. Because not a single wagon driver in town would agree to bring me here from Slutzk, I got up and walked here on foot."

News From the Front

הַעִדֹתִי בָכֶם הַיּוֹם אֶת הַשָּׁמַיִם וְאֶת הָאָרֶץ

"I call the heavens and the earth today to bear witness against you"

(Devarim 30:19)

In the last year of the Sfas Emes' life, war broke out between Russia and Japan. The Russian Czar issued an order to draft Jews into the army. Many Gerrer chassidim were among those drafted and sent to the front.

The Sfas Emes was fearful for the fate of all these Jewish lives. As long as these soldiers were fighting on the front lines, the Rebbe did not lie down on his bed. He would sleep on the floor at night, his clothes damp from all the tears he shed for his people's troubles.

The Rebbe received many letters from his chassidim at the front. From the trenches, they wrote their Rebbe both Torah thoughts and the day-to-day events of their lives. One brilliant young man wrote the Rebbe a long Torah discourse. The Sfas Emes wrote him a letter in return, beginning this way: "'I call the heavens and the earth today to bear witness against you.' The word 'ha'idosi' ('to bear witness') comes from the root meaning *adi*, or adornment. I have adorned heaven and earth with you — with Jews such as yourself!"

One Precious Minute

וּבָחַרְתָּ בַּחַיִּים

"And you shall choose life"

(Devarim 30:19)

When Naftali Trop, *rosh yeshivah* of Radin, fell critically ill, the yeshivah students prayed constantly for their beloved rebbe to recover. One of the boys had a novel idea. He began a campaign to collect "life" for the *rosh yeshivah*. The students donated days and even weeks of their own lives so that R' Naftali might continue to live.

After the campaign was over, the student who had begun it went to see the Chofetz Chaim. He told the Chofetz Chaim that the boys had volunteered to donate precious days of their lives for R' Naftali, and even ventured to ask the Chofetz Chaim if he would like to participate in the campaign as well.

The Chofetz Chaim sat lost in deep thought, considering how much he could donate for the *rosh yeshivah's* sake. At last, he looked up and said that he was prepared to donate one minute.

The story spread through the yeshivah as if on wings. Seeing how greatly the Chofetz Chaim valued time, that most precious commodity of all, the next day in yeshivah saw all the students eagerly redouble their diligence in learning.

A Gift From Hashem

וּבָחַרְתָּ בַּחַיִּים לְמַעַן תִּחְיֶה אַתָּה וְזַרְעֶךָ

"And you shall choose life, so that you will live, you and your offspring"

(Devarim 30:19)

The Chofetz Chaim's young grandson once asked, "Zaydie, how old are you?"

The Chofetz Chaim looked at the little boy, but did not answer. Seeing this, the child did not ask again.

A little later, the Chofetz Chaim took several bills, put the money into an envelope, sealed it well, and gave it to his grandson: a present from Zaydie. Presently he asked the little boy, "Why didn't you open the envelope to see how much money I gave you?"

The child answered, "A present from my Zaydie is very precious to me. It doesn't matter how much money there is in the envelope."

"That's the way I felt about your question about my age!" the Chofetz Chaim smiled. "Life is a precious and wonderful gift from *Hashem Yisbarach*. Do we have even an inkling as to the true value of each and every minute of life? What difference does it make how many minutes of life we have received as a gift from *Hakadosh Baruch Hu*? When you get a gift, you don't count it!"

No Strength?

כִּי הוּא חַיֶּיךָ וְאֹרֶךְ יָמֶיךָ

"For He is your life and the length of your days"

(Devarim 30:20)

R' Shmelke of Nikolsburg and his younger brother, R' Pinchas, would learn together as boys. They remained awake through many nights, until the young R' Pinchas felt too tired to go on. He went to fetch a pillow to place under his head in order to sleep a little.

R' Shmelke admonished, "Why have you stopped learning the

holy Torah, exchanging something eternal for something temporary?"

R' Pinchas replied, "Don't you see that I have no strength left to learn?"

"The strength you used to get up and fetch the pillow — that was strength you could have devoted to learning!"

The mother of these two *tzaddikim* used to say, "I have two sons. The first doesn't want to *bentch* (R' Shmelke used to fast constantly), and the second doesn't want to say '*Hamapil*' (R' Pinchas hardly ever slept at night)."

So diligent were the two brothers in their learning that they once learned through two straight days without stopping to sleep at all. When R' Pinchas needed to get another *sefer*, he went down the stairs from the attic in which they were learning — and from sheer exhaustion fell asleep right there on the steps!

פרשת וילך

Parashas Vayeilech

The "Tenth" Man

ד׳ אֱלֹקֶיךָ הוּא עֹבֵר לְפָנֶיךָ הוּא יַשְׁמִיד אֶת הַגּוֹיִם הָאֵלֶּה מִלְּפָנֶיךָ

"Hashem, your G-d — He will cross before you; He will destroy these nations from before you"

(Devarim 31:3)

The life of a Jewish man was once saved through a remarkable display of *hashgachah pratis*. Here is his story.

"When the 'White Army' ruled Russia after World War One," the man begins his tale, "it was the first time in many years that the Jews enjoyed freedom. The Jews who dealt in diamonds and jewels became especially prosperous. I was one of them.

"Every morning, I went to my office in the diamond exchange at 8 a.m., and stayed there all day. One morning I decided to go to the office early. As usual, I had with me a briefcase full of diamonds and jewels. As I walked along, I heard someone call out. Turning my head, I saw a man standing at the door of a small shul, looking for a tenth man to make up a *minyan*. He called to me to come in. As I had a little time to spare, I went in to become the tenth man.

"However, as I walked into the shul I saw that there were only three other men there besides myself and the man who had called to me — and who was now standing in the doorway again, calling out for a 'tenth' man.

"'What's this?' I complained. 'I'm not the tenth, I'm the fifth. This will take all morning!'

"'Don't worry,' the fellow told me. 'Many Jews pass this way each morning.'

"I began to recite *Tehillim*. During the next ten minutes, he managed to get one more man for the *minyan*. I got up to leave, but he pleaded, 'Listen, today is my father's *yahrtzeit* and I have to say *Kaddish*. Please stay! I'll try to organize a *minyan* quickly.'

"'I can't wait,' I said. 'I have to be at my office at 8 o'clock — which is right now!'

"Forcefully, he said, 'Listen, I'm not letting you go. I have *yahrtzeit*, I have to say *Kaddish*. The minute I have ten men, we'll *daven*, and you can go.'

"Not wanting to enrage him further, I reluctantly returned to my place and continued saying *Tehillim*.

"Another ten minutes passed, during which time he managed to snag another two men. Again I started for the door. But he stopped me, saying sternly, 'Listen to me now: If *you* had *yahrtzeit* for your father, you'd want me to stay. Right? And I would stay! Now I want you to do the same thing for me!'

"Hearing this, I decided that part of my morning's plans would have to be abandoned. Whatever happened, I would stay!

"At about 8:30, we finally had a *minyan*. I thought the man would say some *mishnah* and then *Kaddish*, but no — he began from the beginning of *davening*. Impatiently, I glanced at my watch. I would be very late getting to the office today, I thought.

"I kept looking around to see whether anyone new had joined us so that I could leave, but the ten men remained ten men. When we finished, the man with the *yahrtzeit* served cake and drinks and then let us go.

"I began to make my way to the office, carrying my briefcase of jewels. I was two doors away from my building, when a man I knew came sprinting toward me, waving frantically.

"'Hurry! Get away from here!' he screamed wildly. 'The Communists took over the government today. Some of them came in and killed the Jews in the diamond exchange, and now they're gathering up the booty. Run for your life!'

"And that's exactly what I did. I stayed hidden for several days — and, as you can see, with Hashem's mercy I managed to escape from Russia. You can imagine what would have happened to me had I left that *minyan* early."

R' Baruch's Letter

וַד׳ הוּא הַהֹלֵךְ לְפָנֶיךָ הוּא יִהְיֶה עִמָּךְ לֹא יַרְפְּךָ וְלֹא יַעַזְבֶךָ

"Hashem — it is He Who goes before you; He will be with you;
He will not release you nor will He forsake you"

(Devarim 31:8)

The Jews of Morocco had moved out of the Jewish section into other neighborhoods, where they discarded their special Jewish dress and began to learn from the ways of the gentiles. Enlightenment and French culture became widespread among them. Many Jews — especially the younger set — became uprooted from their heritage. They grew distant from their Torah and scorned the rebuke of their parents and rabbis.

This spiritual holocaust was promoted by the French "Alliance" schools whose goal was to spread "culture" among the Jews. This organization built a network of secular schools throughout the developing lands, including Morocco.

By way of these schools, a secular attitude seeped into Jewish homes. "Enlightenment" became a byword. Many Jews began to imitate the French and their culture.

It is not surprising, then, that many opposed R' Raphael Baruch Toledano when he was appointed Chief Rabbi of Meknes. They saw in this fiery and uncompromising man an obstacle in their chosen path.

One such Jewish activist, a leading opponent of R' Baruch, wanted to introduce many aspects of French culture into the community. R' Baruch stood like a stone in his way, rising up against anything that seemed contrary to the spirit of the Torah.

In return, the activist tried in every way to foil R' Baruch's plans. He expressed opposition to R' Baruch's opinions and actions at every chance he got. His ultimate goal was to find a way to remove R' Baruch from his rabbinical post and thereby remove his influence over the people.

One day, the man received news that made him dance with joy. He had the perfect weapon with which to finally get rid of R' Baruch!

The Jewish court was recognized by the government and considered a government bureaucracy. Therefore, as a government employee, R' Baruch was not permitted to engage in business.

When his opponent heard that R' Baruch had just published a *sefer* and was selling it to the public, he thought he had found the perfect chance to accuse him before the authorities and ruin his good name. He was quick to spread the news of the Rabbi's terrible "crime": "Attention! A government employee, who must work only at his job, is conducting a private business!"

The slander did its job well. Within a few days, R' Baruch was summoned for an investigation. His staunch supporters, concerned about their beloved rabbi, wished to accompany him and testify on his behalf. But R' Baruch saw no need for this. Placing his trust in Hashem, he went to face his interrogators with a tranquil heart.

Back home, his family waited fearfully for the results of the investigation.

R' Baruch was called up by the official in charge of his case, and accused at once of conducting a book business. "You are betraying your position!" the bureaucrat barked.

Instead of answering, R' Baruch handed the official a letter. It was from the city's governor, granting R' Baruch permission to sell his *sefer*.

Taken by surprise, the bureaucrat stammered in confusion, "Of course, you have full permission to sell your books if you wish. There is no problem, no problem at all!" And he let R' Baruch leave immediately.

The furious official summoned the activist who had made the accusation against the Rabbi. Had the official acted as the other man had wanted, the governor's wrath would have fallen on his own head. No wonder he was enraged!

Abashed, the activist left. Not only had he not succeeded in ruining R' Baruch, but he had managed to lose the government's favor as well. For his efforts, he had received a stinging slap in the face.

As for R' Baruch, his thoughts on the way home were filled with wonder. "When I published my *sefer*, I had no special reason to request permission from the governor to sell it. Many rabbis publish *sefarim* without a thought of getting a permit! But Hashem planted the notion in my mind to have this letter prepared, and it has now foiled my agitator's plot!"

When R' Baruch's family and supporters heard what had happened, they realized afresh that a special *hashgachah* watched over him. *Hakadosh Baruch Hu* rewarded His beloved R' Baruch by leading him always along the correct path.

A Most Unusual Mishloach Manos

וַיִּכְתֹּב מֹשֶׁה אֶת הַתּוֹרָה הַזֹּאת וַיִּתְּנָהּ אֶל הַכֹּהֲנִים בְּנֵי לֵוִי

"Moshe wrote this Torah and gave it to the Kohanim, the sons of Levi"

(Devarim 31:9)

R' Shlomo HaLevi Alkabetz grew up in dire poverty. Then, as a young man, he became engaged to the daughter of R' Yitzchak — a man of wealth and property.

As Purim approached, R' Shlomo's mother called him over with a worried frown.

"As you know, my son, it is the custom, along with the *mishloach manos*, to send the *kallah* a nice gift — a piece of jewelry made of gold or precious stones. How will we follow this custom, when we have nothing?" She sighed deeply.

R' Shlomo did not want to distress his *kallah*. For some time he sat sunk in thought. Finally, he answered, "Don't worry, Mother. Leave it to me. With Hashem's help, by Purim I'll manage to get her something very nice!"

The weeks passed. And then it was Purim.

"Mother," said R' Shlomo, "please prepare the cakes and other baked goods for the *kallah* and her family. The gift is ready!" As he spoke, he handed her a package.

His mother was radiant with joy. Opening the package, she blurted in astonishment, "You're sending a commentary on *Megillas Esther* to your *kallah*?"

"She has plenty of jewelry and fine stones from her rich parents," R' Shlomo said. "But a commentary on the *Megillah* that I composed myself is something she will not receive from anyone else."

When they opened the *mishloach manos* and found the precious commentary within, R' Yitzchak's family's joy knew no bounds.

"Blessed is He and blessed is His Name!" R' Yitzchak exclaimed happily after reading what his future son-in-law had written, "for the merit of having such an outstanding *talmid chacham* fall to our lot. He is worth a thousand jewels!"

Later, when he published the commentary, R' Shlomo named it "*Manos HaLevi*," because it had served its first purpose as a *mishloach manos*!

Why His Eyes Could See

וַיִּכְתֹּב מֹשֶׁה אֶת הַתּוֹרָה הַזֹּאת וַיִּתְּנָהּ אֶל הַכֹּהֲנִים בְּנֵי לֵוִי הַנֹּשְׂאִים
אֶת אֲרוֹן בְּרִית ד' וְאֶל כָּל זִקְנֵי יִשְׂרָאֵל

*"Moshe wrote this Torah and gave it to the Kohanim, the sons of
Levi, the bearers of the Ark of the covenant of Hashem, and to all the
elders of Israel"*

(Devarim 31:9)

Moshe Rabbeinu wrote the Torah on the last day of his life. In his commentary, *Sha'arei Chaim* on the *Sha'arei Teshuvah* (*Sha'ar Shelishi, Os* 28), the *Smag* states that even a very old man is forbidden to stop learning Torah.

It is said that when R' Shßmuel Hominer showed this commentary of the *Smag* to R' Isser Zalman Meltzer, R' Isser Zalman said, "Let me tell you an amazing story that I heard while in Slutzk.

"I once went to see a certain *talmid chacham* who was blind. He showed me twelve *sefarim* that he had written. Then, mentioning a certain *dvar Torah* in one *sefer*, he said, 'That is the last *chiddush* I wrote.'

"I asked him what he meant.

"'I worked hard,' the blind man told me, 'and, with Heaven's help, came up with many original thoughts. When I grew old, this became hard for me, and when I had finished writing down this *chiddush* I decided that I would stop working so hard to learn Torah and would learn in a more relaxed way instead. Suddenly, I lost my vision.

"'I went to see great doctors. After a host of tests and examinations, the greatest doctor of them all told me, "We cannot give you new eyes, but I am amazed that you have been able to see until now. The tests have shown that you should have been blind for the past ten years. The fact that you have been able to see all this time is incredible!"

"'The doctor didn't understand the reason,' the blind man continued, 'but I do. As long as I labored over the Torah, I continued to see, to learn, and to come up with original Torah thoughts. When I decided to stop laboring, my eyes stopped seeing. This should teach us how a man must put all his strength into learning Torah and doing mitzvos and good deeds — even in his old age!'"

Sofrim, the scribes who write *sifrei Torah*, can make mistakes. Therefore, it is important to proofread every *sefer Torah* very carefully, to eliminate any errors.

The following story, which highlights this point in a remarkable way, was told by R' Yaakov Dovid Weintraub of Bnei Brak, grandson of R' Avraham Sofer, the story's hero. It was later published in the book, "*Tefillin U'Mezuzos Kehilchasan*," a guide for Jewish scribes.

It was the twelfth day of Elul. In cities and towns throughout Poland, in bustling *batei midrash* and in overflowing hearts, Jews were preparing for their upcoming trips to see their Rebbes, with whom they would spend the impending High Holy Days.

Chassidim and men of action — men who spoke little and did a great deal — were already immersed in the work of this special time of the year. They filled their days with Torah and good deeds, and stole hours of the night to do the same. Who could sleep with the shofar blast echoing in the chambers of his heart?

R' Yaakov Dovid of Radomsk had been living for years in Plavna, a small town on the banks of the Wort River, not far from the large city of Radomsk. He, too, would have liked to find a few extra hours — or even a few extra minutes — at night, but he could find none. He spent all his time involved in Torah and holy service. "His nights were like his days for learning Torah and doing his holy *avodah*. His actions were hidden and were ruled by fear of Heaven." This was the accolade given to the Rebbe by one of his own teachers, R' Menachem Mendel of Strikov. The Radomsker's fame spread far and wide as a holy man whose prayers brought miraculous salvation to those who sought them.

Winter and summer, the Rebbe would rise to begin his work at midnight. He would learn Torah, review *mishnayos*, and dip into the *Zohar* and *Chovos HaLevavos* until the morning light. He would greet the dawn with *Tehillim*, which he would recite with great sweetness and warmth, his eyes dripping tears onto verse after verse until the time came for a quick visit to the *mikveh* and then *Shacharis* in shul. Afterwards, still wrapped in his *tefillin*, he would continue his in-depth learning of *Shas* and its commentaries until midday, when he would finally revive himself with a little food.

This is the way he conducted himself all his life. This night, the twelfth of Elul, was no different. It was the *yahrtzeit* of the holy R'

Bunim of Peshischa, the Rebbe who had left his indelible stamp on Polish Jewry and opened for them the floodgates of wisdom and fear of Heaven. R' Bunim's disciples, and the disciples of his disciples, lit bonfires in every Rebbe's courtyard throughout Poland in honor of the Rebbe who, blind in his last years, had taught his students that one did not need human eyes in order to see, or even a flesh-and-blood body in order to live.

On this night, his chassidim recalled what had happened when R' Bunim had been in his final illness and near the end of his life. Lying in his bed, R' Bunim heard the sound of bitter weeping. It was coming from his devoted wife and rebbetzin.

"Why are you crying?" the Rebbe had asked in surprise, summoning his last reserves of strength to speak. "After all, I lived my whole life only in order that I might teach myself how to die." A short time later, the Rebbe's soul departed this world.

"All his life he learned how to die," his chassidim whispered years afterward, "but he did not succeed. See, the Rebbe lives on. His light has not been extinguished, nor will it ever be."

R' Yaakov Dovid of Radomsk was a disciple of a disciple of R' Bunim. The great Rebbe's fire burned in his own veins. On that twelfth day of Elul, R' Yaakov Dovid completed his day's work, consigned his soul to Hashem for the night, and closed his eyes for a little sleep. It would soon be midnight, when he would rise once again to perform Hashem's holy work.

But he did not even get an hour's sleep. Just a few minutes later, R' Yaakov Dovid woke with his heart pounding from a dream.

In his dream he saw his father-in-law, the holy *tzaddik* R' Avraham Sofer, who had been living in the nearby city of Radomsk for many years. R' Avraham had been a disciple of R' Bunim of Peshischa and a close friend of R' Shlomo of Radomsk. He was also a *sofer stam* who devoted himself body and soul to his holy work. He had once written *tefillin* for his great rebbe, R' Bunim.

In the dream, he told his son-in-law, "Please, son, get up and travel to the nearby city of Radomsk. When you get there, go to the Gerrer shul, where you will find the last *sefer Torah* I wrote. Open it, and please erase the extra *vav* that I wrote in *Parshas Bamidbar*, in *pasuk* so-and-so. That is the only error in the entire *sefer Torah*. Please ... with my apologies ..." R' Avraham disappeared, and the dream ended.

R' Yaakov Dovid jumped out of bed, confused and bewildered. The Peshischa chassidim labored all their lives to keep their feet on the ground. They were not especially attuned to dreams. How, then, had his father-in-law appeared in his own?

R' Yaakov Dovid knew his father-in-law's pious ways and the care he took with the holy work he did. Every drop of ink that R' Avraham used was infused with love and awe for Hashem. He also knew what the holy *Zohar* has to say about an extra letter, Heaven forbid, in the Torah, and of the *tzaddikim* who were pushed out of their place in the Heavenly yeshivah because of an extra *vav*. Nevertheless, he still did not understand how R' Avraham had come to appear to him in a dream on the night of his great rebbe's *yahrtzeit*.

If what his father-in-law had said in the dream was true, why didn't he fix the problem himself? And if it was hard for R' Avraham to get to the shul, why not ask that the *sefer Torah* be brought to him? After all, the holiness of a *sefer Torah* is not valid if it contains an error, Heaven forbid. How had R' Avraham suddenly come to learn that there was an error in this particular *sefer Torah*? And, most of all, why send the message to his son-in-law in this strange way? Why not deliver it with one of the many travelers between Radomsk and Plavna?

Cutting his thoughts short, R' Yaakov Dovid ran as fast as he could to the home of his good friend, who was also a student of R' Avraham Sofer. Together the two hastened down the road to Radomsk.

They reached the city with the dawn. Their first stop would be R' Avraham's house, in order to find out whether or not the dream had been true. Then they changed their mind. The dream had not asked R' Yaakov Dovid to pay a visit to his father-in-law's house, but rather to correct the error in the *sefer Torah*. Perhaps R' Avraham had not sent the message via a human messenger because of a great need for haste. Accordingly, the two hurried directly to the *beis midrash*.

Respectfully, they lifted out the *sefer Torah* and laid it on the *bimah*. Turning to *Parashas Bamidbar*, their eyes raked the words for the error. They found it at once, glaring out at them. The dream had been accurate. Pulling out a sharp knife, R' Yaakov Dovid lifted the extra *vav* from the parchment.

With trembling hands, he returned the *sefer Torah* to the *aron kodesh*. It had not been a trivial dream, but a true one — though many things were still unclear to R' Yaakov Dovid. With pounding heart, he and his friend left the shul. Then the two raced down the street toward R' Avraham Sofer's house, eager to hear an explanation of the dream from his own lips.

As they reached the house, R' Yaakov Dovid noticed the large crowd gathered outside the door. People had come from every corner of the city to participate in the *levayah* of R' Avraham Sofer, who had departed this world on the night of his great rebbe's *yahrtzeit*.

Suddenly, the answers to all the questions became clear: Why had R' Avraham appeared in a dream instead of fixing the error himself? How had he learned about the mistake that had been hidden from him during his life? Why hadn't he sent word with a human messenger? His holy soul had left his body that very night — but had found its passage blocked by the extra *vav* in the last *sefer Torah* he had written. R' Avraham had hastened to appear to his son-in-law in the depths of the night, to plead for his life.

Step by step, R' Yaakov Dovid walked behind his great father-in-law's bier on R' Bunim of Peshischa's *yahrtzeit*, his eyes cast down and his mind a thousand miles away.

The Children's Dance

הַקְהֵל אֶת הָעָם הָאֲנָשִׁים וְהַנָּשִׁים וְהַטַּף ... לְמַעַן יִשְׁמְעוּ וּלְמַעַן יִלְמְדוּ

"Gather together the people — the men, and the women, and the small children ... so that they will hear and so that they will learn"
(Devarim 31:12)

R' Yosef Chaim Sonnenfeld, Chief Rabbi of Jerusalem, used to conduct a different kind of *hakafos* on Simchas Torah: a "children's *hakafos*." The venerable Rav himself would gather together all the Old City's children and lead them in dance. In a long line, boys of all ages would dance and sing and leap after R' Yosef Chaim, to their joy and delight.

R' Yosef Chaim would line them up, instructing each boy to hold firmly to the lad in front of him. Moishele clung to Dovidel's hand, who held on to Yitzchakel's back, who clutched Tzviki's belt. In this way, he taught the youngsters a valuable lesson: If we hold on tightly to one another, we will forge a mighty chain from which no one will

ever fall to the wayside! From time to time, the Rav would turn around to check that his "chain" was still firm and holding.

Then, holding on to each other with the aged Rabbi at their head, the children would burst into song and begin to circle the *bimah*. The older boys kept the words going while the tots raised their voices in enthusiastic melody. And when they had finished circling the *bimah*, they went outside to dance around the shul itself. And when they had finished circling the shul, they went out into the street to dance circles around the Batei Machseh neighborhood — and all of Jerusalem's Old City, as it says, "Go around Zion and encircle her." From every street children came streaming to Batei Machseh to dance with the Rav.

Whenever R' Yosef Chaim, in dancing around the shul building, came to an obstacle such as a large rock or an abandoned barrel, he would not go around it but would instead climb over it, with a childish jump. Then he would go merrily on his way, the delighted children jumping and dancing after him.

The boys learned a lesson that would last them the rest of their lives: We do not go around obstacles or compromise with them. If something stands in a man's way, he must surmount it and continue on the straight path onward!

Then they would all return to shul, where they continued to dance around the *bimah* for hours, every step filled with youthful joy and boundless energy.

The Path to the Heart

וּבְנֵיהֶם אֲשֶׁר לֹא יָדְעוּ יִשְׁמְעוּ וְלָמְדוּ לְיִרְאָה אֶת ד' אֱלֹקֵיכֶם

"And their children who do not know — they shall hear and they shall learn to fear Hashem, your G-d"

(Devarim 31:13)

Amid the crowd of people waiting patiently to see the Gerrer Rebbe, to ask for his blessing or his advice, were two men of unusual aspect. One of them was an elderly chassid in a wheelchair. The other was a young man dressed in casual clothes and with the overall appearance of being a secular man. He, as it turned out, was the elderly chassid's son.

When the father and son entered the Rebbe's room, the Rebbe

welcomed them warmly. He remembered the old chassid from years back, when they had lived in Poland before the Holocaust.

"Rebbe," the aged man said feebly, but with great emotion, "I feel that my end is near, so I have asked my son to help me come up to Yerushalayim to see the Rebbe's face one more time."

The Rebbe gazed in turn at the old man and his son, and then said to the latter, "I see that you cling to the mitzvah of honoring one's father, which is very good. Still, you must know that there is another Father Whom we are all obligated to honor. And that is our Father in Heaven."

Silence reigned in the room for a long moment, as the young man considered the Rebbe's words.

"Tell me," the Rebbe said. "In what way are you prepared to honor your Heavenly Father?"

"I will honor him," the young man said, inclining his head respectfully, "in any way that the Rebbe commands me to."

"In that case — put on *tefillin* every day!" the Rebbe said radiantly.

"And from that day on," the young man says, "I never let a day pass without putting on *tefillin*." As a result, he grew closer and closer to *Yiddishkeit*, until he became a *shomer mitzvos*.

This is just one example of how the Gerrer Rebbe found the pathway to every person's heart, to lead them on the road to truth.

The Best Student of All

כִּי לֹא תִשָּׁכַח מִפִּי זַרְעוֹ
"For it shall not be forgotten from the mouth of its offspring"
(Devarim 31:21)
"See now, this is a promise to Israel that the Torah will not be utterly forgotten by their offspring."
(Rashi)

R' Chaim Shmulevitz related that, as a youth attending the yeshivah in Grodno, he spent a few days traveling to the Novaradok Yeshivah to see his uncle, R' Avraham Yaffen.

One day during his visit, R' Chaim went over to his uncle and asked him to point out the best boy in the yeshivah. The *rosh yeshivah* pointed at a certain boy and said, "That one is the deepest thinker in the yeshivah."

Then he pointed at another student and said, "He is the most diligent of all the boys in the yeshivah."

"And that boy," continued the *rosh yeshivah,* pointing at someone else, "is outstanding in his *yiras Shamayim* ... and that one in his *bekiyus.*"

R' Chaim pressed, "But, overall, who is the best student in the whole yeshivah?"

His uncle took him over to a corner of the *beis midrash,* pointed at another boy, and said, "He is the best in the yeshivah."

Surprised, R' Chaim asked, "But when you praised all the other special boys and their outstanding traits, you didn't mention this one at all!"

"True," said R' Avraham. "But this boy is the 'seeker' — the one most 'thirsty' of them all ... thirsty for Torah and spiritual elevation."

It later came to light that the boy R' Avraham Yaffen had pointed out as the "thirstiest" of all was none other than R' Yaakov Kanievsky, author of the "*Kehillos Yaakov,*" who learned in R' Avraham's yeshivah in his younger days.

"It Has Cost Us Dearly"

לָקֹחַ אֵת סֵפֶר הַתּוֹרָה הַזֶּה
"Take this book of the Torah"
(Devarim 31:26)

While serving as Rabbi of Brisk, R' Yehoshua Leib Diskin managed to do away with a practice that had been instituted there by the government.

Whenever a Jewish man was required to swear an oath in the secular courts, a clerk would take a *sefer Torah* from a local shul and have the man swear by it. This practice, in R' Yehoshua Leib's opinion, was a bad one. It took away from the honor due to the Torah. So he stood up and announced: "No more taking *sifrei Torah* to the courthouse!"

Not long after that, a Jewish resident of the city was required by the court to swear an oath. As usual, the court clerks went to fetch a Torah from the shul. But a surprise was waiting for them.

"Sorry," they were told. "By orders of the Rabbi, no *sifrei Torah* may be given out."

The clerks returned empty-handed.

When they reported the new development to the judge, R' Yehoshua Leib was summoned to court to explain his behavior.

"Is it true," demanded the judge, "that Your Honor does not permit taking a Torah scroll to the courthouse?"

"Yes!" answered R' Yehoshua Leib.

"And what is the reason for this?"

"We are very protective of our Torah. It has cost us dearly."

"What do you mean?"

"The *sefer Torah* has cost us hundreds of thousands of Jewish lives. For the Torah's sake, our blood has been spilled. We have been tortured, burned, and murdered. For the sake of a single letter, thousands and thousands of souls have been sacrificed!"

This moving explanation, coming from R' Yehoshua Leib in a burst of holy fervor, made a deep impact on the judge. In the Rabbi's presence, he announced that he was transferring the present case to R' Yehoshua Leib's jurisdiction, so that he might judge between the two parties. And R' Yehoshua Leib would later relate that from that time on, the judge would often send him complicated cases that had first been presented in his own court.

R' Chaim Shmulevitz's Journey

לָקֹחַ אֵת סֵפֶר הַתּוֹרָה הַזֶּה וְשַׂמְתֶּם אֹתוֹ מִצַּד אֲרוֹן בְּרִית ד'
אֱלֹקֵיכֶם וְהָיָה שָׁם בְּךָ לְעֵד

*"Take this book of the Torah and place it at the side of the Ark
of the Covenant of Hashem, your G-d, and it shall be there for you as
a witness."*

(Devarim 31:26)

After more than six years of danger and wandering from place to
place during World War Two, the Mirrer Yeshivah finally received permission to enter the United States.

The trip from Shanghai took about four weeks. Despite delays
and obstacles, there was no dimming the sense of freedom that
came on the heels of the open miracle that had rescued the
yeshivah. But R' Chaim Shmulevitz did not allow himself to become
caught up in the emotion of the moment. All through the long trip,
he sat on deck diligently learning from the *sefer "Shev Shemaitsa."*

He recorded his original thoughts during that journey in a pamphlet that he later entitled *"Toras HaSefinah"* ("The Torah of the
Ship"). The pamphlet contains thirty-two extraordinary original
thoughts. They form a remarkable new chapter in R' Chaim's *chiddushim* on the topics of love for Torah, labor for Torah, fear of
Heaven, and trust in Hashem.

While the others paced the deck, impatient for their first sight of
their new home, R' Chaim sat at ease, totally absorbed in the depths
of the *sugya* he was learning. An awesome concentration was
stamped on his face as, beside him, one of the students stood gaz-
ing out at the endless horizon of the sea.

"Where are we?" the boy wondered out loud.

"In *Shemaitsa gimmel*," R' Chaim answered at once.

R' Meir Dan Plotzky, author of the *"Kli Chemdah,"* traveled to
London to raise funds for various Torah institutions.

Once, after a most disappointing day spent visiting a series of
wealthy London businessmen, R' Meir Dan returned wearily to his

lodgings. He would soon have to rush away to Belgium, and from there to America.

He found R' Michoel Levi waiting for him. Levi, a Londoner, bore regards from his elderly father, then 80 years old. In his father's name he apologized to R' Meir Dan for not being able to come in person, being too frail to leave home.

The *gaon* apologized, too, saying that he was in a hurry to continue his travels. "Unfortunately, I have no time today for a personal visit," he said regretfully.

But he soon heard something that made him change his mind. In his younger days, the older R' Levi had discovered a manuscript written by Rabbeinu Chananel on *Maseches Pesachim*, and had sent it to the printers of the "*Ram*" *Shas* in Vilna. R' Meir Dan hurried to meet him, saying exultantly, "For the man to whom we all owe such thanks — the man who has given us such a precious gift as this — there is no honor too great!"

פרשת האזינו

Parashas Ha'azinu

An Unquenchable Thirst

יַעֲרֹף כַּמָּטָר לִקְחִי תִּזַּל כַּטַּל אִמְרָתִי

"May my teaching drip like the rain, may my utterance flow like the dew"

(Devarim 32:2)

"The Torah that I gave to Israel is life for the world — like this rain, which is life for the world ... Because everyone is happy with it"

(Rashi)

R' Eliezer Yehudah Finkel, *rosh yeshivah* of the Mirrer Yeshivah, had an unquenchable thirst for hearing original Torah thoughts from his many students. The students were very precious to him, and he remembered all their divrei Torah for years afterward.

A young man who was a student of his once came to see the *rosh yeshivah* with happy news: His wife had just given birth to a baby girl. R' Eliezer Yehudah congratulated him warmly, then gave him a shrewd look and said, "You no doubt wished for a son ... Being a sensible man, you probably did not wait until the days between the birth and the *bris* to prepare a *dvar Torah*. You already have something up your sleeve! *Nu*, let me enjoy a few words!"

The *rosh yeshivah* was intensely interested in every original thought expressed by every mind that absorbed itself in Torah. He even paid some of his students for the privilege of hearing their *chiddushim*. Word spread around Jerusalem: Whoever lacked money for fish on Shabbos should go to the *rosh yeshivah* with some brilliant insight in learning — and his Shabbos was assured.

To R' Eliezer Yehudah Finkel, his students' *chiddushim* were like life-giving dew.

Bein hazemanim — the weeks between the end of one *zeman* at yeshivah and the beginning of the next — were especially packed with pleasure for the *rosh yeshivah*. Young men came in droves, seeking acceptance to the yeshivah. Each one came armed with a pearl to add to the *rosh yeshivah's* collection. There were days when ten *bachurim* would be lined up at his door, promising the *rosh yeshivah* an especially happy day.

On R' Yosef Dov Soloveitchik's wedding day, his father turned to him and said humorously, "Yosef Dov, you must prepare 'Torah.' Prepare well ... R' Eliezer Yehudah is probably coming to the wedding, and that is his bread-and-butter. He's been getting ready for this night. You'll see, Yosef Dov — he will not be satisfied with just a little!"

There was a very good student in the Lithuanian Mirrer Yeshivah who, unfortunately, was drafted into the Polish army. This came as a terrible blow to the *rosh yeshivah* — until he had an inspiration.

"Open a branch of the Mir in the army!" he told his student.

The student gaped. A yeshivah in an army barracks? How was that possible?

"Each month," R' Eliezer Yehudah explained, "you will send me a letter with original thoughts in halachah that the Jewish soldiers have come up with. In return for each such letter, I will send you the amount of money that every *bachur* in the Mir gets for learning here." In this way, the *rosh yeshivah* hoped, the yeshivah would spread its influence even into the Polish army — and the drafted youth would exchange his military "bench" for a yeshivish one.

Each month, a letter came to the *rosh yeshivah's* house marked with the stamp of the Polish army's military censor. The letters contained the Jewish soldier's Torah thoughts. And each month, the *rosh yeshivah* sent the money he had promised his student.

One month, the money did not arrive as expected. The young man contacted R' Eliezer Yehudah, who explained, "The *chiddush* that you sent me this month is based on principles that you wrote to me about last year. You can't buy two checks with the same set of principles."

A former student once came to see R' Eliezer Yehudah. They had not seen one another for thirty years, and the student was greatly moved by the meeting.

After greeting his visitor warmly, the *rosh yeshivah* asked, "Have you come up with any *chiddushim* since we last saw one another?"

The student gave a beautiful talk on a Torah topic. When he was done, the *rosh yeshivah* shook his head. "That is no *chiddush*! I heard that *dvar Torah* from you at your own *tena'im* — thirty-five years ago!"

A student of the Chevron Yeshivah came one day to discuss Torah topics with the *rosh yeshivah*. When the Rebbetzin came in to serve lunch, the visitor rose quickly to leave, apologizing for taking so much of the *rosh yeshivah's* time. But R' Eliezer Yehudah would not hear of his leaving. The man sat down again, and as the *rosh yeshivah* ate his meal, the visitor regaled him with highly enjoyable *divrei Torah*.

As the man left, the Rebbetzin spoke to him at the door.

"You have a great *zechus*! Your Torah has revived the Rav's spirit. Eating is difficult for him — he finds it extremely boring. But while you were telling him *divrei Torah*, it was different. The food suddenly tasted sweet. Come back here every day!"

Find Me a Minyan!

כִּי שֵׁם ד' אֶקְרָא הָבוּ גֹדֶל לֵאלֹקֵינוּ

"When I call out the Name of Hashem, ascribe greatness to our G–d."

(Devarim 32:3)

R' Yaakov Yosef Herman was a Torah pioneer in America. His scrupulous observance of the mitzvos and his personal outreach drew many people onto the path of Torah. His daughter describes her father's concern with never missing even one *tefillah* with a *minyan*:

Papa went to shul morning and night to *daven Shacharis, Minchah*, and *Ma'ariv* with a *minyan*. Neither heat nor cold, rain nor snow, not even illness, deterred Papa from performing this mitzvah.

When Papa returned home [from a trip to Europe to visit various *gedolim* in their homes], he told us, "I did not miss a *minyan* though I traveled by boat, train, and plane through many countries. Where there is a will, you can always find a way to do a mitzvah."

On his way home, after spending time in several cities in Poland, he arrived in Leipzig, Germany. From there he was scheduled to travel to London. Papa realized that if he followed his itinerary and traveled by train, he would miss *davening Ma'ariv* with a *minyan*.

On the spur of the moment, he decided to travel by plane. In 1931, plane travel was expensive and hazardous, and few people used this new means of transportation. Papa boarded the tiny plane, which flew into the horizon with few passengers aboard. The trip was a very rough one but within a short time Papa arrived in London.

When he disembarked from the plane, the customs officer checked his passport and noticed that Papa had no visa to enter England. However, he was so impressed that Papa had arrived by plane that he allowed him to enter the country without a visa and remain for his allotted time.

It was already quite late at night when Papa knocked at the door of Rabbi Eliyahu E. Dessler, author of the famous work of *mussar, Michtav MeEliyahu,* who was then residing in London. Rabbi Dessler greeted Papa warmly, as he ushered him into his home. "Reb Yaakov Yosef, now I have an opportunity to repay a little of the *hachnasas orchim* you showed me when I was in New York. Tell me what I can do for you to make you comfortable."

"I need a *minyan* for *Ma'ariv,*" Papa said quickly.

"It's very late, but I will see what I can do," Rabbi Dessler said graciously. He went from door to door, until he succeeded in gathering a *minyan* of his neighbors.

After *Ma'ariv,* Papa said thankfully, "This is real *hachnasas orchim,* Reb Elya!"

R' Shlomo Zalman Auerbach observed every detail of halachah with great devotion. He did not skip over the tiniest letter of Jewish law, even if it came with a price tag of great bother and exertion, to the point of making him weak and ill.

For example, he took immense care to always *daven* with a *minyan.*

On the last Thursday morning of his life, R' Shlomo Zalman walked out of his house wrapped in his *tallis* and *tefillin,* determined to go to shul for *Shacharis.* Almost immediately, he stumbled and fell. The young man who was accompanying him tried to persuade him to return home, but R' Shlomo Zalman was adamant: He was going to shul.

Halfway there, he murmured, "I feel terribly cold all over. My legs feel like stones."

His companion urged, "Maybe the Rav will agree to go home?"

"No!" R' Shlomo Zalman said forcefully. "I must hear *Kerias HaTorah* and *daven* with a *minyan*!"

During *Shacharis*, R' Shlomo Zalman felt unwell again. He grew dizzy. His devoted son, R' Baruch, was quickly summoned to his side. Frightened, he pleaded with his father to go home. But R' Shlomo Zalman shook his head. "I have not yet heard the Torah read."

Only after the *davening* was ended did he finally return home. It was the last public *davening* of his life — one for which he had sacrificed himself with all the strength that was left to him.

A Little Boy's Problem

כִּי שֵׁם ד' אֶקְרָא הָבוּ גֹדֶל לֵאלֹקֵינוּ

"When I call out the Name of Hashem, ascribe greatness to our G–d."

(Devarim 32:3)

"When I will call out and mention the Name of Hashem, you 'ascribe greatness to our G-d' and bless His Name."

(Rashi)

R' Yisrael Salanter's 5-year-old grandson was once standing and sobbing.

"Why are you crying, my dear?"

"Because I want to eat."

"So why don't you eat?"

"Because I have to make a *berachah*!"

"So? Don't you know the *berachah* for this food?"

"Yes, I know it. But there is no one to answer *amen* to my *berachah*, so how can I make it?"

Hide and Seek

הֲלַה' תִּגְמְלוּ זֹאת

"Is it to Hashem that you repay this"

(Devarim 32:6)

R' Baruch of Mezibozh's young grandson was once playing a game of Hide and Seek. He hid, and his friend had to search for, and find, him.

The little boy waited a long time in his hiding place, but nothing happened. Finally, he stepped out — and saw, to his disappointment, that his friend was not searching for him at all, but was playing with some other game. Upset, the child went to tell the story to his holy grandfather.

When the Rebbe heard the tale, he burst into bitter tears. He wept for a long time. His chassidim were upset and bewildered by the Rebbe's weeping. They did not understand the reason for it.

At last, the Rebbe turned to them and cried, "Don't you understand that this is the distress that the *Shechinah* feels? *Hashem Yisbarach* conceals Himself from our nation and wants us to search for Him and discover Him and His handiwork, until the entire world is filled with knowledge of Him. Instead, everyone turns his attention to his own personal property and his own concerns, and we forget completely to search for Hashem. So the concealment goes on — and the *Shechinah* is distressed."

The Bar Mitzvah Suit

שְׁאַל אָבִיךָ וְיַגֵּדְךָ זְקֵנֶיךָ וְיֹאמְרוּ לָךְ

"Ask your father and he will relate [it] to you, your elders and they will tell you."

(Devarim 32:7)

As a young boy, R' Elazar, son of R' Elimelech of Lizhensk, loved antics and wild tricks. There were hardly any signs of spiritual greatness to be seen in the boy. When people mentioned this to his father, the holy R' Elimelech responded, "Let us merit seeing the day of his bar mitzvah."

Elazar grew up and approached the age of mitzvos. When the preparations for his bar mitzvah began, his father expressed a wish to be present while the boy's new suit was being sewn.

The tailor was summoned to R' Elimelech's home. The Rebbe instructed the tailor to direct all his thoughts while sewing the suit to the honor of the Creator of the world. The tailor spread the material out on the table, and the Rebbe closely followed every move he made. Soon the tailor was cutting the fabric.

When he reached the shoulders, R' Elimelech turned to the tailor and ordered, "Please say: 'I am hereby cutting out the shoulders of this suit for R' Elazar, so that he may move his shoulders only for the sake of his Creator, may His Name be blessed!'"

When the tailor reached the sleeves, the Rebbe asked him to say, "I am hereby cutting these sleeves for R' Elazar, so that he may raise his arms only to honor the Creator, may His Name be blessed!"

And so the Rebbe continued with every part of the suit.

The bar mitzvah day arrived. Elazar put on his new suit for the first time. From that moment, everyone who saw him sensed a different spirit moving the boy — a lofty and elevated spirit. And from that day on the youth grew ever higher in Torah and mitzvos, until the time came when he was one of the *tzaddikim* of his generation!

Seder Night With the Ba'al Shem Tov

כְּנֶשֶׁר יָעִיר קִנּוֹ עַל גּוֹזָלָיו יְרַחֵף יִפְרֹשׂ כְּנָפָיו ... ד' בָּדָד יַנְחֶנּוּ

"Like an eagle arousing his nest hovering over his young, he spreads his wings... Hashem alone guided him"

(Devarim 32:11-12)

When the Ba'al Shem Tov began his trip to Eretz Yisrael, he was accompanied by his *sofer* and his daughter, the *tzadekes,* Aidel. In those days, the voyage took place overland until Istanbul, capital of Turkey, and from there by boat to the port of Yaffo.

The Ba'al Shem Tov had many adventures before he reached Istanbul, two days before Pesach. By that time, there was no money left in his purse. His Heavenly intuition and *ruach hakodesh* had deserted him as well. He did not know where to go or to whom to turn for help.

Erev Pesach arrived. The Ba'al Shem Tov sat in the *beis midrash* while his daughter went to the river to wash their clothes. As she scrubbed, tears coursed down her cheeks, because that night would be the *Seder* night and they still had nothing.

Just then, a ship came into the port. Down the gangplank came a rich and important Jew. Seeing the crying woman, he asked her what was the matter. She explained that her father was a *tzaddik,* and that they were en route to Eretz Yisrael and had no place to stay for Pesach. The rich man invited them to spend the *Yom Tov* with him.

As dusk was falling, the Ba'al Shem Tov lay down to sleep in the room he had been given in the rich man's home. He continued to sleep when it was time to *daven Ma'ariv,* and slept on even after his host returned from shul to start the *Seder.* He asked Aidel to wake her father, but she replied, "No, I cannot do that under any circumstances." So the rich man entered the Ba'al Shem Tov's room himself to wake him.

He was shocked by what he saw. The Ba'al Shem Tov's face was glowing in his sleep like a burning flame, while twin rivers of tears ran down his cheeks.

The man understood that he was in the presence of a holy man, and did not wake him. A little while later, the Ba'al Shem Tov awoke on his own. He stood up and *davened Ma'ariv* with tremendous devotion, for his Heavenly sense had returned. Then he sat down to the *Seder,* which he conducted with immense enthusiasm for many long hours. When he reached the *pasuk, "L'oseh niflaos gedolos levado"* ("To the One Who performs great wonders alone"), the time was approaching dawn. The Ba'al Shem Tov recited the *pasuk* with awesome energy, in a clear, loud voice.

It was only after the *Seder* was over that the Ba'al Shem Tov revealed that a terrible decree had been made against the city's Jews — and that he had dedicated himself to nullify it. And on the following day, word came that the grand vizier, who hated Jews, had persuaded the sultan to murder many of them. The Ba'al Shem Tov had prayed devotedly for the decree to be rescinded — and at the moment that he had cried out, "*L'oseh niflaos gedolos levado*," the grand vizier had been killed ... and that was the end of his evil decree.

A Different Perspective

לוּ חָכְמוּ יַשְׂכִּילוּ זֹאת יָבִינוּ לְאַחֲרִיתָם

"Were they wise they would have comprehended this, they would have understood from their end."

(Devarim 32:29)

When R' Shmuel of Kaminka was near the end of his life, there was a certain widow in his town whose only cow — from which she earned a living for herself and her children — died. R' Shmuel undertook to help her, and he did not rest until he had collected money to buy her a new cow. He rejoiced greatly over this, and asked repeatedly, "Does this cow give milk? And how much?"

R' Shmuel's daughter was surprised. "Father," she said, "why all this fuss over a cow? Why your great interest in such a thing?"

"I will tell you a parable," R' Shmuel replied. "This is comparable to a person who earned his living selling sheep's fleece. He gathered the fleece in a big box and took them to the market to sell. On his way, he spent Shabbos in a wayside inn. The innkeeper asked him to give him some fleece in exchange for the cost of his lodgings.

" 'That's too much trouble for me,' the traveler replied. 'It's not worth my while to open the box and then repack everything inside, all for one sheep's fleece.'

"The next day, the man continued on to the marketplace — but was unsuccessful in his business. He returned to his own city along with all his unsold merchandise. On his way, he stopped at the same inn.

"He turned to the innkeeper and asked, 'Would you accept a sheep's fleece in exchange for my lodgings?'

"The innkeeper agreed. The merchant asked his assistant to open the box, choose a nice fleece, and then repack the box. The assistant protested, 'Why is it that, on our way down to the market, you refused to sell him a fleece — and now you are not only willing to sell it to him, but actually went so far as to offer it to him yourself?'

"'Why don't you understand?' the merchant said. 'Then, I was on my way to market. I was filled with hopes of making a nice profit. It was not worth my while to trouble myself so greatly over one fleece. But now, returning empty-handed, the trouble is well worth my while, even for a single fleece.'

R' Shmuel turned to his daughter. "This is the situation we have here," he said softly. "You, my daughter, are young. You have your whole life ahead of you in the 'marketplace' of this world, and time to do a lot of 'business.' Therefore, this mitzvah seems trivial to you.

"I, on the other hand, am an old man and have not accomplished a thing. Therefore, even a small mitzvah becomes a great thing in my eyes."

The Slammed Door

לִי נָקָם וְשִׁלֵּם
"Mine is vengeance, and it will repay"
(Devarim 32:35)

R' Nachum of Horodna was self-appointed guardian of all the poor and brokenhearted people in his town, and would personally see to their needs. From time to time he would go to the town's inn to collect *tzedakah* from its guests, just the way he collected regularly from the townspeople themselves on behalf of the poor.

One day, he knocked on the door of a room at the inn. A lawyer who lived in that town happened to be in the room, enjoying a discussion with a high Jewish government official from Petersburg. When the lawyer opened the door and saw R' Nachum standing there, he knew immediately why R' Nachum had come.

"I have no time for you now," he said hastily. "Please leave!"

But R' Nachum did not leave. Softly, he said, "I will not ask you for more than a donation for the town's poor."

Furious, the lawyer stepped back and slammed the door in R' Nachum's face.

The story became known all over town. Everyone was outraged to hear that the lawyer had so insulted their beloved rebbe. "How could a Jew act this way?" they berated the lawyer. "To insult the man that everyone loves and holds holy?"

But R' Nachum himself did not dwell on the insult. He did not speak to anyone about it, and eventually the incident was forgotten.

The lawyer was himself a defendant in a serious case — which he seemed poised to lose. There was only one thing he could do: Ask his friend, the high official from Petersburg, to intercede for him and save him from his troubles. Without hesitation, the lawyer made the long trip to Petersburg. He went straight to the home of his acquaintance, planning to speak to him there before the man went to his office.

The lawyer gave the porter a note to hand his master, informing him that he was there and asking to be admitted. The porter entered the house with the note — but returned just a minute later to say, "The master is busy. He has no time to see you now."

"Did you tell him who I am?" the lawyer asked urgently.

"Yes, sir."

The lawyer was taken aback, to say the least. He pressed a coin into the porter's hand. "Try again. Please."

But the porter shook his head. "The master has no time. But I can do this for you, sir. After lunch when the master returns from his office, I'll go back in and remind him of your visit."

With no other choice, the lawyer agreed. He returned in the afternoon — only to be told once again that the master refused to see him.

The lawyer walked slowly back to his inn, frustrated and upset. What had happened to make his friend act this way?

Without the official's help, the lawyer's case would not go well for him. He decided to throw himself at the other man's mercy, to humiliate himself and plead his cause. The next morning, he returned to the house and waited until the master walked out. Removing his hat, the lawyer called out in an ingratiating voice, "Your Honor — hello!"

The official averted his eyes and did not answer. Climbing into the waiting carriage, he left without a word.

Confused and distressed, the lawyer watched him drive away. His old friend had turned his back on him. What should he do now? Who else could help him? He did not want to leave Petersburg empty-handed. His trial date was fast approaching, and who knew how long he might end up sitting in jail.

There was no choice. All he could do was make one last-ditch attempt to melt the official's heart. He would grovel in the dust when his friend came home from his office. He would cry at the man's feet and beg him to have pity.

The lawyer waited. When the official's carriage drove up to his house and the man stepped out, the lawyer threw himself at his feet. Hot tears fell as he pleaded for help.

It was only then that the official spoke, revealing the reason behind his remote manner.

"If you had the nerve to slam the door in R' Nachum of Horodna's face, you deserve to have doors slammed in your own face!"

The lawyer tried to justify himself, but the other man made an impatient gesture.

"I will not listen to excuses! There is only one thing you can do, if you wish to set foot in my house. Return to Horodna and beg R' Nachum to have pity and forgive the insult you did to him. I will not believe you unless I see a note written in his own hand, saying that he has forgiven you. Without that note, there is no reason to return here. My door will be closed to you. I will say to you exactly what you said to R' Nachum that day: 'I have no time for you'!"

Abashed and ashamed, the lawyer left Petersburg and made the long trip back to Horodna, in Lithuania, to try and obtain the forgiveness — and the note — that he needed.

R' Nachum, ever merciful and compassionate, received him pleasantly and was quick to forgive him. As he sat down to write the note, he remarked, "I was never insulted, and I did not take the incident to heart."

Note in hand, the lawyer returned quickly to Petersburg, where he found the doors open to him as in former times. The official did his best to help him with the "higher-ups," until the lawyer was acquitted of all wrongdoing in the case against him.

The Clock

וְחָשׁ עֲתִדֹת לָמוֹ
"And swiftly future events [shall come] toward them."
(Devarim 32:35)

After the Chozeh of Lublin departed this world, his son, R' Yosef, inherited the Rebbe's silk Shabbos clothes, his belt, and the clock that had always hung in his father's room. On his way back to his own town, R' Yosef was forced by heavy rain to stop for shelter in the home of a Jewish villager. The rain lasted for several days. After it ended, R' Yosef prepared to continue his journey.

"You owe me money for lodging here these past few days," the villager insisted.

"I have no money," R' Yosef replied, "but I have some valuable things in my knapsack." He took out all the items that he had inherited from his father, and gestured at the villager to take his pick.

The villager consulted his wife. They decided to take the clock, which would show them the correct time to milk their cow each morning.

Some years later, R' Yissochor Dov of Radoshitz happened to stay at that same villager's house. He was given the bedroom where the Chozeh of Lublin's clock hung. R' Yissochor Dov did not close his eyes once. He spent all night dancing instead!

"What was all that strange behavior about?" his host asked in the morning.

The Rebbe answered with a question of his own. "Where did you get that clock?"

"From a Jew who stayed here once. He gave me the clock instead of money for staying here. If I remember correctly, his name was R' Yosef."

"I guessed at once, "R' Yissochor Dov said, "that this clock belonged to the Chozeh of Lublin. Other clocks toll the hour mournfully, letting us know that the end of our lives is near. But this clock, the Chozeh's clock, peals joyfully, letting us know that *Mashiach* is coming closer! That was why I rejoiced and danced all night long."

All a Man Needs

כִּי יָדִין ד' עַמּוֹ

"When Hashem will have carried out judgment upon His people"
(Devarim 32:36)

"When He will execute judgment against them with these chastisements"
(Rashi)

In his old age, R' Zusha of Hanipoli suffered many physical ailments. His assistant asked him, "How can the Rebbe recite the blessing, 'Who has given me all that I need,' when he has nothing but pain and suffering?"

The Rebbe answered, "What does my sinning body really require? A little suffering, to purify it! This, then, is all that I need, and it is appropriate for me to recite this blessing with great joy."

A man once came to see R' Yisrael of Ruzhin. After describing all his aches and pains, he burst into tears and said, "I suffer so much! What does Heaven want from me?"

R' Yisrael replied, "There was once a Jew who came before the Heavenly Court. He had many sins to accompany him, and only a few mitzvos. When these were weighed on the balance scale, he was found wanting. Then the defending angel stepped forward and said that the man had suffered a great deal in his life — and that this suffering must be taken into account as well. The suggestion was accepted. The man's suffering was laid on the scales, which made the two sides almost even.

"But something was still missing to tip the scales completely in the man's favor. By a tiny hairsbreadth, they were still weighed down against the man. He was sent to *Gehinnom*. And as he went, he wailed, "Master of the Universe, everything is from You! Didn't you have another tiny bit of suffering to give me, so that I might be spared the fate of *Gehinnom*?"

The "Professor"

מָחַצְתִּי וַאֲנִי אֶרְפָּא

"I struck down and I will heal"

(Devarim 32:39)

A chassid was once stricken with a serious illness, and became very involved in seeking a cure, consulting with doctors and investigating different medicines — to no avail. Finally, he came to see R' Mordechai of Neshchiz, to ask the Rebbe's advice and to receive his blessing.

"Go to a certain professor in the city of Hanipoli," the Rebbe told the chassid. "He will cure you."

Without wasting a second or counting the cost, the chassid undertook the trip. As there were not yet railroads in those days, the chassid immediately hired a wagon to take him to Hanipoli. The distance from Neshchiz to Hanipoli was considerable and the trip took a long time. As soon as he arrived, the chassid began to inquire as to where the professor lived.

The people of the city were surprised. "This is a small village. There is no professor here," they told the traveler.

"Perhaps there is a renowned doctor?"

No such doctor, he was told.

"Any sort of medical man?"

Again, the answer was "No."

The chassid was bewildered. How could the Rebbe have sent him all this way for nothing? Could such a *tzaddik* have spoken of something that did not exist?

There was nothing to do but to turn back. After all the hardship and expense of the long trip, the chassid was forced to travel back home. Once again, he went to see the Rebbe of Neshchiz. He related everything that had happened. "There is no professor in Hanipoli, no doctor — no nothing!"

When the chassid had finished speaking, the Rebbe asked, "In that case, what do the people of Hanipoli do when one of them, Heaven forbid, falls sick?"

"What can they do?" answered the chassid. "They have no choice but to trust in Hashem to have pity on them and send a cure."

"*That,*" said the Rebbe, "is the 'Professor of Hanipoli' that I was telling you about! The One Who helps the people of Hanipoli will also help you."

And so it was. The moment the man left the Rebbe's room he felt himself growing stronger. Soon the illness departed, until he was completely recovered.

The Illegal Funeral

הַרְנִינוּ גוֹיִם עַמּוֹ כִּי דַם עֲבָדָיו יִקּוֹם וְנָקָם יָשִׁיב לְצָרָיו

"Sing, nations, the praises of His people, for He will avenge the blood of His servants; He will bring retribution upon His enemies"

(Devarim 32:43)

During R' Shalom Sharabi's lifetime, a cruel Arab ruled over Jerusalem — a man who lost no opportunity to incite his people against the Jews. He would also tax the Jews heavily when the thought struck him. One such tax was for *halvayas hameis* — Jewish funerals. Unless they paid a steep amount of money, the Jews of Jerusalem were not permitted to bury their dead.

One day, an elderly man died. He was alone in the world and had not left behind any money. The *Chevrah Kaddisha* went to R' Shalom Sharabi for advice.

"Conduct the funeral without paying the tax!" R' Shalom said forcefully. "I will join you."

As the funeral procession made its way to the Mount of Olives, the Arab ruler watched from the window of his home. Suddenly, his eyes flashed fire.

"How can this be? A funeral without my permission!"

He thrust his head through the window bars and shouted furiously, "Stop! If you keep walking, I will send an Arab mob to tear you to pieces! I'm warning you!"

R' Shalom did not react at all to the ruler's tirade. He gestured at the others to keep moving. The funeral procession continued on its way.

The ruler tried to turn his head — and found it stuck between two bars! Try as he might, he could not remove it. Terrified, he found his entire body shaking violently.

"This is the Jewish *chacham's* revenge," he thought wildly. In deadly fear he awaited the funeral procession's return from the Mount of Olives. The moment he spotted them, he cried out, pleading, "Please, Rebbe, save me! I won't do a thing to you!"

"If you promise that the funeral tax will be abolished and that there will be no more weeping and wailing among our Jewish brothers because of the wild mob you incite against us — the bars will return to their usual place and you will be able to take your head out!" R' Shalom called back.

"I promise! I promise!"

The bars moved back at once, and the ruler was free. He breathed a long sigh of relief ... as did the city's entire Jewish population.

Amazing Memory

שִׂימוּ לְבַבְכֶם לְכָל הַדְּבָרִים אֲשֶׁר אָנֹכִי מֵעִיד בָּכֶם הַיּוֹם

"Apply your heart to all the words that I testify against you today"

(Devarim 32:46)

"It is necessary for a person that his eyes, ears, and heart be directed to words of Torah."

(Rashi)

One morning, after *Shacharis*, a bookseller entered the shul where the *Taz* was *davening* and spread his wares across the tables. Then he stood back and waited for the *talmidei chachamim* in the shul to come and browse through his *sefarim* and perhaps buy some of them.

The *Taz*, who always regretted that he had no money with which to buy *sefarim*, nevertheless came to inspect the bookseller's goods. "Maybe I'll find some secondhand *sefer* here for a cheap price," he thought.

The *Taz* examined all the *sefarim* but did not find one that he did not already know from beginning to end. Then the bookseller pulled out a new *sefer* — by the looks of it, something very special. When the *Taz* picked the *sefer* up, he felt a longing to own it. But when he heard the price, he was forced to give it up.

The bookseller, seeing the real pain in the *Taz's* face, decided to forego his profit. Yet even then, the price was still too steep for the *Taz*. At last, the bookseller offered to lend him the *sefer* for a day.

All through the next twenty-four hours, the *Taz* pored over that *sefer*, which was entitled, "*Sefer HaAgudah*." The next day, he returned it to the bookseller, saying, "I've studied the whole *sefer*. Here is money for letting me borrow it."

All the quotes from the *Sefer HaAgudah* that the *Taz* later brought down in his own writings came from his phenomenal memory, where they remained etched since that single day when he had had the *sefer* in his possession!

❧

R' Meir Simchah of Dvinsk, the *Ohr Same'ach*, had an incredible memory that befuddled all who knew him. Then, in his old age, something happened that seemed likely to expose the "secret" of his remarkable memory.

R' Tzvi Yemini, rabbi of Vilan, came to see R' Meir Simchah to discuss certain Torah topics with him. The guest offered his *chiddushim*.

Running his eyes over the pages, R' Meir Simchah exclaimed, "I wrote something on this very *sugya* thirty-two years ago!"

Turning to R' Yemini, he added, "If you'd care to open that left-hand drawer and take out the notebook there, then turn to page 29, you'll find what I wrote on this subject."

R' Yemini took an old notebook from the drawer and flipped through the pages until he found the one that R' Meir Simchah had mentioned. R' Meir Simchah began reciting, word for word, the passages he had written there, including sources and comments. His stupefied guest held the notebook and read silently along with him. The *Gaon* of Dvinsk did not leave out a word of what he had written thirty-two years before!

At that moment, there was a knock on the door. A woman came in with a halachic question. R' Meir Simchah closed his Gemara, but left his finger inside to mark the place where he had been learning. Then he stood up — the Gemara still in his hand with his finger inside, and went into the next room to review the woman's question. Over the next moments he took several halachah works down from their shelves and riffled through the pages until he found the place he wanted ... all with one hand. The other still grasped the Gemara.

"Where does the Rebbe get the strength, at his age, to keep holding that heavy "Vilna *Shas*" Gemara?" R' Yemini wondered aloud. "Couldn't the Rebbe put it down on the table until he finishes dealing with the woman's question?"

R' Meir Simchah glanced at his guest in astonishment.

"What is the question?" he asked. "It is an explicit *pasuk*: 'Will you lift your eyes from it and it is no more.' One moment, even a tiny one, of distraction from learning erases it from a person's memory!"

The Choice

וּבַדָּבָר הַזֶּה תַּאֲרִיכוּ יָמִים

"And through this matter shall you prolong your days"

(Devarim 32:47)

Sukkos was fast approaching, and in all of Berditchev there was not a single *esrog* to be had. R' Levi Yitzchak ordered men to go out to the crossroads and see if a Jew passing there might have an *esrog*.

Standing at the crossroads, they indeed found a passing Jew who had an *esrog*. But the man did not live in Berditchev and was hurrying home to his own town for Sukkos. The others offered to buy his *esrog* from him, but the man refused. After all, he too was a Jew and obligated in the same mitzvah. The men convinced him to return with them to see R' Levi Yitzchak.

R' Levi Yitzchak asked the man to sell him his *esrog* — in vain. Then he asked him to spend the *Yom Tov* in Berditchev, but the man again declined. It is a mitzvah to rejoice on Sukkos and to gladden the hearts of one's family. They were waiting for him at home. R' Levi Yitzchak promised him wealth and a good livelihood, *nachas* and peace of mind — but the other man stood firm. Hashem had blessed him with everything he needed, and he was on his way home!

"If you spend Sukkos here with us," said R' Levi Yitzchak, "you will be near me in the World to Come!"

Upon hearing this, the man at last agreed to stay. R' Levi Yitzchak was very happy, as was the entire community in Berditchev

— and the traveler himself. To be beside R' Levi Yitzchak in the World to Come was no trivial thing.

R' Levi Yitzchak sent out a secret message to his townspeople: No one was to let the traveler into their *sukkah*. On the first night of Sukkos, the man left shul and returned to his lodgings. In his room he found a lit candle, wine for *Kiddush*, challah, and some food. He was taken aback. Wasn't there a kosher *sukkah* in this place? Going out to the yard, he saw a fine *sukkah*, in which his host and family were happily sitting and eating. But when the man asked to join them, his host refused.

"Why?" asked the bewildered guest. "Why won't you let me sit in your *sukkah*?"

He was offered no explanation.

The man went to the neighbors, whom he found also sitting in their *sukkah* enjoying their meal. But when he asked if he might join them, he received no reply. He went from house to house, from *sukkah* to *sukkah*, seeing many happy families, but was forced to remain outside. At last he understood that the Rav must be behind all this. He went to R' Levi Yitzchak and poured out his pain: "Why have you done this to me? Am I not a good Jew? Why can't I eat in a *sukkah*?"

"Heaven forbid," answered R' Levi Yitzchak. "Of course you are a good Jew! Just absolve me from my promise to have you beside me in the World to Come, and you'll be welcomed with open arms."

Stunned, the man began to debate with himself. On the one hand, the *sukkah*. On the other, the World to Come. This was no simple matter. All one's life a man strives to attain the World to Come, and he had managed to acquire not just *Olam Haba*, but an exalted place there, near this *tzaddik*.

On the other hand — the mitzvah of *sukkah*. How could a Jew eat outside a *sukkah*, especially on the first night of the holiday?

He debated and debated — and then decided. *Hashamayim shamayim laHashem*, Heaven is for Hashem. The World to Come would arrive in its own time. Meanwhile, all of Israel were eating in their *sukkah*s tonight. He, too, was a Jew and was obligated to eat in a *sukkah*. He informed R' Levi Yitzchak of his decision and absolved him of his promise. Then, light of heart, he went inside to sit in the *sukkah*.

After the *Yom Tov*, R' Levi Yitzchak called for the man to come and see him.

"I am returning to you what I promised," he said. "I did not want you to get *Olam Haba* the way a merchant acquires a piece of merchandise. I wanted you to earn it through your own actions! Now that you have agreed to give up the place that I promised you in the World to Come for the sake of a mitzvah — now that you have shown such self-sacrifice — you are indeed worthy of being beside me in *Olam Haba*!"

R' Salman Makes a Kiddush Hashem

עַל אֲשֶׁר לֹא קִדַּשְׁתֶּם אוֹתִי בְּתוֹךְ בְּנֵי יִשְׂרָאֵל

"Because you did not sanctify Me among the Children of Israel."
(Devarim 32:51)

R' Salman Mutzafi once returned money to its non-Jewish owner, in a way which caused a great *kiddush Shem Shamayim*. The story is reminiscent of the one in which R' Shimon ben Shetach did the same thing, causing a gentile to exclaim, "Blessed is the G-d of Shimon ben Shetach!"

In his youth, R' Salman Mutzafi was close to Menachem Daniel, the richest Jew in Iraq. A Muslim sheik once came to Daniel's office to pay back a debt of 350 dinar. But the sheik mistakenly paid more than that.

When the mistake was discovered, R' Salman went out to the sheik's place of business in the marketplace and returned the difference to him.

Astounded at R' Salman's honesty, the sheik, deeply moved, began to shout, "See this Jew? He has come to return these *dinars* to me! Would an Arab have returned the difference?"

A *kiddush Hashem* — par excellence!

פרשת
וזאת הברכה
Parashas
Vezos Haberachah

Hungry for Torah

תּוֹרָה צִוָּה לָנוּ מֹשֶׁה מוֹרָשָׁה קְהִלַּת יַעֲקֹב

*"The Torah that Moshe commanded us is the heritage of the
Congregation of Yaakov."*

(Devarim 33:4)

*"The Torah 'which Moshe commanded us,' it is a heritage for 'the
Congregation of Yaakov.' We held on to it — and we will not abandon it."*

(Rashi)

As a young married man, R' Yaakov Yitzchak of Peshischa lived
with his in-laws near a blacksmith's shop. Passing the shop, he
would see the sparks flying from the white-hot metal as the blacksmith pounded it. R' Yaakov Yitzchak saw in this a symbol for Torah
learning: Even mighty steel, if heated sufficiently, can be bent at will.
So, too, does Torah — which is likened to fire — influence its learner
for the good.

In the mornings, the sound of the blacksmith's hammer blows
would reach R' Yaakov Yitzchak's ears. Jumping out of bed, he
would *daven*, and then sit down to learn Torah.

Then, one morning, he thought, "That blacksmith gets up so
early in the morning for a purely physical reason. I should get up
even earlier to do Hashem's work!"

Accordingly, the next morning he woke up before the blacksmith. When the blacksmith entered his shop, his ears met the sweet
sounds of Torah coming from his neighbor's house.

"That young man is not learning for his livelihood," the blacksmith thought. "Nevertheless, he is already awake and busy
learning. I, who am earning a living for my wife and children, should
get up even earlier than he!"

The next day, the blacksmith got out of bed earlier than R' Yaakov Yitzchak. Waking up to the sound of his hammer blows, R' Yaakov Yitzchak was upset. He decided to get up even earlier on the following morning.

The blacksmith gave up the contest.

In later years, when R' Yaakov Yitzchak merited the title, "The Holy Jew," he would often say, "For a great deal of what I have accomplished, I am grateful to that blacksmith!"

R' Avraham Mordechai of Gur was spending the summer in the health spa at Marinbad, when he received word that his youngest son, Pinchas Menachem (later to become the Gerrer Rebbe), had just begun speaking full words.

The Rebbe immediately sent a special telegram to his brother-in-law, R' Yitzchak Dovid Biderman: "Since I have heard that my son, Pinchas Menachem, has begun to speak, I am hereby naming you my messenger in teaching him *Torah tzivah lanu Moshe* and *Shema Yisrael*, as our Sages, may their memory be blessed, have taught."

From childhood through old age, R' Tzvi Elimelech of Dinov, author of the *Bnei Yissoschor*, was a model of diligence in learning Torah.

For many years, whenever he was called upon to lead the *davening* on the *Yamim Noraim*, R' Tzvi Elimelech would recite all the long *tefillos* by heart. He once explained how he came to be able to do this.

As a child, R' Tzvi Elimelech suffered from severe pain in his eyes. His condition became so bad that the doctors said his vision would be endangered if he did not stop reading for a certain period of time. The boy loved learning so much, however, that he did not stop.

Seeing the way his child ignored the doctors' warning, his father went so far as to make him leave the house several times a day, just to get him to stop learning. Young Tzvi Elimelech did not stop, however. He would sit outside, more often than not in the dark, straining for any stray glimmer of light — and reading.

Finally, his anxious father resorted to something really drastic: He put his son into a dark woodshed. Here, surely, the boy would not be able to learn, and his eyes would rest.

But the boy did not rest. He paced back and forth in the dimness of the woodshed, seeking something to satisfy his hunger for Torah. At last, beneath a pile of wood, he found an old, dusty volume. It was a *machzor* for the *Yamim Noraim*.

With no other choice, R' Tzvi Elimelech learned from the *machzor*, reviewing it so many times that he soon knew all the *tefillos* by heart!

A man who owned vineyards once described to R' Yehoshua Leib Diskin the various new techniques that had been developed in the grape-growing business: new methods of promoting growth, transportation, storage, etc.

To his astonishment, R' Yehoshua Leib showed him that all these "new" methods have already been described in the *Talmud Yerushalmi*, in *Maseches Shevi'is*, in the commentary of the *Rash* of Shanz.

Moreover, the Gaon of Brisk, who had no practical farming experience, offered the vineyard owner various ideas that proved very productive indeed!

A young American discovered his glorious heritage and became an observant Jew. He began to learn Torah and to do mitzvos, and even when he returned to his parents' home he continued to observe Hashem's Torah and to learn it very diligently.

His elderly father was very distant from *Yiddishkeit* and had no idea what it was all about. He retired from his work at that time, and wandered around the house with nothing to do. Watching his son poring over his Gemara, the father was very impressed. His son's life seemed to be so full of content and values. Finally, one day he approached his son.

"Teach me a page of what you're learning," he said.

"This will be very hard for you," the son replied. "In order to understand Gemara, you first need to know Hebrew, and you don't even know the *aleph-beis*. And there's a second language involved: Aramaic!"

But his father was determined. In spite of everything, he asked his son to teach him at least one page of Gemara. The son began to teach him. However, his visit was a short one and they could only continue during his infrequent subsequent visits. In this way, it took a full year of learning together before they finished the page.

When they were done, the father cried jubilantly, "I want to make a party. I've finished learning a whole page of Gemara!"

"There is a custom of making a party for the *siyum* of a *masechta*," the son admitted, "but not on a single page!"

But the father was insistent. He would throw his party.

At a loss, the son went to R' Moshe Feinstein to ask if such a thing — a *siyum* on one page of Gemara — was acceptable.

"Make a *siyum*," R' Moshe instructed. Then he added, "I will come take part in the *simchah!*"

And so it was that a *siyum* was made on a single page of Gemara learned by a man with his son over the course of a full year. R' Moshe attended the *siyum*, heaping praise on the elderly father who had not let any difficulty get in the way of achieving his goal.

The next morning, the old man did not wake up from his sleep. He had died in the night — the kind of death they call "the kiss of Hashem." In the *hesped* he delivered, R' Moshe declared, "There are those who purchase their *Olam Haba* in a single hour ... and there are those who purchase theirs with a single page!"

Not in the Budget

יוֹרוּ מִשְׁפָּטֶיךָ לְיַעֲקֹב וְתוֹרָתְךָ לְיִשְׂרָאֵל

"They shall teach Your laws to Yaakov and Your Torah to Israel"

(Devarim 33:10)

R' Ezra Attia, *rosh yeshivah* of Yeshivah Porat Yosef, had a single burning goal: to ignite a spark of Torah among Sephardic Jews. He hoped to educate special individuals who would eventually become the Torah leaders of their communities. In different ways he worked to draw Sephardi youths off the street and into the arena of

Torah. R' Ezra would do his utmost for each individual youth, especially if he was of a poor family, in order to establish him on the path of Torah.

A youth from Baghdad came to Yeshivah Porat Yosef with clear talent, but with just as visible signs of poverty. After a short talk, R' Ezra learned that the young man's parents were elderly and depended on their son for their livelihood.

R' Ezra tested the youth and found him filled with potential. The *rosh yeshivah* recommended at once that he be accepted to the yeshivah and that he be given a respectable sum of money each month. However, the yeshivah's administrators protested that they could not admit the young man, as the budget would not allow it.

R' Ezra approached the administrators and said, "Please remove this amount from my monthly salary and use it to support this student."

R' Benzion Chazan, one of the yeshivah's administrators, was so moved by this that he said, "Take some of my salary, too!"

In this way, the youth was accepted into the yeshivah, where he grew in time to become an outstanding *talmid chacham*.

❧ ❦ ☙

R' Leshinsky set out for the Nachalas Ganim neighborhood early one evening to deliver a *daf yomi shiur*. It was raining hard, and he decided to wait a little while for the rain to stop. However, the wait stretched and the rain continued to fall.

Since he was near the *Chazon Ish's* house, R' Leshinsky went to ask him whether or not he should walk to the bus station in the heavy rain — the station was some distance away — or give up the plan.

"How many students do you have in your *shiur*?" the Chazon Ish asked.

"There are three men."

"Do you think they will all come out in the rain today?"

"Only one man will come today. The other two live far away and will certainly not venture out in this weather. But the third man is the *shamash* of the shul and lives there in any case. He will certainly be there today."

"In that case," the Chazon Ish urged, "run to the bus and go deliver your *shiur*!"

Noting R' Leshinsky's surprise, the Chazon Ish added, "Do you think that a *daf yomi shiur* for one Jew has just the effect of teaching him one more page of Gemara? That single page changes the Jew into a totally different person!"

Word for Word

וְלִזְבוּלֻן אָמַר שְׂמַח זְבוּלֻן בְּצֵאתֶךָ וְיִשָּׂשכָר בְּאֹהָלֶיךָ

"And of Zevulun he said: Rejoice, Zevulun, in your departure, and Yissachar in your tents."

(*Devarim* 33:18)

R' Shimon Sofer, *Av Beis Din* of Cracow and the son of the Chasam Sofer, related the following story about his grandfather, R' Akiva Eiger:

Rabbi Akiva Eiger was once traveling home from Poland after attending his son's wedding. When they stopped for the night in one of the villages along the way, R' Akiva Eiger asked his host for a *sefer* to learn from, as his baggage had not yet arrived.

"My *sefarim* are not with me at the moment," the host answered. "My son, who is learning in town, is using them. Only one *sefer* is here now — the *Rashba*."

Glancing through the *sefer*, R' Akiva Eiger noticed that it was missing a page. He turned to his host and offered, "I will copy over the missing page for you, in return for your kindness to me."

And he proceeded to write down, from memory, word for word, the entire contents of the missing page of the *Rashba*. Then he continued to learn from the *sefer* for the rest of the night.

By morning, the news had spread: The renowned *gaon*, R' Akiva Eiger, had spent the night in the village. Outstanding Torah scholars and men of stature came streaming out to meet him — only to find that R' Akiva Eiger had already left to continue his journey.

His host showed them the page of the *Rashba* written in R' Akiva Eiger's own hand. Checking carefully, the men found that not a single letter from the original text was missing!

When telling over this story, R' Shimon Sofer would add, "I am not relating this so that you will be astounded by R' Akiva Eiger's marvelous memory — but by his tremendous love for Torah, which left everything he learned so deeply engraved in his memory. In his eyes, it was as though the Torah had been handed down on Sinai that very day, and he sat poring over the *Rashba's* words all through the night."

R' Yechezkel Sarna, *rosh yeshivah* of Chevron, lived abroad for a period of time while fund-raising for his yeshivah. He called a meeting of all the people who had contributed money to the Chevron Yeshivah.

Among the contributors was one man who had given a large amount of money to help move the yeshivah from Slobodka to Eretz Yisrael. In the years since, he had lost his wealth and become a pauper. R' Yechezkel hesitated about inviting this man to the meeting. In the end, he did not invite him, lest the man be embarrassed.

In the middle of the meeting, to everyone's surprise, the man showed up uninvited! He requested permission to speak.

"My dear brothers," he said. "You must know that this world is like a wheel. I, too, was once a rich man. Then the wheel turned. Today I struggle for a piece of bread to eat, and there is no trace remaining of my former vast wealth. The only thing left to me of all my former property is what I contributed to help the yeshivah move to Eretz Yisrael. And that is one merit that I am not prepared to sell for all the treasure in the world!"

He looked around at the assembled guests and continued, "This is what I suggest to you, gentlemen, from my own experience: Whatever you can give to *tzedakah* now — hurry and give it, without hesitation, for no man can know what lies in wait for him around the corner. What we seize and give to *tzedakah* is what will stay with us forever!"

His words left a profound impression on his listeners, and the fund-raising campaign drew to a very successful close.

Precious Nights

וְלִזְבוּלֻן אָמַר שְׂמַח זְבוּלֻן בְּצֵאתֶךָ וְיִשָׂשכָר בְּאֹהָלֶיךָ

*"And of Zevulun he said: Rejoice, Zevulun, in your departure,
and Yissachar in your tents."*

(Devarim 33:18)

*"Zevulun and Yissachar made a partnership. Zevulun ... would
earn profit, and put into the mouth of Yissachar [i.e., and
support Yissachar with the money he earned]. And [the men
of Yissachar] would sit and engage in [the study of] Torah."*

(Rashi)

Even in his youth, R' Yehudah Tzadka learned Torah night and day. Each year, he would add on hours to his learning schedule. During the day he learned in the *beis midrash* of Yeshivah Porat Yosef, and at night he learned until the early hours of the morning in the Be'er Sheva shul in Jerusalem's Beis Yisrael neighborhood.

Because of the high cost of oil, most shuls were forced to cut down on the lighting they were able to offer at night. But the *gabbai* of the Be'er Sheva shul let those learning there at night have all the oil and kerosene they wanted for their lamps. He would sometimes say that, if he chanced to glance out of his window at the shul in the depths of the night and saw the lamps still burning for those learning Torah, his heart would overflow with joy, knowing that the voice of Torah did not cease in his shul.

All through his life, whenever R' Yehudah Tzadka would pass that shul, he would be filled with nostalgia for the long and precious nights of Torah he had enjoyed there.

R' Chaim's Seudas Mitzvah

אַשְׁרֶיךָ יִשְׂרָאֵל מִי כָמוֹךָ עַם נוֹשַׁע בַּד׳ מָגֵן עֶזְרֶךָ

"Fortunate are you, O Israel. Who is like you! A people delivered by Hashem, the shield of your help"

(Devarim 33:29)

R' Chaim Kreisworth (later Chief Rabbi of Antwerp, Belgium) once prepared *Sheva Berachoh* for the *seudah shelishis* Shabbos meal at his home in the Achvah section of Jerusalem. The *seudah* was to be held in honor of R' Shlomo Wolbe (later *mashgiach* of Yeshivas Be'er Yaakov), who had just married the daughter of the late R' Avraham Grodzenski, *mashgiach* of the Slobodka Yeshivah, and granddaughter of the great R' Yitzchak Grodzenski of Warsaw. R' Isser Zalman Meltzer was invited to the *seudas mitzvah*, as were the *roshei yeshivah* of Chevron and their students.

Just a few hours before the guests were due to arrive, the "*Etzel*" — a group of anti-British Jewish rebels — blew up the police station at Machaneh Yehudah. The Chevron *roshei yeshivah* immediately sent word that they would not be able to attend the *Sheva Berachos* after all, because it was likely that the British would impose a curfew after their arrival at R' Chaim's home, and then neither they, nor their students, would be able to leave.

R' Chaim was very distressed. All the tables were already set and the meal prepared. Suddenly, R' Isser Zalman Meltzer and his wife, Baila Hinda, appeared at the door.

In order to come to R' Chaim's house, they had been forced to pass the very police station that had just been bombed. Walking in, R' Isser Zalman remarked, "Yes, it was difficult to come to this *seudas mitzvah* — but not to have attended such a *simchah* would have been harder still!"

Word was sent to the Chevron Yeshivah that R' Isser Zalman had arrived — and the *roshei yeshivah* and their students came at once to join in the *simchah*.

The Donation

זֹאת הָאָרֶץ אֲשֶׁר נִשְׁבַּעְתִּי לְאַבְרָהָם לְיִצְחָק וּלְיַעֲקֹב לֵאמֹר לְזַרְעֲךָ
אֶתְּנֶנָּה

*"This is the land which I swore to Avraham, to Yitzchak, and to
Yaakov, to say, 'I will give it to your offspring'"*

(Devarim 34:4)

R' Moshe Basan had a deep and abiding love for Eretz Yisrael.
Because he himself was prevented from moving there, he put a great
deal of energy into helping those who did live there. On his table
stood a large *tzedakah* box for donations to benefit the Jews of Eretz
Yisrael. Everyone in the community knew of their rabbi's love for the
Holy Land, and helped him collect money for this purpose.

One day, a respected member of the community came to see R'
Moshe.

"Mazel tov!" he cried joyously. "My wife has just given birth to a
son! I have come to invite his honor to be *sandak* at the *bris*."

R' Moshe was overjoyed at the news, and blessed the new father
with *nachas* from his son.

"Unfortunately," he added, "I will not be able to participate in the
bris, as I have already been invited to be somewhere else at that
time, and have promised to go."

The new father was crestfallen. Then he had an idea.

"Your Honor," he said, "I am prepared to donate 200 *dinar* right
now for the Jews in Eretz Yisrael — if only the Rav will grant my request and be *sandak* at my son's *bris*."

He was certain that R' Moshe would not refuse this generous offer. Surely he would cancel his prior commitment.

But the Rabbi thought otherwise. "No, no — I cannot cancel my
promise."

R' Moshe stopped speaking, and sat lost in thought for several
minutes. Then he took his wallet from his pocket, and before his visitor's astonished eyes proceeded to count out 200 *dinars* and
deposit them in the *tzedakah* box sitting on the table in front of him.

"Y-your Honor," stammered the stunned visitor, "I can understand that you are not able to fulfill my request. But why did you put
200 *dinar* into your *tzedakah* box?"

Smiling, the Rabbi replied, "You promised to donate 200 *dinar* for the Jews of Eretz Yisrael, on the condition that I would serve as *sandak*. Now that I am unable to do so, should these Jews in Eretz Yisrael suffer a loss? Because I am the one who prevented you from donating the money, *I* am obligated to lose that amount — not the Jews in Eretz Yisrael!"

Deeply moved, the new father took out his own wallet and immediately put 200 *dinars* of his own into the *tzedakah* box.

"Now that I've given the donation," he said, "the Rav can take his money back."

But R' Moshe was quick to reject his idea. "No! Once I've given, I won't take it back. In the merit of our donations, Eretz Yisrael will be rebuilt and we will merit living there speedily, in our days!"

A Remarkable Old Age

וּמֹשֶׁה בֶּן מֵאָה וְעֶשְׂרִים שָׁנָה בְּמֹתוֹ לֹא כָהֲתָה עֵינוֹ וְלֹא נָס לֵחֹה

"Moshe was one hundred and twenty years old when he died; his eye did not dim and his moisture did not leave [him]."

(Devarim 34:7)

A fund-raiser from the Novaradok Yeshivah came, as usual, to the city of Karlin Pinsk to collect money for the yeshivah. He went to see one of the Torah greats, author of the halachah work *Beis Dovid*, who was then more than 90 years old. Though he was becoming more and more forgetful, he still continued to learn Gemara by heart every day.

When the fund-raiser walked in, the Beis Dovid greeted him, then asked, "How can I help you?"

The fund-raiser said that he had come to raise money for the Novaradok Yeshivah, as he did each year.

"How much do I give every year?" the Beis Dovid asked.

The fund-raiser mentioned the amount. The Beis Dovid took out his wallet and gave him the money. Then he sat down to learn from memory, as his eyesight was too weak to let him learn from a *sefer*.

The fund-raiser sat at one end of the table, watching the Beis Dovid's radiant face and listening to his pleasant voice reciting the

Gemara, Rashi, and *Tosafos* — moving from page to page with wondrous precision.

After a time, the Beis Dovid turned to the fund-raiser and asked, as before, "How can I help you?" The fund-raiser answered that he had already received a donation, but was just staying a little while.

"I have grown very forgetful lately," the Beis Dovid said. "But I do remember, *baruch Hashem*, the entire *Shas* — as well as I remembered it as a youth!"

The fund-raiser was deeply moved by this revelation. Later, when he visited the Chofetz Chaim, he related the entire incident to him.

Some time afterward, the Beis Dovid departed this world. A eulogy was given for him in Radin, and the Chofetz Chaim asked that fund-raiser to publicly describe the scene he had witnessed.

"But who am I," protested the fund-raiser, "to eulogize the Beis Dovid?"

"I will give the eulogy," said the Chofetz Chaim. "You will describe the incident first."

And the fund-raiser did so, to the wonderment of all who heard him.